The Rebellious Sisterhood

Female artists...taking their world by storm!

Artemisia, Adelaide and Josefina plan to break
the mold the male-centric art world has placed
them in. They each have ambitions and are willing
to fight for their rightful place—they know their
worth, even if society doesn't.

From their base in Seasalter, Kent, the women
use the only tool in their arsenal to have their
voices heard: their paintbrushes. On their mission,
might these rebellious women also find something
they weren't looking for—men to fight for
and love them?

Read Artemisia's story in
Portrait of a Forbidden Love

Read Adelaide's story in
Revealing the True Miss Stansfield

And Josefina's story in
A Wager to Tempt the Runaway

All available now!

Author Note

Josefina and Owen's story is about living your best life even when it requires hard choices and a change of plans. It's about balancing who you are with what you owe the people you love. For Josefina, that means balancing her promises to her father with being true to her own dreams. For Owen, it's coming to terms with the past and the reality that he can't change who he is, but he can love himself as he is.

Here are a few historical notes:

1. The inn The Crown is later known in Seasalter as the Blue Anchor. It is unclear exactly when the name change went into effect, so I opted to go with The Crown.

2. St. Alphege Church, where Owen got his education, is still there.

3. The beach at Seasalter is pebbly, more of a shingle than a sandy beach (although Artemisia and Addy in previous books do manage to find some sandy spots).

4. Baldock House, which Owen purchases around 1813, was really owned by William Baldock, who died with a smuggling fortune in 1812.

5. William Baldock ran the Seasalter Smuggling Company for years before his death, and you can read up on him at the Blue Anchor website.

6. It is true that oysters from the Whitstable-Seasalter area were exported to the Hapsburg Court.

7. It is true that oysters make admirable reefs.

8. It is true the year in the book saw remarkable flooding in many Kent areas excluding Seasalter.

BRONWYN SCOTT

—

A Wager to Tempt the Runaway

HARLEQUIN®
HISTORICAL™

Recycling programs
for this product may
not exist in your area.

ISBN-13: 978-1-335-50625-2

A Wager to Tempt the Runaway

Copyright © 2021 by Nikki Poppen

This edition published by arrangement with Harlequin Books S.A.

For questions and comments about the quality of this book,
please contact us at CustomerService@Harlequin.com.

Harlequin Enterprises ULC
22 Adelaide St. West, 40th Floor
Toronto, Ontario M5H 4E3, Canada
www.Harlequin.com

Printed in U.S.A.

Bronwyn Scott is a communications instructor at Pierce College and the proud mother of three wonderful children—one boy and two girls. When she's not teaching or writing, she enjoys playing the piano, traveling—especially to Florence, Italy—and studying history and foreign languages. Readers can stay in touch via Facebook at Facebook.com/bronwynwrites, or on her blog, bronwynswriting.blogspot.com. She loves to hear from readers.

Books by Bronwyn Scott

Harlequin Historical

Scandal at the Midsummer Ball
"The Debutante's Awakening"
Scandal at the Christmas Ball
"Dancing with the Duke's Heir"

The Rebellious Sisterhood

Portrait of a Forbidden Love
Revealing the True Miss Stansfield
A Wager to Tempt the Runaway

The Cornish Dukes

The Secrets of Lord Lynford
The Passions of Lord Trevethow
The Temptations of Lord Tintagel
The Confessions of the Duke of Newlyn

Allied at the Altar

A Marriage Deal with the Viscount
One Night with the Major
Tempted by His Secret Cinderella
Captivated by Her Convenient Husband

Visit the Author Profile page at Harlequin.com for more titles.

For Carol, who lived and loved to the fullest,
who put family above all else and who convinced
me to buy the red dress in the window.
We'll always have Italy.

Chapter One

Seasalter, Kent

Wildness born of midnight and madness coursed through Josefina, filling her with the hot, exhilarating thrill of a mission accomplished, and beneath a full moon no less! She threw back her head and howled in victory at that bright moon as the last of the crates were offloaded from the boats on to the discreet beach of Shucker's Cove.

Padraig O'Malley, the smuggling captain, laughed and tossed her a bag. 'Josefina, catch.'

Josefina hefted the little washed leather bag in her hand with an appraising glee. One could never have too much money. A year on the road, painting from town to town, had taught her that. She tested the weight of the coins within. Enough. There was enough inside to make a nice addition to the stash of coins she had hidden beneath her mattress back at the art school.

'Well, Fina, is it enough? Do you want to count it

out in front of me?' Padraig the Irishman chuckled at her obvious assessment of the payment. He flung a casual arm about her and took a swig from his flask. He was in high humour; the shipment had come in easily and without trouble. 'You'll notice the other boys, Fina. They take their payment without question.' He laughed.

'Well, I'm not one of the boys, now am I?' Josefina gave her hair a coy toss over her shoulder, flirting. Padraig was the leader of the Seasalter gang. He decided what shipments they took and when. He also decided how they were dispersed, what they were sold for and who got what share of the take. It paid to be friendly to him.

'No, you're certainly not.' He passed her the flask and she took a healthy swallow. 'Although you can drink like them.'

Josefina shoved the flask back at him against the hard breadth of his chest. Padraig was all muscle and brawn, a burly man. 'You like that about me,' she flirted, dancing away from him. She was aware there was a great deal more he liked about her. It was best to keep him at arm's length when he was flush with drink and success. Nights like tonight, men like Padraig thought themselves kings of the world and all those in it. She knew how to handle such men, but she'd prefer not to have to.

Josefina ducked away into the night, losing herself among the dispersing crew members. 'Goodnight, Charlie, goodnight, Thomas, goodnight, Ned,' she called until she was out of sight, alone on the Faversham Road leading to the art school, where her bed waited for her. She had her very own room and three warm meals a day until May and all she had to do was paint one picture.

Josefina tossed the little bag in her hand, listening to the coins clink. How satisfying to have money of her own, a roof over her head and food for the winter, all provided by her own efforts. And how different. Her life was not the one she'd led a year ago. Life was simpler now, freer. She was her own master. She went where she chose and stayed as long as she chose. She ate, she drank, she painted what she chose. She saw the world in all of its raw beauty, not the rose-filtered version she'd been raised on. She was twenty-four, a child no more. No one told her what to do, although there were plenty of people from her past life who had tried, who would still try. Men like Signor Bartolli. Only no one knew where she was.

She liked it that way. Liked it enough to have walked away from the luxury of her father's villa and all the comforts provided by his wealth and fame. His death had freed her and she'd fled the moment the cage door was open. If she'd learned anything from her father's life, it was that gilded cages were still cages. He'd spent his life kowtowing to patrons, painting what they desired in order to secure his wealth and reputation. He lived where they lived. He did not get to travel as he desired and had never seen the places of his own dreams: the pyramids of Egypt, the tropical islands of the Caribbean, the painted natives of the Americas. But she would. She would see it all, paint it all for him. Just as she'd promised him before he died.

Josefina looked to the stars, indulging in the fantasy that her father looked down on her from the lofty heavens. What would he think if he really could see her now? Would he applaud her decision to disappear, to seize and shape her own destiny? Would he be appalled that she'd walked out on the luxury he'd spent his life providing to live the life of a vagabond, wandering the dirt roads of a backwater like Seasalter at midnight, her worldly wealth clutched in her hand?

She hoped not. She hoped he would understand her choice. She'd chosen to keep her promise to him and to herself. She was never going back, even if it meant she had fewer dresses to wear and none so fine as the ones left behind in her wardrobe. Even if it meant she had to count her pennies and join smuggling rings, working her way through her adventures from place to place. She didn't want to be the pampered daughter or wife of a rich man, a princess in a tower. She wanted to be free.

That's what she told herself late at night in her warm dormitory room when the doubts crept in. She *wanted* to be free. Freedom was *her* choice. Only lately, it didn't seem to be enough. She tossed the bag again. She had shelter, food, the chance to make some money. In exchange, come May, she was free to go, free to set sail for the Americas. She had everything she desired. What more was there? She had enough. More than enough.

He had seen enough. The little fool thought to compound a crime against the Crown with walking home alone at midnight. Owen Gann didn't need a telescope to see the stupidity in that, not even from the distance of the widow's walk atop his Seasalter manor house situated along the marshy Kent coast. Tonight, he stood atop the walk and kept his own discreet vigil as Padraig O'Malley's free-traders unloaded their monthly shipment, his telescope never leaving the deep pocket of his greatcoat.

He had no quarrel with smuggling. Growing up in Seasalter, he understood intrinsically that for many it was a necessity in order to make ends meet. Once, he'd been one of them. These days, he preferred to make his money honestly by daylight and without fear of criminal repercussions. Apparently, that was just one of the many differences between him and *her*. He was full of caution and restraint. She was without either.

From the cove, her laughter carried up to him, proof that she lacked all caution, all fear. The moonlight caught her in profile, her head thrown back to the evening light, her silhouette lithe and dark, dressed in trousers that flattered her figure even at a distance, her identity unmistakable against the moon: Josefina Ricci, the Italian protégée of Seasalter's leading artist, Artemisia Stansfield, the Lady St Helier. Damn and double damn. She was the last person who needed to be on the beach tonight engaged in illegal transactions beneath a full moon for all to see, excisemen and riding officers included.

Josefina Ricci was a thrill seeker, that had been clear about her from the start. But Owen had not thought she'd go as far, however, as to embrace crime. He might be understanding of smuggling, but the Crown was not. He reached into his pocket for the telescope, sweeping the beach once more to be sure the smugglers were safe. The cove was hidden and there were no excisemen on duty in this part of Kent at present. He knew the smugglers' informants must have reported that no trouble was expected, but still, one couldn't be too careful. And someone *did* have to be careful on Josefina's behalf if she wouldn't be careful on her own. That person wasn't going to be Padraig O'Malley. O'Malley was notorious for his daring, although 'daring' wasn't what Owen called it—he called it recklessness. He looked to the sky and swore again. Padraig should have known better. The night was too bright for any but the most intrepid of free-traders or the most desperate.

Given that it was January and seas were rough, the Seasalter smuggling company surely fit the latter if not the former. Winter was slow for free-traders, the Channel a chancy proposition, storm ridden for months with dangerous gales, one of the two main sources of income for Seasalter families. Oysters were the other. While oysters could be harvested in January if the seas cooperated, the lack of reliable winter smuggling income—also weather dependent—made for long, empty stretches around here, broken up only by the art school's annual Christmas party and his own 'Oyster Ball' in February to provide the folks with enough gaiety to get through the final phase of winter.

Assured the beach was secure, Owen put away the telescope. Safe beach or not, it didn't change his opinion. The landing tonight was too dangerous, but then, he had the luxury of such an opinion. O'Malley did not. Owen remembered the days when he didn't have the luxury either, of the long winters growing up when his family struggled through the cold harvesting months, October to April, augmenting the off-season of spring and summer with smuggling and some fishing, and then the years when support for his family had fallen singly on his own young shoulders.

In those days, the fraternity of smugglers had been the saving of his family. He would not turn his back on them now that he had money of his own and no need of their services. They had been there for him and he'd be there for them. Those men out there on the beach tonight might not have a choice, but *she* did. He'd like to know what possessed Josefina Ricci to be out there howling at the moon—an action as incautious as the landing itself.

And the sight of her doing so called to him, deep down in his bones.

Even though he didn't want to admit it.

Even though part of him was angered by her recklessness in joining O'Malley—how *dare* she take such a chance after all Artemisia had done in bringing her here?—the other part of him revelled, albeit cautiously, in it. The part of him that had made a habit of taking to his widow's walk with his telescope on smuggling nights to protect the gangs from a distance. He liked to tell himself he'd adopted the ritual because he owed the smugglers, because he had a reckless younger brother whom he'd nearly lost. But he suspected there was more to his increased recent vigilance than that.

Josefina reminded him of his brother, Simon. She, too, was a free spirit, a breath of fresh air in any room she entered. Like Simon, she was reckless. She simply couldn't help it. Recklessness was part of who she was. Even the circumstances surrounding her arrival had been reckless—her presence in Seasalter the result of a wager Artemisia Stansfield, the art academy's headmistress, had made with her arch nemesis, Sir Aldred Gray, over female talent when it came to painting.

The tale was Artemisia and her sister, Adelaide, had plucked Josefina at random from among the Covent Garden street artists for rehabilitation, for redemption, and for revenge after Sir Aldred had remarked a woman couldn't paint as well as a man—and a woman *certainly* couldn't instruct another to paint as well as a man could. It had been meant as a slur against Artemisia's academy and Artemisia had reacted immediately, wagering Sir Aldred on the spot that she could take an itinerant artist from the market and turn them into an artist capable of winning a prize at the Academy's spring show. A hundred pounds was on the line, but Owen knew it was about more than money. Pride and reputation were on the line, as well.

Watching Josefina tonight, Owen wondered, though, if the redoubtable Artemisia had finally bitten off more than she could proverbially chew. Did she know that her new protégée was running with Padraig O'Malley's smuggling gang? Looking back, perhaps he shouldn't be so surprised. Certainly, the signs of wildness had been there since her arrival.

The first night he'd seen her had been at the school's welcome-back-from-the-holiday gathering. She'd been a veritable spark, the heart of the party. Everywhere he'd looked, she was there, the red of her dress always catching the corner of his eye, her laughter bright and clear, cutting across myriad conversations to reach his ears. He'd stood up with her for a few of the informal country dances that night after furniture had been pushed back and carpet rolled up.

She'd been a laughing, living flame that night, igniting anything in her path and she'd done it every day since. It was rumoured she'd drunk freely at a local gathering at the Crown, Seasalter's only inn, after a successful smuggling run, danced on the tables with Padraig O'Malley and even let the smuggling captain kiss her. It had been a public kiss surrounded by laughter, nothing a man ought to be jealous of, yet it had stirred him. Owen wanted to be the one dancing on scarred tables with her, the one sharing a flask of cheap spirits with her, the one kissing her at midnight. He knew it was not well done of him, but there it was. He was jealous of her, of Padraig. He was likely ten years her senior; he didn't swig from flasks and take chances beneath a full moon. But sometimes when the moon was full like tonight and the heft of his burdens weighed upon him, he wished he could.

What would it be like to be that young again? That free? No one counting on you? Able to go where you wanted, when you wanted? To howl at the moon and not care what anyone thought? These days he was closer to forty than he was thirty. He ran an oyster empire that shipped shellfish to London *and* the Hapsburg Court. He had a string of oyster factories along the Kent coast: Seasalter, Whitstable, Haversham.

He'd come a long way from the boy who'd run with smugglers at fifteen so he could buy medicines for his sick mother, harvesting the Gann family oyster beds at sixteen alongside his father and taking on the responsibility of raising his brother at seventeen when his father died. He spent his twenties enacting the possibilities he saw around him, adding another link to the heavy chain of responsibilities he already carried.

He was no longer Owen Gann, the Oyster Man, but Owen Gann, the Oyster *King* of Seasalter, of all of Kent—a title he'd worked his life for so that no one under his care would ever suffer for the lack of money as his mother had suffered. But even noble goals had their price. That goal had cost him—a price he was reminded of when he looked at Josefina Ricci and his blood began to sing and his mind began to hum with yearning. Not for days gone by to be repeated, but for the days ahead to be different—less ledger work and more…something else. Something he couldn't put a name to, something the wild Josefina Ricci had come to embody.

A cloud crossed the moon, blocking his view of the smugglers below, Josefina's vibrant flame lost from sight as she took to the road leading to the art school a full two miles away. Owen stood awhile longer in the dark, debating his options, although he was already sure of his conclusion. He would not rest easy while Artemisia's protégée was abroad in the night. He ought to be working. He had an enormous investment underway to complete a process of vertical acquisitions that had been years in the making, but his ledgers would get nothing from him until she was safely home. He would not be able to live with his conscience otherwise.

Owen turned and made his way down the steps. If he was quick, he could intercept her at the Faversham fork. Surely his ledgers could survive one night without him. Evening accounting was what rich men did, he'd come to learn. They counted their money and then figured out how to make more. He wished the prospect of that still stirred him the way it used to. But at some point, maybe a man had enough and maybe he'd reached it.

Chapter Two

Josefina had reached the fork in the road when a form stepped across her path, blocking the moon with its size, a tall, broad-shouldered man. For a moment, a sense of alert caution swept her. Her first instinct was that Padraig had followed her. Josefina gripped the handle of the knife worn at her waist. She wouldn't call her caution fear; she refused to be afraid of a man—it gave him too much power. Moonlight picked at his hair, glinting white gold, and the grip on her knife relaxed. She knew this man and he wasn't Padraig. In fact, he was quite Padraig's opposite.

'Mr Gann, what an odd time of night to be abroad.' He was dressed in boots, a greatcoat and waistcoat, but beneath those layers his shirt was undone, open at the neck as if he'd already been in for the night. In where? In a mistress's bed? Was he coming home from some- where? It wasn't impossible that Kent's most eligible bachelor had a lover squirrelled away somewhere, just perhaps…improbable? He was as upstanding as they came. One could not imagine he would allow himself to engage in anything as sinful or delightful as carnal pleasure. Neither concept seemed to be in his vocabulary.

'You as well, Signorina Ricci.' He gave the pointed reply and fell into step beside her. They might have been out for an afternoon stroll. 'Does Lady St Helier know one of her students is abroad in the night?'

Josefina tossed her head. 'I am hardly one of the girls. The oldest among them is sixteen.'

'And you are so much older, is that it? Worldly wise enough to be out alone on the Faversham Road in the dark?' Gann chuckled, a low, dubious baritone in the night. 'What would you have done if I was a less than honourable character?' He leaned close to her ear in a conspiratorial gesture and she smelled the sage and rosemary of his soap. He was honourable *and* fastidious. 'What if I'd been an exciseman? Or Padraig O'Malley? A pretty head toss is seldom enough to convince their sort to stand down.'

Josefina grimaced. 'You saw?' Her mind played back all that was included in that statement. He'd seen not just smuggling, but Padraig on the beach with his flask and his familiarity.

Gann gave a negligent shrug that lifted his wide shoulders. He wasn't built like a gentleman; he was big, broad and blond. 'Anyone could have seen. Only the desperate take a shipment under a full moon. Are you desperate, *signorina*, or merely reckless?' His words were tinged with derision and rebuke.

'You disapprove,' Josefina challenged. Disapproved of smugglers. Disapproved of Padraig O'Malley, perhaps even of sucking a little joy from life in a moment's thrill. They'd come to the place where the path to the school veered from the road. He disapproved and yet he was here. 'Did you come to scold me or to see me home safe?'

'Perhaps both, *signorina*.' Gann gave her a small smile as he stepped away from her. 'I assume you can make it from here without falling into any trouble?'

It was on the tip of her ready tongue to say she could have made it all the way without help, but he'd already left her, his broad back and blond hair disappearing into the night. Josefina wished he'd disappear from her thoughts as easily, but he seemed insistent on remaining, all of which focused on the single salient point that he'd come to walk her home at midnight. How interesting. He barely knew her. What he did know of her was through Lady St Helier and limited to a dance or two at the welcome-back party, hardly the stuff on which to build anything beyond an acquaintanceship. Certainly not enough on which to make demands of protection.

Not that she was looking for protection or for anything other than passing acquaintance. She had her knife for protection and her time in Seasalter was limited to mere months. She had a world to see come May when the weather cleared and now she had money for travel. She was not looking for attachment. *Was he?* Had something more than acquaintanceship prompted his nocturnal outing? Was that something more of the decent or indecent variety?

A woman must always ask these questions, even if the man appeared upstanding. It was one way in which a smart woman could shield herself. Back at home, disappointing interactions with Signor Bartolli, a man she'd thought was her friend, had taught her that. *Disappointing* was a mild word for what had ultimately happened between them. He'd offered marriage in exchange for access to her father's name and reputation posthumously. He'd been more interested in her connection to fame than he had been in her. He'd definitely not been interested in no as an answer, making it clear in several ways including threat and force that his offer was merely a rhetorical question. Men offered nothing, not even protection, for free. She did not think *free* was a word that figured in Gann's vocabulary either. He was wealthy and men with wealth knew its worth and the worth of all things. Everything was endowed with a price. The world was one giant ledger book to such men. But the world was so much more than that.

Gann was not her type at all. The scold in his voice tonight was proof enough of that. Owen Gann hadn't an adventurous bone in his body. He liked sure things. Businessmen didn't become rich because they took risks. Their risks were calculated, hedged against careful odds. She knew he'd spent his life in Kent. She was out seeing the world. He opposed recklessness for its own sake; she embraced it. He could not be less like her if he tried. And yet she fell asleep with one thought whispering across her reasoning: he'd come to walk her home.

* * *

He'd come to tattle on her! The next morning, the sound of voices in the school's receiving parlour stopped Josefina in her tracks, her breath catching in alarm. She flattened herself against the hall wall, careful not to be seen from the parlour—at least not until she was ready. She needed to have her arguments in place first. From her vantage point, however, she could see them—Lady St Helier and *him*: Owen Gann. What a queer sense of gentlemanly honour he had to walk her home last night and betray her the next day. A gentleman was supposed to keep a lady's secrets.

Was this why Lady St Helier had asked her to come to the parlour? So that Gann could confront her with her crimes? What would Lady St Helier think? Would she ask her to leave? Josefina experienced a moment of panic over the prospect. She didn't want to leave the security of the school in the dead of winter. She was miles from anywhere. It would take a few days to walk to London, although a horse or coach could make the trip in a long day. It would be an inconvenience to be sure. She would end up spending her hard-earned savings surviving the winter with little left over for travel in the spring.

These were very practical reasons, she told herself, for not wanting to leave Seasalter yet. But her conscience forced her to be honest. Was it only practical reasons that prompted her panic? Or was it that after three weeks here, she was already getting comfortable? Lulled into complacency by hot meals and a warm bed? Surely not. She dismissed the notion. She had a promise to keep to her father. She would not falter now, not after coming so far, and neither would Lady St Helier. She squared her shoulders with resolve. The wager meant too much to her tutor. To turn out her hand-picked protégée would be to concede. From what Josefina knew of Lady St Helier, she was not a woman who conceded anything, especially to a man. Josefina blew out a steadying breath. She was not going to be expelled, no matter what Owen Gann had come to say.

'I don't know what could be keeping Josefina. I told her to be prompt.' Lady St Helier's voice drifted into the hall.

'It's no matter. I have time.' Gann paused. 'Perhaps it is the proposition that delays her. Perhaps she is opposed to it?'

Proposition? Josefina furrowed her brow. She knew of no such thing. What she did know, though, was that the conversation didn't sound as if Gann had come to tattle. Her curiosity was piqued, too much to claim a headache and send her regrets with a maid. She could not walk away from the parlour door now. Josefina smoothed her skirts and stepped into the parlour, mustering a polite apology as she entered. 'Lady St Helier, my apologies for being late.' She made a little curtsy, keeping her eyes on the floor. Her father always said a little display of humility never went amiss. At any rate, it was far better to look at the floor than to catch Owen Gann's eye. There was always the possibility he might intend to expose her later.

Lady St Helier gestured for her to take a seat. 'Do you remember our guest, Mr Gann? You met him at our little party when you first arrived.'

'Yes, I remember him.' Now she had no choice but to look his way. He was dressed most properly today; his shirt was done up, his patterned waistcoat buttoned, his cravat tied intricately. Gone was the man in haphazard dishabille who had walked beside her at midnight. This man's boots were polished, his breeches pressed and… Well, never mind about his breeches. A girl ought not to notice how tight a man's breeches were or how muscular his thighs might look showcased in all that well-fitted buckskin. One could not notice such things in the dark at midnight. Daylight, however, changed all that. In the daylight, without the length of a greatcoat to disguise anything, she was finding it difficult *not* to notice those thighs.

Josefina forced her gaze to remain on his face—surely that ought to be safer. But there was no safety in the late-morning gleam of perfectly styled gold hair, or the sharply chiselled angle of a clean-shaven jaw. There certainly was no safety in the blue gaze that met hers, steady, even and laughing. She stiffened. He was laughing at her, very secretly, but it was there in those eyes. She took the upper hand, letting him see she was not bothered by his presence. 'What brings you out this morning, Mr Gann?'

'You do, actually, Signorina Ricci.' He smiled, his eyes continuing to spark.

'I can't imagine why,' she replied coolly. This was

all a game to him. He was teasing her, dangling her secret between them in this private contest that reshaped basic conversation with innuendo. She would not have thought he possessed a teasing spirit, stick-in-the-mud that he was. Except for when he'd danced with her, he'd spent the night of the party talking with the older men in a corner.

'Can't you, now?' He chuckled and let the silence linger too long for comfort, long enough to draw attention to the tension between them.

Lady St Helier's gaze moved between them over the rim of her teacup. She set it down and cleared her throat. 'I've been thinking about the painting for the wager with Sir Aldred, Josefina. After assessing your work, I've decided you should do a portrait. It would allow for the best showcasing of your natural and acquired talents. Mr Gann has agreed to serve as your subject.'

Josefina stared at Lady St Helier, disappointment washing through her. 'I'd thought to do a landscape.' Landscapes were her specialty.

'I want a portrait for the wager. It is *my* wager, after all.' Lady St Helier's answer was politely pointed and Josefina's temper flared despite having known the conditions. Of course, it was Lady St Helier's decision. But that did not ease the sting of memory. How many times had her father been given similar commands? This was what it meant to have a patron. One took orders, one set aside their own creativity in exchange for room and board and occasionally fame.

'Certainly, my lady. It was just a suggestion.' Josefina fixed her gaze on her lap. Perhaps this was just the prick she needed to ensure she didn't become complacent. She'd not come all this way to fall prey to the same predicament that had trapped her father. Seasalter was a short-term arrangement. She would help Lady St Helier win the blasted wager and be on her way in the spring. As she'd planned. As she'd *promised*.

'Lady St Helier won the portrait category a few years back.' Gann tried to make peace. 'You could not ask for a better mentor.' She speared him with her gaze for his efforts. She'd had mentors before. Her father's artistic circle had been full of them, men she'd looked upon as uncles, helping her hone her craft. Those same men had offered her positions in their workshops when her father had fallen ill. One or two of them, Signor Bartolli among them, had offered more. But she'd not been interested in either apprenticeship or marriage. Both led to the same result, a surrender of her freedom. She'd end up as her father had, beholden to others for her livelihood.

Lady St Helier rose to make her exit. 'Now that's settled, I'll leave you two to work out the details. Once the setting and some initial sketches have been done, you and I can consult on your approach, Josefina.'

Gann waited to speak until Lady St Helier had gone. 'Perhaps it's not the portrait you object to, but the subject.'

'Not disappointed, merely surprised by the…um…

nature of your business here this morning,' she put it delicately.

'You find a social call odd?' He grinned. He was playing with her again, but she was ready for him this time.

She nodded towards the two unused teacups on the tray. 'Social calls in England require the drinking of tea. You had none.'

'I never drink the stuff.' Gann chuckled, that same edgy baritone that had rumbled near her ear on the road last night. 'By the time I could afford such a luxury, I had no taste for it. And you, *signorina*? Is tea not an Italian taste?'

'Not really. It's coffee we like, done in the Turkish style.' Turkish coffee, strong and hot, drunk from the Venetian cafés lining the canals with her father's friends as they watched gondolas glide past. The world came to Venice, even these days when people whispered of its decline. Perhaps that's why her father loved Venice above all other places. Venice brought the world to him when he could not go out to the world.

'I've heard of it.' Gann gave her a slow smile, his gaze contemplative. 'From the look on your face, I can tell it is a pleasure not to be missed.' He grew serious. 'You thought I came to tell Artemisia about your prank last night.' His voice was low, private, so that they would not be overheard. Even now, he was being careful with her secret.

'Yes, I did.' Josefina met his gaze openly. 'It's not a prank, though. It's work.'

He did not flinch from her scold. 'It's dangerous, whatever you call it. You are not from here, perhaps you do not understand. Smugglers can be hung or transported and there is little mercy for them. The Crown has hung children for smuggling. It will not hesitate over a woman, especially one who isn't English. The Crown does not care to have money taken from its treasury and that's what smuggling does.'

Josefina gave a toss of her head. 'I can hardly imagine the sum is so substantial.'

Gann fixed her with an arched blond brow. 'A few years back, smuggled tea alone cost the Crown as much as seven million pounds in lost revenues.' *Touché*. The sum was staggering. She should have known better than to challenge him on a money matter.

'Perhaps that will give you pause, *signorina*, the next time O'Malley asks you to go out. This is not trivial business to the Crown. They catch so few smugglers that they must make harsh examples of those they do catch.' He paused and reached for a lemon cream cake from the tea tray. 'I don't come for the tea, but I do like the cakes. My sister-in-law, Elianora, makes them at the bakery. I confess to a bit of a sweet tooth.'

A baker? Josefina found that interesting. A rich man had a baker for a sister-in-law? But then, he hadn't always been rich, had he? That had been an interesting note dropped into the conversation and then glossed over.

He bit into the spongy cake and watched her in the

ensuing silence. 'I want your word that you won't go out with the crew again. It's not safe.'

'We won't be caught,' Josefina argued, reluctant to admit to the danger he called out. 'The cove is hidden and Padraig says the riding officer is in our pocket.'

'One of them is,' Owen corrected, finishing the little cake. 'Not all of them are. Lieutenant Hawthorne certainly is not. He's new, he's ambitious and, at the moment, he's alone in his command without our fellow to temper him. Meanwhile our man is wintering in town on orders of the Crown. He won't be back until spring.' Owen grimaced. 'That's not the only reason it's not safe. I would not recommend running around anywhere with Padraig O'Malley at midnight. It could lead to all nature of unintended consequences.'

Such as informing Lady St Helier? Josefina's temper flared. He was trying to order her life with a bit of patriarchal blackmail. She would not tolerate it. She rose, putting an end to their conversation. 'For future reference, Mr Gann, I do not like to be told what to do, especially by someone who has no right to tell me. I am painting your portrait. That is all.'

'You misunderstand, *signorina.*' His tone was stern as he rose to meet her challenge, his height towering in the small room. 'I do not mean to impose my will, but since Lady St Helier is not aware of your associations she cannot offer any guidance or caution, which I am sure she would if she knew what you were up to. In her absence, I feel it is imperative to remind you that you are a representative of this school and of her.

She has given you a great opportunity. Do not make her regret it.'

That reminder did make her conscience fidget, not that she would ever let Gann see it. She did not want to bring scandal to the school, but she needed the money and she needed the thrill. 'I appreciate your concern, Mr Gann. I assure you I can take care of myself on all accounts.' She gave him a nod and turned to go, stopping at the door. 'Last night, Mr Gann, you asked me what I would have done if the man in the road had not been yourself.' She looked over her shoulder, meeting Owen Gann's impenetrable blue gaze. 'I would have gutted him.'

Chapter Three

'I hear you're having your portrait painted.' Simon Gann lowered his large fisherman's frame into the leather chair across from Owen's desk. A cosy fire popped in the hearth behind him as the carved mahogany mantel clock chimed a peaceful eight in the evening. All was well, or nearly so. Owen did admit to some curiosity and concern over his brother's visit.

'Isn't it a bit late for a social call?' Owen joked once he was assured the call had nothing to do with ill news regarding his sister-in-law and newborn niece, just weeks old. He saw less of his brother than he'd like these days. Simon was busy with his life as a baker, a husband and now a father.

'It was Ellie's idea that I come.' Simon still grinned at the mention of his wife's name a year after the wedding. 'She says a man needs a little time away from his daily routine.'

That was generous of her, given that the bakery opened before dawn to bake the morning bread and she had a newborn on her hands. It was insightful, too, Owen thought. Simon and Ellie lived in the set of rooms above the bakery with Ellie's father. It was a comfortable but small space, made smaller by the arrival of an infant. 'I imagine it feels good to have a moment to yourself,' Owen said. 'Babies are sometimes noisy blessings.' That didn't stop him from smiling, too, over the thought of his little niece. She wasn't even a month old and she was already breaking hearts.

Simon's brow frowned for a moment. Realisation struck and he laughed. 'Oh, no, Ellie didn't mean me. She meant you. She thinks you're working too hard.'

It wasn't untrue. Between the upcoming Oyster Ball in February and the vertical acquisitions project, his ready resources, both mentally and fiscally, were stretched at the moment. 'I always work hard,' Owen dismissed the concern. 'Are you sure she didn't mean you?' he teased and Simon chuckled.

'Well, she might mean us both, at that. My Ellie is a perceptive woman. It is nice to have a moment's peace with another man for company,' Simon confessed. 'Even with the squalling, I've no complaints. My daughter is an angel and my wife is a saint. She's up twice a night with the babe and still rises to see to the morning bread and the rest of us.' He shook his head in fond disbelief that such a paragon was his. 'I don't know how she does it.'

'I could make it easier for her, for both of you. My offer is still good. There's plenty of room here for a family,' Owen said. 'Ellie wouldn't have to worry about housekeeping and there'd be help with the baby.'

'We wouldn't want to be underfoot,' Simon refused politely.

'You wouldn't be and it would only be temporary if that's what you're worried about.' Owen could argue as amicably as Simon could refuse. He strode to the decanters on the sideboard and poured two glasses of brandy, handing one to his brother. 'We can build you a house in the spring. The lot near the church is still for sale and it would be close to the bakery, too.'

Simon shook his head. 'I appreciate it, but Ellie and I are happy as we are.' He took a swallow of the brandy and smiled thoughtfully. 'Do you remember growing up, you and I thought the baker's quarters were the most luxurious accommodations we'd ever seen. The Foakeses had four whole rooms, they were always warm from the oven, and smelled like biscuits and bread.'

Owen nodded. In their youth, the Foakes house had been all a home should be, warm and yeasty, where no one went hungry. There was always the assurance of bread, even the assurance of dessert after supper every night. How different that was compared to the dark, often cold one-room fisherman's hut he and Simon were raised in where there was no assurance of supper, let alone dessert.

Simon stretched expansively in his chair, his arms wide. 'Now I'm living that dream, Owen.' He winked contentedly. 'And I have the bonus of going to bed with the baker's daughter every night. I wouldn't trade my lot for all the tea in China.'

Although he almost had. Owen sipped his own drink, leaning against the sideboard. Simon had travelled the Near East looking for spices, looking to make his own fortune a few years ago rather than go into business with his brother and ride off Owen's coattails. Such a foray had nearly cost Simon his life. His ship had gone down and Simon had been marooned on an island off the east coast of Africa long enough to be thought dead. His brother had been through hell in those months, trying to survive. Owen did not begrudge him an ounce of the happiness he now had.

'Have you and Ellie given any more thought to opening a bakery in London?' Simon and Ellie had hopes of establishing Ellie as a premiere provider of sweet delicacies to the ladies of London. Ellie was an extraordinary baker. The idea was sound. If Simon wouldn't take money or a home from him, perhaps he could at least give his brother some business advice. 'I could have my man in town look for a property. There's plenty of time to be ready for the Season.'

'Yes, we're still thinking about it, but, no, you needn't put your man on it. We can handle that, too,' Simon demurred. 'I think Ellie was right. You do need to get out if all you do is spend your nights worrying over me and Ellie. You need something or some*one* to occupy your time or you'll nag me to death.' It was said good-naturedly, but Owen recognised it wasn't necessarily untrue. He was in a rut. Life lacked a certain spark these days. Making money and looking for ways to make more had lost some of its lustre—even his coveted vertical acquisitions project had lost some of its shine and he was desperate to reclaim it.

Simon leaned forward. 'You're used to taking care of people, Owen. You've been doing it since you were a boy. First Mother, then me. Now it's your workers, the smugglers. You take care of all of us. Perhaps it's time to see to yourself.' He gave Owen the knowing look of happily married men everywhere as he offered his advice. 'A wife and children would fill this house right up and your life, too. No more long nights alone with only your ledgers for company.' Simon had never put it so bluntly before.

'I have a family, Simon. You, Ellie and the baby.' They were the only people in the entire world he trusted to love him for himself, the people who knew him in all his incarnations, rich or poor, and they loved him regardless. There were others for whom he could not say as much. 'Besides, I think it might be rather difficult to find someone who will suit me, who would be happy living a life "between."' For women seeking status—the daughters of baronets and second sons— to marry him meant to have access to the wealth and comfort that eluded their fathers, but his wife would not possess a title. No matter how much money he made, they would always live outside the *ton*. Sons of oystermen could rise only so far. To the *ton*, he'd always be a novelty, someone to invite and gape at. On the other hand, a hardy woman like Simon's Ellie would be too intimidated. The oystermen of Seasalter thought him a demi-god, too lofty to approach on a daily basis, too different from them despite his lowly origins, yet for London society he'd never be lofty enough.

Simon made a derisive noise in the back of his throat. 'You're still not smarting from Alyse Newton's snub years ago, are you?' He tossed back the remainder of his drink in a show of solidarity. 'You came out the winner there. You're far wealthier now than you were when you were courting her. She probably regrets it every night.'

Owen gave his brother a wry smile. Alyse Newton might regret certain aspects. She was Lady Stanley now, wife to a diplomat who hauled her from post to post every two years doing England's business in the most inclement corners of the empire, although rumour had it Lord and Lady Stanley were in town this year between posts. Inclement posts aside, she had her title. He did not wish her ill. He hoped whatever sacrifice she'd made, it was worth it. A title was the one thing Owen couldn't give her, although he'd been prepared to give her so much more: his heart, his love. He'd not put them on offer since. He'd not been enough for a woman like Alyse.

Simon rose and glanced at the clock. 'Why don't you come down to the Crown with me for a nightcap? We've drunk the good stuff, now let's go drink the bad like the old days. I thought I'd look in on the men down there before heading home.'

The offer was tempting. A cold walk, more time

with his brother, a chance to rub elbows with the ordinary men of Seasalter, to try to prove yet again he was one of them. Owen shook his head. 'I can't afford another night away from the ledgers.'

Simon raised a blond brow. 'You took a night off?'

'Last night. The smugglers were running.' Simon knew of his vigil.

'Ah, taking care of all of us again.' Simon grinned.

'They took care of us once,' Owen said, feeling as if he had to defend his decision.

'Yes, they did and thank goodness for them or we might have starved.' Simon cocked his head. 'It's more than that, though, isn't it? You miss them.'

Owen gave a snort. 'I *owe* them. I do not miss making illegal money when I have plenty of ways to make it legally.' He clapped his brother on the shoulder. 'I thank you for the visit and the invite. You can tell your wife I am fine and that you've discharged your duty admirably. Be sure to kiss that niece of mine for me.'

Simon slanted him a dubious look. 'Are you sure you won't come?'

Owen nodded. 'I'm sure.'

The house was quiet after Simon left. Owen was acutely aware of every crackle of fire, every tick of the clock. Sounds that had intimated cosiness when Simon had been there now emphasised how alone he was. He wasn't just alone, he was lonely, which was quite a different thing altogether.

The columns of the ledgers blurred before him. Owen passed a weary hand over his eyes. What was all this for if Simon would not take a pound from him? If Simon didn't need his money, didn't need all he'd worked for? After all, Simon had his own funds set aside from his voyage, driven by his own need for self-sufficiency. There was no mother or father for Owen to support in their old age. His wealth had come too late for that. There was his niece, little Rose, of course. Perhaps Simon would allow him to spoil her.

Maybe this was the reason his business ventures had lost their appeal, becoming merely perfunctory. There was no *need* for more money. He had enough for whatever might come his way. There was no one to spend it on, no one who needed him. Well, that wasn't quite true. His workers needed him. They relied on his factories and the oyster harvest to see them through. But deep down, he knew it wasn't the same. His workers needed what he could provide for them. They didn't need *him*. Anyone with money would do. He could sell the factories to another fair-minded man and that man would suffice for them.

It was a sobering thought to realise he was merely an interchangeable piece for many. It was just as disconcerting to have reached the pinnacle of one's success and wonder what it had all been for. It was akin to forgetting why you'd wanted to climb the mountain in the first place after reaching the summit. Owen shook himself and rose, pushing away the megrims with the ledgers. This was the night talking, nothing more. He would get no more work done this evening. He would read something edifying and turn in with the hopes of rising early and concluding his work before his appointment with Josefina Ricci tomorrow.

The thought of Josefina brought a wry smile to his face as he climbed the stairs, a book tucked under one arm, a lamp in the other. Was she retiring early tonight as well in anticipation of a busy day tomorrow? Somehow, he doubted it. She seemed to live in the present, to move from moment to moment, not looking too far ahead. Perhaps even now she was at the Crown amid those drinking to Simon's new daughter. Perhaps Padraig O'Malley was there, too, an arm slung about her as it had been on the beach. Would she be flirting with him? Stealing his flask? Would O'Malley follow her home and end up gutted for his efforts?

'I would have gutted him.'

Owen could still see her face, all seriousness, as she'd offered her parting shot this morning. There'd been no hesitation. In the moment of danger, she seemed very certain of herself. Her answer had been in deadly, doubtless earnestness. Did she know her response from experience? He hoped not, yet she was very much a woman alone who had no one to rely on but herself. The world could be a very unforgiving place for such a woman. It was such a woman who perhaps needed a protector more than anyone else. He thrust the thought aside at the top of the stairs before it could take on dangerous proportions. He would *not* be that protector. She'd made it clear she didn't feel the need for one. She'd also made it clear that he had no claim to her. Of course. Sitting for a portrait did not qualify him to a claim in any regard. Still, perhaps he could keep watch at a distance, like he did for the smugglers. He would be waiting. Just in case.

Chapter Four

She did not want to keep him waiting. It wasn't professional and she'd already done it once. She didn't like to be predictable. Josefina trudged up the gravel drive leading to Owen Gann's home, trying to avoid most of the mud and puddles that populated the winter roads in Seasalter—a near impossibility, she was coming to learn. English winters were vastly different from Venetian winters: colder, wetter, damper. It was true San Marco's piazza flooded at times, but she'd never felt a wetness like England's, that went straight to a person's bones and stayed there. Today, the rain had relented, leaving the sky heavy with steel-grey clouds that promised a few hours reprieve at most.

Sometimes she wondered if she'd ever be warm again. Josefina sidestepped a puddle, laughing at herself. But of course she would, in May, when she set sail for the Americas and the Caribbean with its fabled turquoise waters and white sand beaches. For now, though, blue sky and bluer water seemed a fantasy.

She rounded a turn in the drive and Owen Gann's house came into view, a brick structure that only nominally answered to the description of 'farmhouse.' Manse was more appropriate. Her artist's eye took in the symmetry of the building; the balance of the home was broken in equal halves by a portico at the centre for coaches to drive beneath and disgorge their passengers. Each side sported six perfectly spaced white-shuttered windows, three up and three down, with the left side of the home ending in a single-storeyed brick square denoting the kitchen. Certainly an elegant building for a place like this. It even outshone the farmhouse Lady St Helier and her husband called home.

It was clean, too. She could see that close up as she approached the front doors, white without a speck of mud on their pristine panels and the brass knocker on the right gleamed. Even the white shutters on the windows were clean and the ivy that framed the windows did so in a controlled crawl. Owen Gann took pride in his home. The home of his adulthood. This was not a poor man's manse if she'd understood the brief reference he'd made earlier. She supposed in some places an ancestral home might linger in a family even after the coffers were depleted, but not here in Seasalter, where there weren't any noble families or country squires. Josefina made a mental note as she raised the brass knocker. This was a home he'd acquired.

A man dressed in the uniform of a country butler answered her knock and ushered her into a drawing room, where a fire burned and Owen Gann waited.

She'd hoped to be the one waiting on him. To be alone in the drawing room would have given her a chance to take his measure in more subtle ways.

He rose as the butler announced her. 'Signorina Ricci, welcome.' He gestured that she should take the seat opposite him by the fire. 'Coffee, please, Pease,' he ordered, tossing a wry smile her direction. 'No tea for us, isn't that correct, *signorina*?' He settled into his chair and crossed a long leg over his knee, studying the small satchel she set beside her chair. 'Is your equipment outside?'

'No, it's all right here.' She drew a notebook from her bag and smiled at his surprise. 'Not everything about painting occurs on an easel, Mr Gann. I can't paint what I don't know and I don't know you, not well enough to paint at any rate.' Here was a man who had everything—wealth and status—yet he strode midnight roads in order to walk home a woman he didn't know beyond passing acquaintance. Here was a man who dressed expensively, but sported a build more commonly found among manual labourers and fishermen, a man who chided her for her risks, but kept her secrets when given the opportunity to expose them. Here was a stick-in-the-mud who had become interesting. None of those pieces added up to anything cohesive. How was she to paint someone who didn't make sense?

The coffee tray appeared, complete with rolls stuffed with a chocolate creme worthy of a Parisian patisserie. 'It isn't Turkish coffee, but perhaps it will do.' Gann poured from a silver pot into two expensive creamware porcelain cups. Their very simplicity made them elegant. Much like the man himself. The expensiveness of his clothes did not equate with gaudiness. No brightly patterned waistcoats for him. She made a note in her book.

'Shall we start as we drink our coffee? I am sure you must be a busy man. Tell me about yourself. What do you do?'

'I sell oysters, *signorina*. I sell them all over England and I ship them to royal courts like the Hapsburgs where English oysters are considered the best in the world.' The stick-in-the-mud was back. How was she to paint a man who sold *oysters*? All she knew of oysters was that her father's friends sometimes joked that oysters were nature's aphrodisiac. Great. That would hardly impress anyone.

'Oysters are how you made your fortune?' Perhaps painting a rich man would be a better angle. She tried to imagine how she would paint him in this house surrounded by his silver service and Wedgwood creamware. Would she position him at the fireplace in the heavily masculine chair he currently sat in, all dark leather and wood? 'Do you have a dog?' She interrupted as the inspiration struck. A dog would be nice, a big one, perhaps a black-and-tan hound whose head reached the arm of the chair, tall and regal and alert like his master.

'No.' Gann speared her with a blue stare that would have rendered the hardiest of debaters speechless. 'I do *not* have a dog.' Too bad. Dogs made unapproachable men seem more human and uninteresting sticks-in-the-mud less so. 'Shall I continue? I believe I was explaining the beginnings of my fortune to you, because you *asked*.' He was scolding her for the rude interruption. It was poorly done of her, Josefina recognised, but somewhere between his dissertation on supply and demand in the oyster fields and buying his first boat, her thoughts had simply strayed away from the conversation and when they'd come back they'd brought a dog with them.

'I'm afraid money matters are hardly interesting to the general public,' Gann apologised, but coldly. He wasn't apologising for himself, but for her.

'Show me around the house.' Josefina jumped up, eager to change the pathetic trajectory of the interview. One could learn a lot about another person by looking at their home and the things they surrounded themselves with.

Gann rose, apparently finding the topic a suitable substitute for his boring fortune. 'I acquired the house in 1812 when it came on the market. It's the nicest house of its kind in this area and it had been owned by a man much like myself, a local rags-to-riches fellow named William Baldock. He herded cows and eventually was an innkeeper, but he died with a fortune some estimate to be worth over a million pounds.'

Now *that* was interesting. 'How did he make *his* money?' she felt compelled to ask. Certainly cows and innkeeping didn't account for it.

Gann gave his low baritone laugh. 'How do you

think a man makes that kind of money in the isolated reaches of Kent? I'll give you a hint—it wasn't oysters.' He ushered her through into the dining room, sliding back the doors that separated it from the drawing room. She was aware of his hand, light at her back as he allowed her to step through ahead of him. Whatever his rough beginnings, Gann had acquired good manners somewhere along the way and good grooming, too. She could smell the clean scent of soap on him and the undertones of starched linen.

A glass-fronted hutch displaying eye-catching pieces of china sat on one wall, a sideboard on the other, and a gleaming table that could seat twelve dominated the centre of the room. Very elegant for the country. Probably the largest table on this end of the Kent coast. Surely he didn't eat in here alone? 'Who do you entertain here?' Josefina was trying to place him in this room and couldn't.

'No one.' He strolled the perimeter, studying the space as if seeing it for the first time. 'This room is seldom used. I think the last time I opened it up was a year ago for Simon and Elianora's wedding. They were married on Christmas Day, a very impromptu affair given that Simon didn't return until Christmas Eve.' He smiled at the memory and then sobered. 'To date, it is the grandest surprise of my life, to have my brother back from the dead. Of course, my new niece runs a very close second.'

Josefina nodded. Artemisia had told her about Simon Gann's miraculous return. She liked Simon.

He was gregarious and always had a smile when she saw him at the bakery. He might look like his brother, both of them tall, broad and blond in the best tradition of Vikings and Saxons, but he lived out loud whereas Owen Gann lived 'within,' she supposed. She'd hoped the interview today might shed some light on that. So far, she was failing to find that light.

They left the dining room, Gann shutting the doors behind them. There were other rooms; the kitchen, a small sitting room at the back of the house that appeared as pristine, as elegant and as unused as the dining room. They toured the enormous, barren, currently unused cellar beneath the house, where Gann speculated a large part of the Baldock fortune had been earned, then a smaller wine cellar close to the kitchen. The final room was his private office and he'd saved it for last as they returned to the front of the house— Gann was too much of a gentleman to suggest they tour the private bedchambers upstairs. She had hopes for the office, the place where his work happened. Surely, this room would reflect his heart.

She stepped inside and breathed in the masculine smell of the study, the remnants of smoke from the fire, the scent of leather-covered furniture. The room had potential, more so than the others. Deep turquoise velvet curtains trimmed in heavy gold fringe framed the windows, a wide, polished desk bearing a stack of open ledgers testified to its use as more than a decoration. Two tall wing-backed armchairs faced the fireplace, an oil of the English countryside hung over it, the only nod to pictures in the room. The requisite sideboard with decanters stood against one wall. A full-length bookcase lined the other, filled with expensively bound tomes, the books on the shelves interrupted occasionally by the showcasing of a costly ornament: a paperweight, a small globe with lapis-lazuli oceans.

Josefina crossed the floor on a hunch, noting the quality woven carpet beneath her feet, another nod to the room's luxury. She gave the lapis-lazuli globe a spin on its gold axis. 'This is pretty, tell me about it.'

She watched Gann give a dismissive shrug. 'What is there to tell? It was here with the house. It was something of Baldock's. I paid extra to the family to purchase the house with all its furnishings.' He gave her one of his wry smiles. 'More efficient that way. I don't have the time or the eye to decorate an entire house.'

She'd thought as much about the furnishings. There was nothing of *him* here, nothing of his taste, nothing of his history. He'd bought and borrowed his status. All legitimately, of course. She gave the globe a final spin and turned to face him. 'Is there anything of *you* in this house, sir? A hobby? A favourite piece of furniture? Do you play the pianoforte in the drawing room? Is there an addition you've made to the house or the gardens?' Hope flared briefly. Perhaps he'd put in a folly or a fountain outside?

'No, the house was quite perfect the way it was. There was no need to change anything.' He gave her a sharp look as he squashed the last of her hopes for useful conversation. She couldn't paint supply-and-demand charts. 'As for pianofortes, music lessons weren't on the agenda in my childhood. We were lucky to have food to eat.'

'You must have had some education. You read and write and work sums,' she argued. Owen Gann was a shrewd, educated businessman. He might not have attended university, but he had far more learning than most.

'Thanks to the generosity of the curate at St Alphege's I was able to receive private tutelage long after most boys around here left school.' The words were as sharp as his look. 'I am sorry you find me of little interest, after all.' He was more stubborn than most. Usually men enjoyed the opportunity to talk about themselves. He was proving reluctant. Defensive almost. She wondered why.

Josefina flipped her little notebook shut, sensing the interview had come to an end. Normally, she would give a client encouragement, but Gann was being intentionally oblique. 'It's not that I find you uninteresting, it's that I find you bland, sir, and a bland portrait will not win any prizes no matter how well executed it might be.'

He gave her a curt nod. 'Forgive me for not being forthcoming enough. I am not in the habit of baring my soul to all and sundry.'

That would have to change if she was to paint something meaningful. She held his gaze, refusing to be rebuked for her probing. 'You don't have to share yourself with everyone, Mr Gann. Just with me. We'll try again tomorrow.' She saw herself out and made her way down the drive to the road, glancing back at the house just once to catch Gann's blond head already bent over his ledgers at his desk. He probably wouldn't leave the office, spending all day in there or, if he did, he'd merely trade that office for another at the factory. Then back to the estate office for the evening. It sounded like a lonely existence.

She began to speculate. Perhaps he took supper on a tray in there as well since he wasn't using the dining room. The man had a large house at his disposal and he only lived in two rooms, his office and presumably his unseen bedchamber. Or perhaps, she mused, he slept in there, too. No matter where he slept, it begged the question of why he'd bought the house in the first place. But that, like so much else about the man, remained shrouded in mystery, assuming there was anything else. Perhaps he *was* bland, a handsome, well-built man with nothing going on inside. She'd met men like that before. But this man was a successful businessman. That didn't happen on its own. One could not be bland about money and be successful. There was more to Owen Gann than met the eye, but how did she find it? How did she paint it?

'He's being difficult,' she complained to Artemisia over a lively supper with the St Heliers. Artemisia had invited her to dine at the farmhouse so they could discuss the interview. Like herself, Lady St Helier believed in the importance of setting the stage for an exceptional painting with excellent research beforehand. 'Either he is truly uninteresting or he is deliberately hiding himself.'

Artemisia's handsome husband gave a short laugh, his eyes sparking. 'I assure you, I've worked with Gann and the man is *not* bland. But he is private.'

'You're not helping,' Artemisia scolded him playfully and something shimmered, palpable in the air between them. Josefina recognised the need to make this a short night.

Darius sobered and fixed his gaze on her. 'You said he gave you a tour of the house.' Josefina made a face. He chuckled. 'Oh, I agree. The public rooms are of no use. William Baldock could come back from the dead and still recognise the place right down to where that little globe sits on the shelf. It hasn't moved in over a decade.' He leaned a little closer. 'Make him take you up to the widow's walk. Make him tell you what he does up there.'

'Why don't you just tell me?' Josefina replied. 'It would save time.' Especially as the Viscount clearly already knew.

St Helier shook his head. 'No, it's not my story to tell. It's his and it's your job to root it out of him.'

Artemisia rose. 'Come with me, Josefina. Let me show you something.' Josefina followed her to the back of the farmhouse where a long glass-walled room had been converted into an artist's studio. Artemisia sorted through a pile of sketches until she found the one she wanted and lit a lamp. 'Do you recognise this?'

Josefina studied the pencil drawing. Even in a rough draft, she envied Artemisia's eye for detail. There was no doubting that the woman who'd set herself up as her mentor was an accomplished artist. 'This is a preliminary of the woman with her horse.' Josefina couldn't recall the names.

'Yes, tell me about the woman.'

'I don't know her,' Josefina stammered.

'Look at the drawing. What do you know of her from that? Look carefully,' Artemisia coached.

For the first time since coming to Seasalter, Josefina felt nervous about her own skill. Would it measure up to the genius of Lady St Helier? She took her time, letting her eyes study the drawing by section, moving slowly from the top left to the bottom right. 'She's defiant, you see it in her eyes. She's a horsewoman, her posture is turned towards the horse as if they are one, as if they understand each other. She is not the horse's master. The proportions suggest they are each other's equal. They are a pair in all ways.' She dropped her eyes to the woman's hands. 'She's unmarried, further proof that she's defiant. She is standing on her own without the shelter of a husband's name or title to protect her from censure. Furthermore, she's wearing breeches, you can just see that at the bottom of the painting, enough to know she's not wearing a riding habit.'

Artemisia smiled approvingly and Josefina felt a warm stab of pride in having pleased her. 'Now, tell me why this painting won its category that year.' That was a little harder to do having only the sketch to go on.

'Because it tells a story.' She knew that, though. Painting was a type of storytelling, history-recording, record-keeping. The problem was Owen Gann wasn't giving her a story *to* tell.

'How do you think I unearthed that story? I will tell you Lady Basingstoke, as she is known now, was not the most forthcoming of subjects until I got her in the stables. I travelled north up to her family's seat and spent a week following her around the stable. When we were in the stables, she never stopped talking about this horse and that, which ones were hot and which one was lame and which one was in foal, and the blood-lines of each. When she came to Warbourne, the horse in the picture, her voice would drop and become soft. One day she said to me, "We saved each other, Warbourne and I. We were both lost causes. In many ways I bet my life on him and he bet his on mine."' Artemisia paused, her own eyes soft on the drawing. 'She told me she pawned the only piece of jewellery she had from her mother to purchase him at auction, that she'd taken the bidding paddle away from her brother and stared down a whole tent of men for that horse. Her brother had been furious. She'd made a spectacle of herself.'

Artemisia turned to her. 'That's the woman I wanted everyone to see in the portrait, a woman who challenged conventions to engage her passion. The point is, Josefina, I had to discover that woman. Lady Basingstoke did not just divulge all of that to me. I had to uncover it by going to the places that meant the most to her. I had to get into her world. You need to get into

Owen Gann's. When you do, you'll see who and what he really is. You'll find the story you need to tell.'

'I went to his home,' Josefina protested. Artemisia's lesson wasn't wrong, but she'd done all that today.

'A home is a man's castle,' Artemisia quoted. 'It's not necessarily his heart.'

St Helier appeared at the studio door, their son in his arms. 'Somebody wanted to say goodnight.' St Helier jiggled the baby in his arms and he giggled at his father's attentions. Artemisia went to them and for a moment the threesome was a circle unto themselves, cohesive and unbreakable as she took the baby from St Helier. The sight made Josefina's throat constrict. It had been a long time since she'd seen a family up close, even longer since she'd been part of one. Even then, it had never been like this for her. It had only been she and her father. But that had been family enough until it wasn't.

'I'm the one that needs to say goodnight.' Josefina could take a cue. St Helier was looking at his wife as if he could hardly wait for his son to go to sleep and his wife's protégée to leave.

'Let me know how it goes with Gann tomorrow.' The baby began to fuss and root at his mother's bodice.

'I will. I'll see myself out,' Josefina offered. 'Thank you for a wonderful evening.' But it was hardly over for her. The St Helier family might be going upstairs to put the day to bed, but not she. She couldn't sleep until she figured out how to get the reticent Owen Gann to reveal himself to her, bared soul notwithstanding.

Chapter Five

He'd been deliberately taciturn with her, making her job difficult, all in order to protect himself. Owen poured himself a late-night brandy and settled into his favourite chair near the fire in his office, declaring surrender as rain battered the windows of Baldock House. No ledger work would get done tonight. Again. His thoughts preferred to roam over the interview—or more to the point the *interviewer*—instead of bank balances.

He'd been rude today. He hadn't wanted her to pretend to be interested, to pretend to care, to pretend this was a real conversation, not an interview for the sake of conducting her business of portrait painting. It would have been too easy for him to get caught up in the flash of her dark eyes, the toss of her black hair, to mistake her natural ebullience for a more personalised flirtation. For heaven's sake, he was thirty-eight years old. He knew how the world worked. Women like Josefina Ricci weren't interested in men like him. He was reserved, conservative, something of a recluse not by choice, but by the necessity of living between worlds, a man who worked hard for his living, his fortune. A man who took only calculated risks. A man who was honest with himself when it came to the fairer sex.

Women wanted more. Alyse Newton certainly had. He had not been enough for her. His fortune had not been enough to override her disgust for his lowly origins. The amount of time he devoted to the necessary maintenance and growing of that fortune had not impressed her. She didn't understand it. As such, they'd had nothing in common. Just as he had nothing in common with Josefina Ricci, a woman who embraced adventure, who never calculated her risks, she merely took them, a woman who travelled, who danced on tabletops. Josefina had been bored by his explanations today about his house and his oysters. A little voice whispered a scold in his head. Perhaps that had been his fault. Perhaps he'd made it boring on purpose. Maybe he hadn't given her a chance.

And rightly so. Giving her a chance was tantamount to all hell breaking loose. He shifted in his chair and took a fierce swallow of brandy. What did giving her a chance get him but trouble and heartache? Giving her a chance to do what? Get under his skin? Torment his body with every toss of her head, every look? Torment his mind with fantasies more appropriate for a younger man? He'd had a taste of that the night of Artemisia's welcome-back party, dancing with her in the parlour, the feel of her in his arms. He'd had another, different taste of her today, a taste of her temper as she'd challenged him, trying to provoke him into startling revelations. It had been just as heady. He'd spent too much time today staring at her mouth while she harangued him, too much time following her about the rooms of his house, too much time fighting a case of rising arousal.

His body was most definitely and inconveniently attracted to her and his mind was not far behind as evidenced by his choices these last few nights: midnight escorts and evenings spent daydreaming into the flames instead of updating ledgers when he had an enormous investment deal looming. She occupied his every thought. Perhaps he could live with that if it went no further than his imagination. He knew better than to let those feelings manifest into something else. He'd convinced himself once that he'd been in love, only to have those feelings quashed with a brutal reminder he couldn't possibly ever be enough for a daughter of a peer. Josefina Ricci might not be the daughter of a peer, but she'd expect a man to be enough in other ways. She'd want a man who matched her in adventure, in live-out-loud passion. She'd made it plain today what she thought about a man who lived in an empty house and curled up with ledgers every night.

It's because she doesn't know you, the little voice whispered. *You can't be mad at her disdain when you didn't give her a chance.*

If she knew him, would she love him? That was the logical question that followed. To what end? She would leave in May, off on another adventure. Not even love was permanent with her. Best not to venture down that path at all and save himself a world of unnecessary hurt. That meant taking certain precautions. He needed to limit his exposure to her. No more days like today where they were alone. Surely, they could conduct their portrait work up in the public vicinity of the school instead of here at Baldock House. In truth, how much time with him did she really need? Just enough time to get a few sketches. He knew enough about portrait painting to know that quite a lot of the process was completed without the subject needing to be present.

The wind howled down the chimney, gusting over the flames in the fireplace. The weather was ratcheting up another notch, enough to worry him. He'd have to go out tomorrow and check the oyster beds. Owen rose and made his way upstairs. Perhaps checking the beds would be a blessing in disguise. He could spend the day on the water engaged in the labour of hard rowing and it would have the added benefit of keeping him out of Josefina's way. He need only see her for a few moments as he explained why he had to break their appointment.

He was waiting for her in the drawing room again, but she noticed the difference in this meeting immediately. These were not drawing room clothes. These were workmen's clothes. Gann was dressed in rough trousers, old boots, a linsey-woolsey shirt open at the neck beneath a shabby hacking jacket, with no cravat or waistcoat in sight. There was, however, worn leather gloves and a knit muffler in his lap, proof that he had other plans this morning.

'Going somewhere, Mr Gann?' Josefina gave a pointed stare to the muffler and gloves.

He rose, unapologetically pulling on the gloves. 'As a matter of fact, I am, *signorina*. After last night's weather, I need to check on the oyster beds.'

'Today? You have to go today? Right now?' Josefina challenged. It sounded like a preposterous excuse for getting out of their appointment. She didn't have time for this.

'I'm afraid so.' Owen Gann was already moving towards the door, already leaving as if his departure was a foregone conclusion simply because he'd decided to break the appointment.

No. Josefina stepped slightly to the right, putting herself between him and the door ever so subtly. If he dismissed her now, it would just prove to him that he could dismiss her again. Seasalter's leading citizen or not, he wasn't going to manoeuvre his way out of their appointment. 'It's no problem,' she said smartly. 'I can see there's no arguing with you.'

'I'm glad you understand, *signorina*.' He had reached her and now found himself in need of stepping around her. 'Perhaps if there's anything you'd like to see here, my man can show you about?' It was an effort at a peace offering—unfettered roaming privileges in Owen Gann's home, but she already knew why he'd offered it. There was nothing here to see, except perhaps the widow's walk, but she sensed it would mean little without him.

'That's not necessary.' Josefina smiled brightly, looping her arm through his as she sprung her snare. 'I am coming with you.' The inspiration had come to her the moment he'd said he was going out. This would be her chance to see inside his world, his real world, not the world he'd purchased from the Baldock estate for display. She moved towards the front door, towing him with her and forestalling any protest he was sure to make. 'I won't be in the way at all. You'll hardly know I'm there.' He gave her a look that said he didn't quite believe that and she shrugged. Well, maybe he was right, but she did promise herself to be on her best behaviour.

She kept that promise, walking beside him quietly, looking at the surroundings, until they reached the shoreline. The waters were grey and choppy today, at least they looked that way to her eye. Owen waded into the water to untie one of the rowboats used by the oystermen to go out to the beds. When it became apparent he expected her to board one of them she could stay quiet no longer. 'We're going out in *that*?' She eyed the water askance, her reference extending to both the boat and the waves. This was far different from the gondolas that glided down the smooth, narrow canals of Venice. But Gann was unfazed.

'Yes, or rather, *I* am going out. You can wait here, although it will be a while.'

'Is it safe?' The boat size didn't seem commensurate to the waves. She might have taken on more than she'd anticipated.

'Yes, I assure you it is. This is nothing. Are you coming?' He was growing impatient.

She didn't dare let this chance slip away. 'Of course I'm coming.'

'Wait right there, I'll carry you.' Gann strode back to the shore and swept her up in his arms before she could protest. She'd promised to not be a burden and now here she was, a literal one. It was hardly the stuff of fairy tales. She'd never been lifted so perfunctorily before and yet she was aware of the effortless strength behind the act as he deposited her over the side of the rowboat and then levered himself in, a reminder that Owen Gann was a big man and a strong one.

He took the oars and they set out, Josefina gripping the gunwales as the boat rode the waves. 'How far are the oyster beds?' Already the shore seemed excessively far away.

'Just a mile out.' Gann nodded to empty, larger boats moored nearby as he rowed, making small talk between the pulls on the oars. 'Normally, we row the boats to those hoys and then take the hoys the rest of the way. But today we don't have the manpower to crew one and we aren't bringing in a large load.'

She was starting to get used to the motion of the boat on the water and her mind began to function again. She wasn't going to drown out here. Gann was too competent and too much of a gentleman to allow it. She told herself Gann wouldn't have gone to the effort of saving her skirts from a wetting at the shore just to let her get entirely soaked now. 'What is so important about the beds?' she asked as he pulled hard on the oars. Winter waters required strenuous effort to keep the boat on course. His strength was on display one more time. Impressive.

'It's been a wet year,' he explained as he rowed. 'There's flooding along the Thames which feeds the estuary and the marshes here and flooding at Maidenhead. We've not experienced the flooding as badly because of the oyster beds. They've built up over the years and made a reef of sorts. But there's been so much rain, I need to be sure the reef has held.' He gave a hard pull on the oars as the boat rose on a grey wave and she fixed him with an enquiring stare. That did not explain the urgency in going out today.

He continued, 'The men who work these beds need me to assure them our harvest will be intact, that their livelihood has not washed out to sea after last night's deluge. Understand, this is not an issue of a single downpour, but an accumulation of them.

'We're here.' Gann pulled the boat to a halt and set the oars. Josefina looked back towards shore. They were a long way out. The only two people in the world. Gann reached for a cage behind him and sent it down into the waters. 'I'd prefer to dive in and see for myself, but given the weather, this will have to do.' He laughed at the look of disbelief she shot him. Dive in indeed.

'Do you dive often?' Perhaps Owen Gann had a crazy side, after all.

'Only when the weather permits. We dive in the summer, those of us who swim. Mostly for fun.' *For fun.* It was difficult to think of him doing anything for fun, yet it was all too easy to let images came to mind of Owen Gann stripped to the skin, his chest bare in the sun—did they get sun in England? She hadn't seen much evidence of it, but in her imaginings the scene was all sunlight and muscle, the muscles that had lifted her into the boat, muscles that rowed against the waves, and hefted the oyster cage into the depths. 'Nothing like the pearl divers off the shores of Arabia.' He laughed and his eyes lit. Another insight and interesting juxtaposition—the oysterman was also a connoisseur of the world. One did not usually equate a worldly education with a simple oysterman, but Owen Gann was proving to be far more.

'Do you find pearls in your oysters?' Josefina wanted to know. He was interesting today and her questions flowed easily as a result. His guard was down. Did he realise?

'Ah, not often. But I have found some, enough over the years to make a decent string. Actually, it's a string started by my great-grandfather, the first Gann oysterman. They're not all matched, of course, it's not like a fancy string you might see in a jeweller's shop.' Suddenly, Josefina wanted nothing more than to see Owen Gann's pearl string. He was being far too modest, far too dismissive of it. Yesterday, when he'd been dismissive, he'd been protecting himself, she saw that now.

She had no idea from what, though. Now he was protecting his string of pearls. Why?

'What do we do now?' Josefina gripped the sides of the boat as a wave rocked them. This was far rougher water than the narrow canals of Venice.

'Now we wait.' Owen smiled in assurance. She was only partially reassured. Perhaps this was nothing for an oysterman who spent his life on the water. To such a man the waters were calm enough today. But to someone who hadn't lived on the water, the wide, grey depths so far from shore were daunting. Still, he wouldn't have brought her out if he'd been worried about the weather.

'Are these your oyster fields or are they open to whoever wants to fish them?' Talking kept her mind off all the dangers that could befall them out here.

'My factory doesn't own the beds, if that's what you're asking. But we are in the Gann bed. An oysterman has his own bed to harvest. His son can take on rights to fish the bed at sixteen. That means he can harvest and sell the oysters.'

'Is that when you started?' She could see him, sixteen, towheaded and gangly, come into his full height but not his full breadth, perhaps more carefree than he was now.

'Yes, on my sixteenth birthday I stood before the oyster guild and claimed my rights to harvest from the Gann bed.'

'It must have been a proud day,' Josefina coaxed, expecting his face to shine perhaps with the memory, a mile marker on the way to manhood, and she wanted to hear more of this story of a younger Owen Gann. But his face remained stern as he momentarily flicked his gaze in her direction before returning to the task of levering the oyster cage from the water.

'It was a necessary one.' The brief words effectively ended that avenue of conversation. More dismissal. More protection. There was something here, something that she'd missed. It was too late to go back for it now. She would make a note to try again later.

Gann set the oyster cage between them and studied its contents, relief spreading across his face. 'Look, everything is fine. The only thing the cage brought up were oysters, as it should. If the reef was breaking, there would be pieces of old, broken shell here, having come loose from whatever they'd attached themselves to.' His excitement grew with his relief. 'Oyster reefs protect the mainland, but also provide a place for other sea life to live.' His blue eyes sparked. 'They're quite beneficial for more than just oyster harvesting.' He broke off with a laugh. 'Have I succeeded in boring you again, *signorina*?'

Hardly. Not today. This man was a revelation. 'I like you this way,' Josefina said honestly. 'Much better than the man yesterday.' This man might even have bordered on fascinating. Not because oysters were fascinating, but because a man explaining his passion, the thing that gave his life purpose, *was* interesting. That man had layers she wanted to peel away, to see the man within, and his secrets, the things he was trying to protect, to hide.

'Watch this.' Gann pulled a small knife from a pocket and selected an oyster from the cage. In two lightning flicks of his blade, the oyster shell lay open in his palm.

'How did you do that?' Josefina's eyes were riveted on his hands. 'Do it again?' He took another oyster and repeated the process. 'Amazing, you're so fast. Slow it down. I want to learn how you do it.' She leaned closer in her curiosity.

'*I'll hardly know you're here.* I think those were your exact words.' He wasn't upset, though. 'You've been full of questions since we set out.' Gann chuckled, but he relented and showed her again. 'You take this little knife and insert it at the back hinge, until you've made a slit and then…' he paused and gave her a serious look '…this is critical, you have to turn your hand so that the blade lifts the shell, like this. Then, you wiggle the flat blade back and forth until you've opened the shell entirely and separated the oyster muscle from the top of the shell.' He presented the oyster to her. 'There you go, that's how it's done. You might come back with the knife for one more pass underneath to sever the oyster from the bottom shell, just so. Now it's ready.'

Josefina met Gann's gaze. 'Ready for what?'

'For eating. Have you not eaten live, raw oysters? Some circles consider them quite the delicacy.' He was daring her again. He'd dared her to get in the boat and now he was daring her to eat this…thing…*raw*. It was the price for his stories, she realised. He'd given her a glimpse into his past today and now she must pay for it. So be it. How bad could it be if people considered it a delicacy? After all, the French ate snails. This could hardly be worse.

She straightened her shoulders, meeting the challenge. 'How do you eat it?'

'Slurp it off the wide end. Chew it perhaps once or twice and then swallow.' He shucked an oyster for himself and held up the shell to demonstrate, slurping down the oyster, liquid and all with enviable ease. 'Your turn.'

She would not be outdone by him. Josefina held his gaze steady and tipped up the shell. She chewed once, the briny taste of it filling her mouth, and she swallowed fast before she could think too much about what she was doing.

Gann clapped his hands. 'Bravo, *signorina*. Well done. So, what do you think of our local gold?'

Josefina wiped her mouth with the back of her hand. 'I think they are an acquired taste.'

Gann laughed. 'All the best delicacies are. Escargot, caviar.'

Josefina smiled. 'Perhaps I will get used to it, then. Do you harvest oysters all year?'

'You can. I'm not sure it's the best idea if there's concern over sustaining the beds.' Owen furrowed his brow. 'Beds can be over-harvested just like land can be overworked. Oysters need time to breed, which they do usually from May to September. There's an old saying that oysters should be eaten only in months with an 'r' in their names, which indicates harvesting between September and April. Sometimes the weather forces us to take January off. It did last year and this year we are being cautious.'

He made a gesture to the waves. 'As you might guess, harvesting in winter out here can be dangerous. While we *can* harvest in the winter, it's often difficult and I do limit it for that reason. I've been experimenting with borrowing some agricultural techniques like fallow fields. We don't harvest during the reproductive season. We harvest October through December out there, then modestly harvest through the winter and make a final push through March and April. It's not what everyone does, but it's what I'm doing for the sake of the oyster crop, the health of our waters and the safety of our workers.' He grinned. 'Have I bored you yet? I failed to bore you earlier, so I felt compelled to try again.'

'A businessman with a conscience, I like that.' Josefina smiled.

He reached for the oars. 'Time to go back and report the good news.'

Chapter Six

On shore, oystermen milled about the beach, waiting for word. At the sight of Owen's rowboat, a few waded into the water to pull it in. Padraig O'Malley swung her up into his arms and carried her to shore while Gann strode through the water among the men. 'If you're looking for adventure, dear girl, he's not the man to give it to you.' Padraig set her down on the pebbly shingle that passed for a beach. 'We've got another drop coming in a week or so,' he murmured. 'I can use you if you're up for it.' He gave her a wink, his hand surreptitiously on her bottom.

'I'm up for it,' she whispered, pointedly removing his hand. 'The smuggling, that is.'

Padraig stepped away good-naturedly, a wide, teasing smile on his face as he moved towards the men to hear Gann's news. 'Let me know when you're up for a bit more—you wouldn't be sorry.'

No, probably not sorry. Padraig O'Malley seemed very capable of showing a certain kind of girl a good time, being big and broad, as big as Owen Gann. But she wasn't sure she was that girl. She'd had lovers like O'Malley before, men who were interested in the pursuit, in a one-night encounter. Those interludes had their purpose. She'd indulged once or twice since leaving home to keep loneliness and grief at bay. But for a woman, such indulgences too often were too risky to become habit. The last thing she needed was an unwanted child or disease now that she was alone in the world with no one to fall back on should she suffer a setback. Padraig O'Malley would soon give up on her and find easier conquests.

Josefina smoothed her skirts and lingered on the fringes of the little gathering, trying to keep her word not to be in the way. Gann would not like her interfering now and calling attention to her presence. But he could not escape drawing her attention. The men gathered about him, interested in every word although his report was short.

They looked to him not just for jobs, she realised, but for leadership, even though such a role put him beyond them. He'd been one of them, once. He understood the oystering life far better than a man who ran his factory from afar. This was yet another image to add to her collection today: the oysterman at the oars, the shucker with deft hands even on a bobbing sea, the young man standing before the guild, now the grown man standing before men who might have been his peers if things had been different. Today, he stood before them not as a peer, but as their leader—an inadequate word, Josefina thought. The men respected him, but he was in some way removed from them. Even in his workman's clothes, he moved in an echelon above mere leader. Yet, their hope was in him, that was plain to see. Owen Gann carried the weight of the community on his shoulders. So went the harvest, so went the community. Only he stood between them and desolation.

After a while, it began to rain, the grey clouds no longer willing to hold off. The men dispersed, back to their huts, back to the Crown. There would be no oystering today, but they'd go out tomorrow. Gann strode back to her side after the last man left. 'I'd offer to see you home to the art school, but with the rain coming down hard, perhaps it would be best to return to my home, which is decidedly closer, and wait for a break in the weather. We can continue our conversation and perhaps have something to eat.'

She'd like that, she realised. The day had passed, the light starting to fade with the coming storm. She wasn't ready to let him go. There were more stories to hear and today he was in the mood to tell them. She wondered if that would change once they returned to the house that was his, but not his, and once he changed out of his workman's clothes. Would the informality that had marked their day disappear amid the formality of his home?

There was one place in Baldock House where informality still reigned. The kitchen. After refreshing herself, Josefina found him there, shirtsleeves rolled up, large competent hands slicing a thick loaf of bread at the long worktable. Something delicious simmered on the stove, filling the room with a fragrant, welcoming warmth. Kitchens were the heart of a home and she thought, seeing him here at work, that this kitchen might be at the heart of Owen Gann in a way the rest of his house wasn't. The warmth here wasn't entirely due to the natural kitchen ambience: worktable, hearth, stove, overhead rack with dangling pots for easy access. How odd to find *any* man comfortable in his kitchen, let alone a man like Gann, who had money to spare for the best of cooks.

Josefina gave an appreciative sniff and let the door swing shut behind her. 'You've been busy.' While she'd been upstairs in a guest room tidying herself and changing out of her damp clothes, Gann had changed quickly and seen to their supper.

He looked up from his bread slicing. 'Cook's day off. She has a sister in Whitstable with a new baby.' His gaze lingered on her longer than usual before he spoke. 'I see you found something to wear.'

Josefina gave a laugh and twirled in her borrowed plum skirts. She liked that reaction, catching him off guard, invoking a response from a man who was so cool, so in control of himself. 'Will it do?' The wardrobe upstairs in the guest chamber had been full of ladies' dresses. The plum gown had fit almost perfectly. She'd also managed to find a hairbrush and a few accessories, too, to tackle her wavy curls made even more so by the rain, and a plum hair ribbon to hold them back.

Gann looked up again from the bread. 'You'll do.' As would he. She rather liked, objectively of course, this version of Owen Gann who wasn't dressed either as a worker or a gentleman, but somewhere in between. Just a man. In a kitchen. An odd juxtaposition, to be sure, and an intoxicating one in its own right. How many women did she know who wouldn't mind having a blond Viking of a man toasting their evening bread? Perhaps she ought to paint him like this. But she discarded the notion as quickly as she formed it. She doubted an upper-crust audience would be attuned to the nuanced messages of such a painting.

Josefina pulled a stool up to the worktable and leaned in on her elbows, teasing him just a bit with a smile. What would he do if she flirted with him? Would it soften him up? Would he laugh with her as he had out in the boat now that his duty and responsibilities for the day were discharged? What might she learn if he let his guard down again for a few more precious moments? 'If you don't like the plum, there's a forest-green gown upstairs I could change into.'

Gann stopped slicing and set down his knife. 'The plum is fine,' he said decisively, almost sternly. 'Are you fishing for compliments?'

'Not compliments. I *am* fishing for answers.' She cocked her head to one side and met his gaze with a coy smile. 'It does make a girl wonder as to why an unmarried gentleman has a closet full of clothes at the ready for a female guest.' She'd speculated on the answer upstairs, of course, after seeing the wardrobe full and functioning. She might even have dallied over selecting a gown. It had been a long time since she'd had clothes to fuss over or choose from. She had precisely three outfits, all of them for work and travel. There'd been triple that many upstairs. 'Do you entertain women in damp clothes often?' Or perhaps he just entertained one woman. The gowns had all been of a size. She liked the plum gown less at the thought it might belong to his mistress. She ought not to care who the gowns belonged to. Gann was allowed his affairs.

Gann reached for a tray and loaded it with the sliced bread for toasting. He deftly slid it into the oven before answering her question. 'I see your sordid little imagination at work, *signorina*.' He gave her one of his wry smiles, the one that said her imaginings were unworthy of her and of him. 'I fear your curiosity will be disappointed. The dresses came with the house. They belonged to one of Baldock's female relations.' He turned to the stove and puttered with the pot, stirring and tasting and stirring some more. Her first impression hadn't been wrong. He was definitely at home in this space.

'You really meant it, then. You did buy this place lock, stock and barrel,' Josefina mused, watching his rather adroit moves. He bent to the oven to check the toast, his buckskins pulling taut across the muscled expanse of his buttocks as he squatted. Gann had an exquisite backside, a discovery previously obscured by his coats. But dressed in only a shirt and buckskins, *very tight buckskins*, there was nothing to keep her eyes from roaming over that particular feature now.

'I did.' He shut the oven, satisfied with the toast's progress, and turned around. 'Fancy that. Did you think I would lie?'

'Most men do.' Signor Bartolli had been willing to promise her the moon in order to win her hand, but she'd learned soon enough he didn't intend to keep those promises.

'I don't.' Gann fixed her with a hard blue stare for a long moment before returning to the mystery pot. She'd offended him.

She believed him, despite what she knew to be a contrary truth in the world—men lied to get what they wanted. A tense silence stretched thin between them. 'What's in the pot?'

The tension eased. Gann grinned, this one a full genuine smile instead of a wry scold as he announced, 'Oyster stew, made fresh from our catch today.' She gave him a dubious look and he laughed. 'Have faith, *signorina*. Oyster stew is far better than raw oysters. It's creamy, warm and filling. More of a soup than a stew, really.'

'You sound like an expert on oyster stew.' In truth, he sounded like a mystery. For every single thing she'd learned about him today, more questions had abounded. Beneath his stuffy exterior, Owen Gann was a riddle of interesting proportions. He *was* stuffy, but he was also proving to be more than that.

'I was raised on it. If it can be done with an oyster, I can do it.' He began laying out dinner things: two sturdy bowls, plates, utensils, a crock of butter, a plate of unshucked oysters, a bottle of cold white wine and two plain goblets. Rustic and domestic. Gann ladled the creamy stew into the bowls and a sense of comfort settled over the kitchen that she hadn't known since she left home.

'Can you teach me to shuck oysters?' She picked one up from the plate and tossed it in her hand. She reached for the shucking knife and awkwardly tried to simulate his movements from the boat.

'No, wait, you have to be careful!' Owen came around to her side of the worktable, swift with concern. 'Wrap your other hand with a towel or you're likely to slice it open.' He was all grim efficiency as he came up behind her and brought his hands over hers, directing her grip. She felt her pulse give a little kick at the nearness and intimacy of their bodies. He smelled of kitchen and clean male. What would he do if she wiggled backwards just a bit? Perhaps she ought not find out when there was a knife involved. But the intrigue remained. Her attempts at flirting earlier had been rebuffed with sternness. For a moment the old Owen Gann had returned. Was he afraid of flirting? Of her? Was it himself he was trying to protect?

'Wedge it under the hinge like so.' His hands directed hers, his strong fingers expertly prising the shell gently apart and working the blade along its length. The shell opened. 'There, we did it.' He set aside the knife and held out his hand. 'Always use a towel. Look, I learned the hard way.' He held up his pinkie where a thin white line ran down the centre.

'Ouch, it looks like that hurt.' Josefina grimaced.

'It did. I didn't listen to my father and nearly sliced myself down to the bone.' Owen stepped away and returned to his side of the worktable. If the closeness of the interaction affected him, he covered it well doing little tasks. He filled the wine glasses and slid the toasted bread and cheese on to their plates. He nodded towards the door. 'Shall we go through to the dining room with our feast?'

'No, let's stay here.' She didn't want to exchange the cosiness of the kitchen for the cold formality of the dining room. She wasn't ready to give up the comfort she felt here and she wasn't ready to give up him. If they went to the dining room, this version of Owen Gann might be replaced by the cold boor she'd encountered yesterday.

Gann nodded, approving of the choice. 'In that case, we'll need this.' He reached for a lamp and brought it to the worktable, setting it in the centre and turning up the wick. 'There, candlelight.' The flame lent another type of ambience to the space, making the kitchen into an intimate space where two people might partake of meal together and more, where secrets might be exchanged.

'Were you raised to cook, as well?' Josefina enquired taking a first, tentative sip of her soup.

'I learned to cook out of necessity.' She recognised that line from earlier. He'd used those words before. 'An oysterman can't stand on ceremony. He has to be able to provide for himself in all ways. A man should be able to cook and sew for himself at least enough to get by. He never knows when he might need the skills.'

'A stew and stitches?' Josefina laughed softly in the candlelit darkness.

'Exactly. Try this…' Gann reached for a small bottle and dribbled a few drops of brown liquid into her stew '…it's sherry.'

'Oh, that's delicious.' Josefina savoured the swallow and took another spoonful, eating in earnest now that she'd decided she *liked* oyster stew. She studied Gann as he applied himself to his own bowl, taking hearty spoonsful and eating with the well-mannered gusto of a man who appreciated a hot meal. She tried to reconcile all she knew of him and failed. 'I admit to having trouble imagining you as a stew-and-stitches man, cooking on a hob over a fire in a fisher's hut.' They'd passed the huts today on the beach, draughty, mean hovels, the most rudimentary of shelters.

'Yet those were my humble beginnings.' Gann's gaze was serious in the candlelight, the flame turning his blue gaze a dark sapphire.

Josefina reached for the wine and refilled their glasses. This was the moment to push forward, to ask about those humble beginnings. What else could she add to the puzzle of Owen Gann, not just for the painting, but for herself? She was aware, sitting here in the lamplit kitchen, that something had subtly shifted for her today. She'd become interested in him, not solely for the extrinsic reward of the painting, but for the intrinsic reward of simply knowing who he was. 'Tell me about those beginnings.'

Gann shook his head as if he were clearing cobwebs. 'Not tonight. You shan't have all my secrets out of me at once. Besides, I don't have company for dinner often. I'd hate to ruin a good meal and good wine with a sad story.' Ah, so he'd noticed her efforts. She'd not been as deft with the wine as she'd hoped or with her questions.

Perhaps he was right, though. The meal was going well and it was indeed a delight to eat with someone. Of course she ate with sixteen someones every night in the great hall at the school, but it wasn't like this. The great hall was noisy, filled with the chatter of sixteen young girls all talking at once. Gann's kitchen was quiet, warm, intimate and it reminded her of home. 'My father and I would eat like this in our kitchen of an evening when his work was done.' Josefina helped herself to another slice of bread and dipped it in her bowl. 'Hearty food and a chance to talk over the day, just the two of us.' How she'd looked forward to that precious hour. No apprentices from her father's workshop running in with messages, no imperious orders from a patron over timelines and expenses. Her throat tightened at the unexpected memory.

'Your father?' Gann asked the question quietly, a thousand other questions underlying it. How did a father allow a daughter to wander the world at will? What caused an Italian girl to make her way to England on her own?

'My father passed away last year.' It was difficult to speak through the tightness in her throat. She'd given up thinking it would ever get easier.

Gann gave a slow nod of understanding. 'I *am* sorry.'

'I am, too.' Josefina took a swallow of wine, letting the coldness ease her throat. She'd lost everything when she lost her father: her family, her home, her position in society and in the community. Even her name, although that had been—to borrow Gann's word—of necessity. Who was she if she wasn't Felipe Zanetti's daughter? She wasn't sure she knew yet. But she couldn't be Josefina Zanetti and roam Europe unheeded. Josefina Zanetti could be found by the likes of Signor Bartolli. She *had* to be someone else and so Josefina Ricci was born. Ricci had been her mother's name and a common name in Italy, unexceptional and unlikely to draw interest.

Gann was studying her intently, his gaze prying into her with methodical certainty like the shucking knife had prised into the oyster. It was a reminder to be careful. The less people knew of her, the more secure her dreams were. How was she to see the world and fulfil her promise to her father, if people knew who she was and where she was? There were those who would think she was better off at home. They would look for her if they knew where to start. She'd confounded them so far. Josefina Zanetti had disappeared the day of her father's funeral. She didn't need Gann or Artemisia getting too curious about her antecedents. 'I don't mean to be intrusive, but why did you leave? Was there no way to stay?'

She met his gaze evenly. 'Not any way that was acceptable to me.' His thoughtful stare was discomfiting. She was used to men being more interested in her face than in who she was. She'd expected the same from Owen Gann when she'd twirled into the room in her plum skirts. Men told pretty girls their secrets all the time and far too easily. But here in this kitchen, he had turned the tables on her. It was she telling him her secrets. It was time to get back to business.

She rose and half leaned over the worktable, letting the flame pick out the mischief in her eye, mischief not even a man like Owen Gann would miss. 'I hear you have an interesting widow's walk, Mr Gann.' She snatched up the wine bottle. 'Perhaps you'd like to show me or will I have to find my way on my own?' Gann wouldn't refuse. He wouldn't want her wandering around his house unescorted, despite the fact that she'd been alone upstairs for quite some time when she'd changed.

'Are you sure you want to see it in the dark?' Gann prevaricated. Ah, he was protecting himself again. He wasn't sure going upstairs with her was in his best interest. Perhaps he wasn't as immune to her flirting as she'd thought. Frankly, neither was she.

'Yes, most definitely.' She came around the table and hooked her arm through his before he could come up with other arguments. 'Lead on, sir.' When he wasn't being a boor, Owen Gann was an attractive man. The widow's walk was turning into a compelling proposition for reasons that had little to do with her painting.

Chapter Seven

The view from the top was breathtaking and cold. One could see across the water to the Isle of Sheppey. The steeple of St Alphege's gleamed white in the distance against the dark sky. The clouds had blown away after the rain and a few stars peeked out. Josefina raised an arm. 'The stars are so close, it's like I can almost pick them. I like that here, I can see the stars. You can't see stars in London.' One could see stars and Sheppey, and something else far more interesting. 'That's Shucker's Cove.' The hidden cove wasn't so hidden from above. A gust of wind blew across the widow's walk and she shivered, the plum wool of her gown no match for a late January wind off the water.

'Shall we go in?' Gann enquired, noting her shiver.

'Please, no, I'm fine.' She wasn't ready to go in yet. The idea that he could see Shucker's Cove from here was interesting. She needed to think of a different word. She'd overused it today with regard to Gann.

He moved away from her momentarily to a trunk

set in the corner of the walk and returned with a blanket. He shook it out and wrapped it about her. 'You'll need this if we're to stay up here.'

'You can see the smugglers from here.' She was thinking out loud now. 'You watched us from the widow's walk last time.' That's how he'd known to meet her on the road. 'Do you always watch the smugglers?' But she answered her own question. 'Of course you do. The house is perfectly situated.' She gave a pleased laugh. 'Baldock made his fortune smuggling, didn't he?' She could see it now, how a smuggler could protect his investment from here. One could see Shucker's Cove *and* the surrounding area. From here, one could see the approaching Coast Guard from the water or riding officers approaching from land.

'You're very astute, *signorina*.' Gann made her a little bow.

But that wasn't all. 'I know why Baldock would have found this useful, but why do you? Why do you watch the smugglers? You're not one of them.' Another gust swept over them and she pulled the blanket tighter. It was cold and late. She'd have to go soon before Artemisia worried, but not before she solved this particular mystery.

'No, not any more.' He leaned on the railing, looking out into the distance. 'I used to be, though.' He shot her a glance, perhaps measuring how she took the news.

'You? A smuggler?' She smiled, wanting to coax the story from him. He turned away, his gaze looking out over the cove.

'When I was about fifteen, my mother needed medicines we couldn't afford on an oysterman's salary. I wasn't old enough to work the beds. But I could work with the smugglers.'

Josefina processed that information in silence for a long while. There was so much there—his warning to her about smuggling, a further glimpse into the tales he'd told her today and a glimpse into those humble beginnings he'd refused to tell her about. And a glimpse into tragedy. 'Was it enough? Did the medicines save her?' Fifteen-year-old Owen had loved his mother enough to risk his own neck.

Owen shook his head. 'Not in the end. Perhaps the medicines bought her a little more time with us. I'll never really know, though.' She heard the hurt in his voice. He'd risked everything for no guarantees. Perhaps that was why he was so reserved, so calculated now about what risks he took, what he revealed. 'I stopped smuggling then, after she died. I'm not one of them any more, but they are my men, my fishers. Who will harvest the oysters that feed my business empire if they're in prison? Who will care for their families if they are taken?'

He was retreating, she heard it in his words. He made his support of the smugglers sound more practical than he meant it, but she wasn't fooled. Owen Gann was an honourable man. His next words proved it. 'I pay a decent wage, but they need smuggling to make ends meet in the off-season. It's a way of life here. Everyone is part of it even if they're *not* a part of it, do you understand? That doesn't make it less dangerous, though.' He gave a stern lift of his eyebrow. '*You* do not have to be part of it. There's no reason for you to take unnecessary risks.'

'Yet *you* continue to align yourself with them.' Josefina gave a defiant toss of her head, challenging him and the wind. She did not like being told what to do, especially by a man who had taken the risks he was advising her against.

'I can afford to. I dare say you cannot.'

'Do they know you watch them?'

'No, but now that you've figured it out, I'd prefer you not say anything to them. It's better that way.' Owen Gann, the silent protector, watching over his people from a distance, just as he'd watched over them today, rowing out to the oyster beds to assure them their harvest was intact.

'I'll keep your secret,' she whispered softly beneath the wind. The concept of a chieftain had died out centuries ago in these parts, but in Owen Gann, she sensed the role was alive and well. If Seasalter had a chieftain, it would be him. She'd not expected to find this discovery beneath the stuffy exterior of her subject when she'd set out this morning. What else might she unveil if she pushed hard enough? Temptation rose with the wind.

'You're a good man, Owen Gann.' Good men were rarities and inspired a certain intoxication all their own. The wine and the late hour moved her to a recklessness she struggled to keep leashed. Late hours were dangerous. The night interposed a false sense of intimacy that lured one towards impulsive gestures often regretted by morning. And yet, what was life without a little temptation? 'Thank you for a lovely evening, the nicest I've had in a long while.'

Josefina stretched up on her tiptoes to reach him and gave in to impulse. She kissed him, once on each cheek, the stubble of his beard brushing her skin with its roughness, the smell of him—sweet sherry and sharp wine—in her nose. It was tempting to kiss his lips, to drink in all of him. She held it in check and stepped back.

'Why did you do that?' His hand went absently to his right cheek, unsure what to make of it.

'It's how Italians say goodnight.' She smiled. The kiss was ambiguous to Englishmen. The French had *la bise*, but the cold, reserved English had nothing like it. She would let him read into it however he liked as she made her exit.

What should he make of it? Everything? Nothing? Was it just flirting? Was it something more or was that just his heated imagination? The power of the moment? Owen played the brief scene back in his mind over and over as he sat before the fire in his chamber, remembrance dancing in the flames.

She'd moved against him without warning, her arms about his neck, her mouth brushing his cheek, once, twice. The rosewater on her skin had been a borrowed scent, perhaps from the guest chamber, not her own.

Her own scent was something wilder, like the woman herself.

For a moment he had contemplated the outrageous, taking the kiss from her, capturing her mouth with his. There had been a slight hesitation in her movements, as if the thought had occurred to her as well, and then it had been gone. She'd stepped back and the evening had been over.

The episode had lasted seconds, but his mind slowed it down, dissected it, savoured it like the tender morsel it was. Good lord, what was the matter with him? He was acting like a moony village boy, building a fantasy out of a simple gesture and a few words. *This is how Italians say goodnight.* A bold gesture and bold words. Englishwomen didn't kiss men of their acquaintance goodnight. Neither did they tramp through mud and row out to oyster beds alone with a gentleman they barely knew. Or slurp raw oysters on the half-shell in a rowboat. His mind flooded with images of the day, of her, each scene imprinted in vivid detail.

He'd *enjoyed* today. It was quite an admission given the strategy he'd devised last night to avoid her and beginning the day trying to leave her behind. Neither stratagem had lasted long. He could not recall the last time he'd enjoyed an ordinary work day or an ordinary meal; his own company had paled ages ago. Then she'd kissed him. Sweet Heavens, he was back to that again. His mind seemed to have it on a perpetual loop.

Somewhere in the depths of Baldock House, the hall clock struck midnight. He'd best get to bed. Tomorrow was another work day at the factory and here at home. Downstairs there was a pile of paperwork waiting for him to complete the purchase of a fleet of ships that would take his oysters throughout Europe. No longer would he have to pay exorbitant shipping fees or rely on others' schedules. It had taken three years to arrange the financing, to arrange the deal that would complete his vertical empire.

Owen waited for the joy of acquisition, the glee of accomplishment, to fill him. No glee, no joy came. There was only a sense of relief, a very different feeling than joy and a slightly emptier one. Perhaps that was the price one paid to keep those he cared about safe.

It doesn't have to be. The little voice spoke in his head. *You're lonely. Why not do something about it?*

Perhaps there could be joy of a short-term nature with Josefina Ricci. She'd expect nothing but comfort. He could offer that. She'd made no secret she was leaving in May. By May, he'd be in London, doing business, shipping oysters, making deals. He wouldn't have time for comfort or anything else then. What had been a detriment last night was suddenly an advantage.

Shame on him! Was he really so lonely he was thinking of propositioning a woman who might feel obliged to him because of her work? All because she'd kissed his cheek? It was midnight foolishness at best. She might be the sort of beauty a man dreamed about, but she wasn't for him. He'd been through this last night with himself, as well. What would he do with all that wildness, all that passion even if he dared to claim it?

That was for the Padraig O'Malleys of the world, not the Owen Ganns. *But once she might have been.* Once, he'd burned with that same passion, that same drive to drink fully from life's cup. Responsibility had made that a rather short-lived period. He rose and made ready for bed, determined to put her out of mind.

Padraig O'Malley's expression bordered on fiercely determined as he faced the group assembled in the Crown's parlour. Private business required a private space, it seemed. His eyes lingered on her a little longer than necessary. Josefina smiled back out of a need to lend him support. The big Irishman appeared to need it tonight. He seemed agitated as he brought the meeting to order. It made her sit up a little taller, take sharper notice of his words. Or was that because of Owen Gann?

These are risks you don't need to take.

Gann would be furious if he knew she was here. No, not furious. She didn't think Owen Gann was ever furious. He was calmness itself. He did not deal in extremes and intensities. Then again, his world was well ordered. Except for that moment two nights ago when she'd kissed him. There'd been disorder then, the potential for passion in the moment. She'd seen that potential flare in his eyes. An instant only.

'We have news from our source.' The words dragged Josefina back to the meeting. 'He says the coast from Seasalter to Whitstable is being watched more heavily after the last drop. The Frenchies weren't as careful as they should have been. Their ship was spotted. It eluded the Coast Guard, but it's alerted them all the same. This is a problem with regard to the next shipment.' A large order of brandy that the gang was counting on for a big sale in London. Usually, Josefina learned, those large shipments made berth at Shoreham because of its close proximity to London, but Shoreham was being heavily watched. When plans had been laid, the obscurity of Seasalter had seemed a good substitute.

'With such a large order, we'll need a different place to store the tubs while we cut the brandy and get it ready to transport. We can't use the cave. It will be the first place anyone looks.' Padraig faced the group squarely, hands on hips. 'That means we'll need to have the Frenchies put in several miles up the coast.'

There were grumbles. Miles up coast meant a journey, time away from home and more risk of discovery. It would look odd for a large part of a small village to suddenly be absent. 'If we don't risk ourselves, we risk the shipment,' Padraig argued with the dissension in the room. 'There's no place here large enough.' He was gruff and, for a moment, Josefina thought he and one of the men might come to blows. Then Padraig softened. 'Perhaps if it's too risky all around, we should bow out. There's still time to reach the French.'

The loss of anticipated income silenced the group. Josefina's gaze flitted from man to man, each one processing what the loss of the delivery would mean to them, to their families: shoes that wouldn't be bought for growing children, clothes, medicines. That money wouldn't be spent on luxuries, but on necessities. They had to take the shipment. If Gann knew of the dilemma, he'd want to help, she reasoned. But these men would never ask for that help so it had to be offered in a way that served Owen's desire for secrecy about his midnight vigils and serve Padraig's pride, too. The words were out of her mouth before she thought better of them. 'What about Baldock House? The cellar was used for storing smuggled brandy before.'

'It hasn't been Baldock's house for years now. Gann isn't a smuggler. I don't think he'd approve.' Padraig gave her a smile that bordered on patronising, it said he didn't expect her to understand the nuances of their community, let alone their history. It was a reminder that she was an outsider. 'I appreciate the idea, though, Fina.'

Josefina rose, not willing to be dismissed. 'Wait, here me out, Padraig.' The men around her murmured. Someone stifled a guffaw. Stupid men, assuming she had feathers for brains. 'Gann doesn't need to know.' His ignorance would keep them all safe. 'The night of the drop is the Oyster Ball. He'll be out of the house and he's not bound to wander down there until you can move the barrels. He doesn't use the cellar. Gann keeps his wines in a different place. No one will even know the barrels are down there. They can stay as long as we need them to. Then we can arrange to distil and move the brandy while he's out on another night.' The more she thought about it, the more sense it made. It kept the drop local and didn't require the men to travel a long distance to meet the ship. 'The cellar door is unlocked and can be accessed from outside the home.' Even better. There was no need to steal a key or to arrange to have the door propped open.

Padraig's gaze had become thoughtful. 'It could work,' he said slowly, starting to think out loud. 'A lot will ride on you, Fina. You need to guarantee he'll be out when we need him to be out. Can you do that? You have time, the drop isn't for another two weeks.'

'He'll be too busy dancing.' She laughed, a bit of warmth flooding her at the acceptance. Men who'd laughed at her earlier were nodding now. Never mind they were taking their cue from Padraig. It felt good to feel like she belonged, no longer just the pretty outsider.

Charlie remained sceptical. 'What about getting it out? We can distil the brandy during the day once it's stored without being seen, but we can't haul it out in daylight or even by moonlight if he's home.'

'I could arrange to have Gann come dine with Lady St Helier and the Viscount,' Josefina spoke up. It was a bold offer, but surely it wouldn't be that hard to arrange, followed by an evening of cards? 'You would have to move quickly, though.' Cards would only last so long and Artemisia and Darius tended to retire early on account of their infant son.

'Fair enough.' Padraig looked pleased with her response and Charlie looked appeased. Padraig gave her a wink. 'We'll count on our lovely Josefina to keep Gann too busy to notice us coming or going. He'll return home none the wiser.'

Which was all to the good, Josefina thought. The less Gann knew, the more help he could be if anything went wrong. He'd be entirely innocent of the whole operation should anyone question him. And he'd approve if he knew. He'd said as much, hadn't he? He felt it was his job to watch over the people of Seasalter, to care for them. He understood how important the smuggling money was to them. If he could have offered, he would have.

'Now that's settled—' Padraig beamed at the crew '—let's drink, first to our success, then we'll find something else to drink to.' He threw an arm about her as a cheer went up at the notion of an impromptu party. 'Well done, Fina. I knew you'd bring us good luck the moment I saw you.'

He pulled out his flask and offered it to her. Gann would hate that, too. She took a defiant swallow as a fiddle tuned up in the common room. It was going to be a loud, raucous night. There'd be drinking and dancing and she was determined to enjoy herself, determined not to think of a quieter evening spent with a quieter sort of man, who, probably, right now, was tucked up behind his big desk, writing in his ledgers while the clock ticked somnolently in the hall, punctuating the stillness of the house. Why ever would she want to be there, when she could be here? And yet, when Padraig grabbed her about the waist and twirled her into a country dance, she couldn't shake the notion this felt wrong. This wasn't where she wanted to be.

Chapter Eight

The sketches weren't right. Josefina stepped back from the drafting table, hoping distance might bring a different perspective and reassurance that she'd only imagined the imperfections. It didn't help. Taken separately, parts of the sketches were right. His hands were right: big, capable hands, roughened by weather and work, devoid of a gentleman's ornamentation—no rings even though he could afford them. But his eyes were wrong. The setting around him was wrong.

She'd drawn him at his desk, beside his desk, the long elegant turquoise curtains in the background, in the chair in the drawing room, but they were just places. They didn't offer any useful insight into him. A setting ought to do that. It ought to tell the subject's story. The person in these backdrops could be any rich man. The Academy would find the work generic and unworthy of a prize. She had to do better. Perhaps she needed some more inspiration. Perhaps she needed to study her subject in his natural habitat again since the unnatural habitat had failed to do him justice. Or perhaps she just needed a walk, some air to clear her head.

Josefina put the sketches away and grabbed her cloak from a peg in the work room and her ever-ready satchel and set out for the shore. She wouldn't dare think of calling on Gann unannounced. He wouldn't approve of such disorderly conduct as an unscheduled call. But maybe she didn't need to see him to be inspired. Perhaps it would be enough to walk in his footsteps.

The shore was busy despite the cold. Children played tag on the pebbly shingle, men worked on boats and nets. Women went about chores and child-watching, all out of doors. Where else were they to do the work of living? As she watched them, it occurred to Josefina there was no choice but to live outside. The huts could hardly be lived in around the clock. Even the few row cottages would be too small for a family of any size to enjoy the indoors for any long period of time. These homes sufficed for evening meals and shelters when the weather gave them no choice.

It occurred to her, too, that this was how Owen had grown up. He and his brother, Simon, had played as these children played: in ragged breeks and thin coats, with pebbles, sticks and shell shards washed ashore and fashioned into whatever their imaginations could conjure. He had lived like this, wild, free, poor, unlikely to rise above whatever his father had been. And yet he had. He had not only risen above his father's humble

station, he'd fashioned a life that was the complete an-
tithesis of the one he'd had. No more poverty, but also
no more freedom, no more wildness. What had he been
like? The wild boy, Owen Gann? It made her smile to
imagine the restrained, reclusive businessman as an
extroverted boy.

She stopped to chat with a few women, but the usually talkative women were taciturn and distracted today
as they gathered together. Their gazes drifted towards
the water edge and the group of men gathered there.
Two blond heads stood out among the crowd. Simon
and Owen. The Gann brothers. The other men, she did
not recognise. They were not Seasalter men. Their coats
were too fine, their boots too clean. And there were
soldiers among them. 'Who are they?' Josefina asked.
The sight of soldiers made her as uneasy as the women.

'Some fancy men from London, business partners of
Mr Gann's,' Charlie's wife whispered in awe. Another
whispered in disdain, 'And some redcoats.' The woman
spat on the ground. 'That Lieutenant Hawthorne is too
nosy for his own good and ours.'

'What are they doing here?' She could guess. Did
it have something to do with the highly anticipated
brandy run? Or perhaps it had to do with the prior run
and the French boat that had nearly been caught. Her
stomach tightened, Owen's warnings coming back to
her.

'The businessmen want assurances that Gann's reputation is clean before they close a big deal. The soldiers
are here to ensure Seasalter isn't a hotbed of smug-

gling,' Charlie's wife explained. The meeting down by the shore had broken up. Men paired up in groups and headed back to the Crown. There was a rustling among the women as they suddenly drifted apart and tried to look busy. Josefina felt exposed, left alone. She froze with a moment's indecision. Did she want Owen to see her or should she hurry back the way she'd come?

Too late. Owen and Simon strode towards her. 'Miss Ricci, what a pleasant surprise. Have you come to sketch the fishermen?' Simon was all cheerfulness next to his brother's more subdued demeanour.

Josefina laughed and gave a toss of her head. 'No, I've come for inspiration. How is your baby girl?'

'Inspiration enough for me. Elianora and I have decided to rent a shop space in London for the Season to sell her cakes.' Simon was in high spirits. 'You must excuse me, Elianora is expecting me at the bakery. Owen, I will see you tonight.'

Simon's departure left her alone with Owen for the first time since their supper together. 'Today's a big day, I hear.' It stung to think the whole village had known of this big day and the purpose for it and yet she hadn't. She'd spent an entire day with him, eaten a meal with him, and he hadn't mentioned it once.

'Yes, it is. I am closing a deal for a purchase of ships, a small shipping line, if you will.' Gann looked every inch the prosperous businessman today with his pristine cravat and expensively cut jacket peeping from beneath a dark blue, many-caped wool greatcoat with polished brass buttons that rivalled military perfection.

She felt dishevelled in her work skirts and warm but well-worn cloak beside his sartorial elegance. Not that he was looking at her. He seemed to be looking beyond her to a point over her shoulder. 'Did you find what you were looking for, *signorina*?' His gaze met hers only briefly before returning to the point over her shoulder. His demeanour was stiff. He was trying very hard to be aloof as if they were still in his drawing room, as if they hadn't shared a meal in his kitchen or experienced a fleeting moment of intimacy during a goodnight kiss on his widow's walk. Was that kiss still on his mind? She wasn't sure that any man had ever thought about her kisses days later.

'Yes. I was looking for you, actually. I was walking in your footsteps.' She looped her arm through his and continued her stroll. 'Tell me, which of these huts was yours?'

He didn't have time for this. He needed to be back at the house overseeing Pease, who was overseeing Cook, who was overseeing the dinner that would be on the table at seven o'clock sharp tonight after a half-hour of preprandial drinks in the drawing room. But here he was, strolling the shingle with Josefina Ricci as if he had all the time in the world. He wished he did. There was something about being in her company that made him forget his cares, as if nothing mattered but this moment and the next. It made her dangerous to him.

She'd taken his arm, but now it was he leading her through the warren of row cottages and huts that comprised the main part of what nominally passed as the village. They came to a stop next to a hut, as ordinary and as ramshackle as the rest. It was nothing special. It hadn't been then and it wasn't now. It was set back, apart from the rest. No one was home, not that he had any intention of knocking and asking to come in. It would put pressure on the family to want to entertain him with resources they couldn't spare and it would bring back memories he didn't want to engage with, not today. He didn't want to step into the one-room abode and see the bed where his mother had died still standing in one corner, or the hearth where he'd cooked so many inadequate meals and fallen asleep next to on so many nights, exhausted to the bone.

'Four generations of Ganns lived here,' Owen said. All the way back to his father's grandfather. Oystermen their entire lives. 'My mother died there.' He was aware of Josefina squeezing his hand, lending her compassion, but the rest of him was in the past, remembering, filling in the pieces. 'My father died two years later of hard work and a broken heart. I raised my brother in that hut after that. Working the oyster beds in season, working odd jobs out of season, cooking meals, keeping us fed.' Those had been hard, but inspiring, years. They'd been the catalyst for wanting to do more, for seeing the potential to do better.

'I am sorry to raise the dead.' Josefina's voice was quiet, her earlier teasing subdued. No doubt she was regretting it. She'd likely got more than she asked for, but once he'd started remembering, started talking, he had not been able to hold back. She made divulgence as irresistible in daylight as she had on the widow's walk the other night. Today he could not blame it on the wine or the hour.

'Who lives here now?' Josefina was studying him with her dark eyes.

'A family named Bexley with three children under the age of six, at least they were when they moved in, but that was years ago.' Before he'd bought Baldock House. He'd been renting a house a little way up the coast that had belonged to a squire who favoured London. Goodness, those children would be full grown now. The daughter would be old enough to marry, the little boy nearly old enough to claim his rights to fish the oyster beds. Three children grown to adulthood in that single room, like he and his brother.

They moved on, a thoughtful silence between them. 'Why don't you do something about it?' Josefina spoke quietly but there was a challenge in the question.

He didn't like the underlying assumption, that somehow he'd turned a blind eye to the situation. He stopped and faced her slowly, giving himself time to put his temper in check. 'Do you think I haven't tried? It's not as easy as you might believe. I can't just throw money at it. If I could just build them all houses, I would.' Goodness knew he'd tried just such a strategy several years back when he was new to the dynamics of money and pride. His money had come up hard against a stone wall.

'They say it's not fitting. How can oystermen live

like equals to foremen and managers?' New houses struck a dangerous blow to the social order that had sustained their little community for centuries. Everyone understood their place. Still, he didn't want Josefina to think he'd simply given up. He was made of sterner stuff than that and he wanted her to know it for reasons he couldn't quite fathom or didn't want to.

'I do what I can. If someone has an ill grandmother, I send medicine, if a family is bad off, I try to see they have what they need, but even then I have to be discreet. A man's pride is a formidable object even when his family stands to benefit.' He had a hundred examples of times when his outright help had been turned down. He'd had to find other more subtle ways to offer it through the church or another third party. 'I was young and brash. I thought money could fix anything, but sometimes it creates more problems than it solves.'

Josefina nodded. 'I know.' It was said in commiseration, sympathetically, as if she did indeed know and it made him wonder—how would she know such a thing? It was a reminder of all he didn't know about her and wanted to.

'How? How do you know?' It was a frank, rude question. One never asked so directly about another's financial background.

Josefina threw him a coy look as they began to walk again. 'That's very direct, Mr Gann. I'll give you points for boldness.'

'I'd rather have an answer.' He smiled back, enjoying the banter. He was good at this, direct negotiating. He'd honed his teeth on such strategy in the boardrooms of London's businessmen. He'd learned early not to take no for an answer if one expected to get anywhere and he'd been rewarded. Businessmen had liked the scrapper from Kent. Women liked it, too, up to a point—a point he'd never be able to cross.

'There's a lot of things I'd rather have, Mr Gann.' She laughed, to divert him, darting ahead with a quick little half-step. It only made him more determined.

He lengthened his stride and caught up to her. 'Call me Owen. No more of this "Mr Gann" business. Were you always an itinerant artist?' There were suddenly a million questions he wanted to ask her, wanted to know.

'No, I wasn't.' She danced away, walking backwards now so she could face him with that teasing smile of hers. The cold air had pinkened her cheeks and the wind had picked her hair free. She was beautiful and out of reach. 'But that's all I'll tell you for now. The rest will cost you.'

They'd left the village and had reached the road. It was decision time. He didn't want her to go. 'Come to dinner tonight, Josefina.' *That* stopped her in her dancing tracks. She pushed an errant strand of hair out of her face.

'I don't have anything to wear. I didn't pack my ball gowns when I left home.' She tried for a joke. He'd caught her off guard and now she was grasping for an excuse.

'There are gowns upstairs at the house. I'm sure

there's something suitable among them, or that Lady St Helier could loan you.'

She shook her head. 'You don't want me at your very important party.' But he did. He was already imagining her at the table, charming the businessmen with her smile, her wit and her boldness. And afterwards, they might go up to the widow's walk, they might continue their conversation and other things.

'I do. Lady St Helier and the Viscount are coming. She's agreed to act as my hostess. You wouldn't be alone at the table.' Now that he'd invited her, now that he'd thought about it, he *wanted* her to be at his dinner tonight.

'I can't.' She was firmer in her response this time.

'Why? What are you doing that precludes an evening of socialising and good food?' He recognised that he was pushing hard now. It was not well done of him. She hesitated and he *knew*. He stepped forward, compelled to stop her with words, with whatever he had. He grabbed her wrist. 'Don't go to him. Don't…'

Don't pick Padraig O'Malley over me, don't go with the smugglers.

It wasn't just the danger he wanted her to reject. There was no run tonight, but they would all gather to drink and dance and get up to general mischief at the Crown. Owen resorted to bribery. 'I think you might find an association with Lieutenant Hawthorne insightful and potentially useful.' Perhaps if he could give her a reason to come besides simply coming for him he could sway her.

She studied him, reading the implied message that there might be help for the smugglers in her attendance. 'Well, when you put it that way, perhaps I might avail myself of a dress from your guest chamber after all.'

The dinner was starting to look more enjoyable. 'I'll send the dress down to the school right away.'

Chapter Nine

Inviting her was the most impetuous, most selfish thing Owen had done in a long while and he did not regret it. Josefina was dazzling. The rose silk brought out the black of her hair and the dark of her eyes. Gold earbobs in the shape of tiny leaves teased at her lobes as her laughter teased from the other end of the table, where she sat beside Lieutenant Hawthorne. Watching her made it difficult to keep his attentions on the dry banker, a Mr Matthews, who sat to his left. Thank goodness St Helier was doing that for him with a few well-placed questions to keep the conversation going.

'You set a superior table, Gann. Quite a surprise to find such culinary excellence is such an isolated place.' The banker's gaze twitched down the table. 'It seems Seasalter has other pleasant surprises, as well. Who knows, this might become the next Brighton. First the art school and the St Heliers taking up full-time residence, now the Italian protégée.' Owen didn't care for the way the banker's glance moved down the table and lingered, the object of his gaze evident. The man was taken with Josefina. 'Quite the community you've got here, Gann. A little undiscovered gem if I don't say so myself.'

Owen didn't like the direction of either of Matthew's insinuations. 'The art community here is all Lady St Helier's doing.' He would insist on credit being given where it was due.

'Seasalter would make a fine resort town,' Matthews said. 'Just a day's carriage drive from London makes it accessible. You could really develop this place. Throw up a few middle-class hotels and inns, get a few bathing machines and just like that you have another seaside resort,' he mused out loud. He leaned towards Owen confidentially. 'Let me know if you ever want to go in on it.'

'No, Matthews, I am afraid it would be a poor investment from beginning to end,' Owen said firmly. He motioned for Pease to refill the man's goblet, hoping to redirect the man's thoughts. 'The beach is too pebbly. It's a working man's beach, hardly conducive to luxurious picnics, and the shoreline isn't right for a harbour. We're more estuary and marsh than open sea,' he reminded Matthews. They'd discussed this today, the importance of eventually building their own harbour for the fleet at Whitstable for just that reason. Even if such things were possible, development of Seasalter was the last thing Owen wanted.

Matthews shrugged, undaunted by Owen's reservations. 'That's what sea walls and promenades are for. Structures can be built to overcome geographic limitations.'

Owen raised a brow. 'And risk jeopardising the wild-life Lady St Helier draws in the marshes? I don't think that would go over well.' Lady St Helier wouldn't want the intrusion of tourists and crowds. Neither would the smugglers. Summer travellers and boaters were not conducive to discreet drops in Shucker's Cove. More importantly, such tourism could negatively affect the oyster beds and jeopardise the livelihood of those who counted on them. No, the charm of Seasalter depended on it being left alone. He was relieved when Artemisia rose from the other end of the table and signalled for the ladies to depart with her to the drawing room. The evening could move forward towards more pleasant topics.

He didn't keep the men long at the table. They'd spent the day together and business had been settled. In truth, the main concern of their business had been settled before the visit. They were here to ensure his money was good enough for them, that Owen Gann wasn't a gauche fisherman. Having a viscount to dine and a table that rivalled any table of the *ton* had sealed that concern. That the table was graced with the refined company of Lady St Helier and the alluring Signorina Ricci had further reinforced for them that his money and his person was good enough for their association. They could comfortably overlook his humble antecedents.

That wasn't to say it didn't gall him that such measures were still necessary a decade after having made the first steps towards his substantial wealth. Money was money. Technically, his pounds spent as well as a duke's, perhaps better since it seemed so many of the aristocracy was perpetually burdened by debt. But he knew better. Money was not money. It mattered who had it. The brine of the sea would follow him always.

In the drawing room, Lady St Helier invited the bankers' wives to take turns at the piano and a polite musicale evening ensued. Matthews, it turned out, was a passable tenor who sang with his wife. Josefina was the last of the women to take a turn. She rose and made her way to the piano and Owen felt as if every man in the room watched her. Or was he the only one who was aware of each movement she made?

She sat down at the instrument, adjusting her skirts. 'This is a Venetian serenade sung by the gondoliers as they pole through the canals of an evening,' she offered by way of introduction, tossing Lieutenant Hawthorne a little smile that had the man positively drooling in his chair. What an imbecile, Owen thought. The King's Finest had his head easily turned. Perhaps it took one to know one. She'd certainly turned *his* head.

Josefina began to sing in soft gentle Italian and soon Lieutenant Hawthorne wasn't the only man in the room entranced. If there'd been any question of her refinement, Josefina's performance would have confirmed it. It was as if they were in Venice itself when she sang. Owen had never been, but he could imagine it: a city built of canals instead of roads, lanterns bobbing on long narrow boats that slid peacefully between the watery lanes, a soft breeze of an evening carrying the gondolier's songs throughout the town. What magic that must be.

But it provoked questions, too. Why would someone ever leave such a place? What was so unacceptable about the offers that would have allowed her to stay? What sort of woman was she that she painted, spoke two languages and played the pianoforte? She possessed the refinements of a well-brought-up young woman, not a street rat. She'd not always been an itinerant artist.

His thoughts had wandered far afield when she finished and he was loath to give them up when the song ended. He would have liked to have stayed in his imaginary Venice awhile longer, but it was time to end the evening and she'd given him the perfect note on which to do it.

'I think it went well,' Josefina said as he shut the door behind the St Heliers. They had lingered a short while after the last guests departed to assure him the evening had been a success. But they were eager to get home to their infant son and Josefina, it seemed, was eager to stay. She'd been the one to encourage them to go, assuring them she would follow shortly. She had portrait business she wanted to discuss first. Owen thought it more likely there was smuggling business she'd want to discuss. Whatever the reason, he was more than happy to have her stay behind.

'I think so, too, thanks to you. I am glad you decided to come.' Owen gave her an easy smile. 'Would you like a drink? A nightcap, perhaps?' How natural it seemed to have her here after just a few visits. How right it seemed to debrief the evening with her as he might with a wife and how foolish it seemed to entertain such fantasies.

'If it's up on the widow's walk, you have a deal.' Josefina tossed him one of her wide smiles and swished her skirts as she set out ahead of him for the stairs. He followed, decanter in one hand, two glasses in the other as those rose silk skirts led him out on to the walk.

There were no stars tonight. The clouds hung low and cold. He poured for them as she hunted out the blanket. 'It would be a good night for smuggling,' he said once they'd settled against the railing, drinks in hand, the blanket about her shoulders. 'I'm sure Lieutenant Hawthorne gave you a useful earful of information tonight.' He clinked his glass against hers, but she seemed subdued.

'He did, but that's not why I wanted to come up here.' The smile she gave him was soft, almost sad. There was a different light to her eyes. 'Tonight reminded me of home and I would linger in the memory awhile longer.'

'To home, then.' Owen nodded. In a way, the evening reminded him of home, too. Not a home he'd lost or left, but a home he'd not possessed and perhaps never would. Tonight had been a glimpse into the what could have been, or what might yet still be if he tried for it again. His unused dining room had been transformed into a beautiful setting for a beautiful meal, people lining the sides of his polished table, silver shining, crystal catching the light, china clinking. What would his mother have given to sit at such a table, to eat such food? Could she even have pictured such luxury? And yet, he wasn't entirely sure when he looked at Josefina that the home he imagined tonight was a place.

'To home,' Josefina whispered and he whispered back in the intimacy of the night, hungry for the pictures she would paint with her words of places he'd never seen and people he'd never meet, 'Tell me about it, tell me about Italy, about your father, about nights like this.'

At his words, the memories rushed forth, needing no further invitation. She'd not been aware they'd swum so close to the surface. Tonight they would not be denied. 'We would host supper parties on the balcony of our town house. We lived on the Cannaregio Canal and the balcony ran the length of the house.'

She could remember that house down to the minutest detail, the peeling pink stucco, the long country table on the balcony, the benches and chairs they cobbled together up and down its length, the mishmash of second-hand dishes her father made look eccentrically artistic instead of incongruous. After enough wine, no one much cared if the china matched. In truth, no one had cared before. They cared only for good food and good friends. 'Those evenings went on late into the night, sometimes even until the sun came up. A few

nights, we served breakfast before they all went home.'
Josefina gave a little laugh at the remembrance.

'It sounds wonderful.' Owen grinned in the darkness.

'It was.' She was warming to the topic now, the memories seeming to lose their sadness. 'I played the hostess. We'd sit for hours, talking about art, arguing about this technique or that or who made more important contributions to the medium: Caravaggio or Tintoretto.' She'd cut her teeth on those discussions. Her education had not been as formalised perhaps as Artemisia's, who'd had the Royal Academy to fall back on, but she'd argue it was just as good. Her education had taken place informally at the hands of her father and his friends. At their knees, she'd learned of the Renaissance masters, how to recognise a Titian, how to mix paint, how to develop perspective. 'The gondoliers would push their boats past, singing, a perfect accompaniment for our evenings. Sometimes we sketched the people in their boats and sent the drawings down. Someone always had a pad of paper at the table.'

'You miss it. You speak of it with such passion. I can imagine I'm there, at the table with you.' Owen's words were soft in the darkness. 'I would miss such a magical place.'

'I miss *him*. He made it magical.'

Had she really said that out loud? She should have said, *It stinks in the summer. There are fevers.* Why hadn't she said something witty to lighten the mood or disabuse him of the magic of Venice? Josefina peered into her nearly empty glass and set it aside. Perhaps she could blame it on the wine and the brandy, but she suspected she would have told him anyway. Owen Gann had a way of bringing out her secrets, things she talked about with no one.

Owen leaned against the rail, his big body angled to face her. 'What was he like, your father?'

'He was an artist, romantic, scatterbrained at times. He'd get lost in his work and forget to eat. He might not pay the bills for months on end. He was eccentric, sporadic, brilliant, loving, kind. He wasn't a usual father, but he was a good one. He bought me my first evening gown and my first pearls. He wasn't afraid of me growing up like some parents are. He encouraged me to embrace my talents and dreams.' She reached for his free hand and matched her fingers to his, lacing them through. She needed to stop this conversation before she told him too much. 'What of your father? Did he encourage you to dream of all this?'

'No, my father didn't know how to dream, only how to work and it killed him when I was seventeen. It was a hard dose of reality. I realised that could be me in twenty years, leaving behind a family who needed looking after if things didn't change and why would they change? They hadn't changed for generations. If anything was going to change, I had to do it. No one was going to do it for me.'

She heard the resolution that lingered in his voice still. After all these years, he was still changing things, for himself, for his people. She heard the angst, too, the boy who'd become the family's breadwinner. At seventeen, she'd been living blissfully in her father's studio while he'd been dredging oysters, doing a man's work. 'He would be amazed at what you've done, this empire you've built.'

Owen's gaze met hers, sharp and shrewd. She'd made a misstep. 'Would he? I think he would say, "Owen, you've forgotten where you came from. We are oyster people."'

'You're still oyster people, aren't you?' she argued gently. That won her a rueful smile.

'Yes, I am still oyster people, but not the way my father understood it and, unfortunately, not in the way bankers like Elias Matthews understand.' He looked out over the quiet waters of Shucker's Cove. 'Tonight was a success, but it should not have been necessary. They came to judge me. My money wasn't good enough on its own. They didn't want to be tainted by associating with an oysterman, a mere fisherman even if he could make them money.' He gave a harsh chuckle.

'You were more than equal to the task.' He'd been a revelation tonight in his fine clothes, at his fine table, his manners as impeccable as his wine. What a chameleon Owen Gann was—one day a cool businessman eager to be rid of her, the next, a simple man in a rowboat, a man who could cook, and a man who could entertain as if he'd never seen the inside of his own kitchen. But it was easy to be a chameleon when one belonged everywhere and nowhere, wasn't it? Who knew this better than she?

She could be anything she said she was. There was no one to gainsay her, no one who knew better, no one who could divine her lies from truths. It was the blessing and the curse of being free. She filed it away with all the other images of Owen, this new image of the man caught in between worlds. Too good for one and not deemed good enough by the other. It was a dichotomy she, as a female artist, was all too familiar with. Too good to be ignored, but too controversial to be accepted—unless she was someone's wife. One couldn't have all that talent running around unleashed, unaccounted for. If not, she'd simply have to be ignored, brushed away like a nuisance of a fly until she was forgotten or lost amid a workshop of apprentices who were more memorable and more male. But the price of that freedom was high, the price of not belonging, of only pretending to for a short time. His eyes held hers and in that moment she understood one thing with raw, unadulterated clarity.

He knew.

Owen shared that price with her. It rocketed through her with all the electrical charge of a lightning bolt. They were both people caught between worlds. The space betwixt was the only space in which they could be free. That he knew and understood undid her. In the face of the evening, the memories it invoked, the sharing of those memories here with him, of realising she was not alone in her isolation, were too much. *She need not be alone.* What if he was also desperate to set aside the seclusion he lived in? A little thrum began to hum through her, the thrum of mutual attraction, of mutual acknowledgement, of anticipation, of expectation and easing. She licked her lips. 'Why did you invite me tonight?'

His eyes lingered on her face, hot blue flames in the cold dark. 'Shall I tell you the truth?' His voice was a low baritone of a whisper. 'You will think me selfish.' His hand skimmed her cheek with its knuckles, an intimate gesture that sent a slow river of warmth straight to her belly. 'I didn't want to be alone.'

'And now?' She hardly dared to breathe for fear of breaking the spell woven by their words, the night and his touch.

'I still don't want to be alone.'

She turned her cheek into his palm, caressing it with the whisper of her words. 'Neither do I.' Invitation accepted. His mouth found hers then in a long, slow kiss that sipped from her as if she were the finest of wines. It turned her insides to *marmelatta* and her knees to a trembling *panna cotta* held together only by the cream that might collapse at any time. Who would have thought the solid, solitary Owen Gann would kiss like Casanova? Or that a simple dinner party would end in his arms and in his bed—there was no mistaking what they'd committed to here on the widow's walk. There would be no hasty tupping against the railing and a walk home in the dark, the space between her legs sore from rough, hurried use.

Owen swung her up into his arms as if she were weightless. She looped an arm about his neck and teased her lover—yes, her lover…he would be that very soon. 'Where are you taking me?'

'To bed.'

The two words sent a shot of excitement through her. Were there any two more thrilling words in the English language?

'Very well then, carry on.' She laughed up at him softly, seductively, noting the way his eyes darkened in response. A different sort of tremor went through her, a reminder that Owen Gann was not a man who made love for pleasure's whim alone.

Chapter Ten

It was a reminder borne out in the bedroom. He placed her on the wide four-poster bed and stepped back to undress with intentional care. First, laying aside his masculine accoutrements: the sapphire pin in his snowy cravat, the gold pocket watch and chain, the matching cufflinks that glinted in their trifle tray, the way his eyes had glinted on the widow's walk with hot, deliberate desire. His coats followed: dark evening jacket, waistcoat of damask ivory…sombre colours compared to this year's brighter hues she'd seen in London. But Owen Gann was a serious man, as sober in the boardroom as he was in the bedroom, it seemed.

The thought of all that seriousness brought to bear in lovemaking made her mouth go dry as deft fingers made short work of his shirt buttons with the same dexterity with which they'd wielded a shucking knife on a rocking boat. She sucked in her breath as his shirt joined his jacket. Sweet heavens, he was a beautiful man, a Viking in the raw indeed. Years of hard labour had left him with a smooth, sculpted expanse of pectoral muscles that tapered to lean hips and an exquisitely defined iliac girdle that disappeared into the waistband of his trousers.

His hands rested there, angling downwards, drawing her gaze towards the manly core of him. His arousal was evident despite the dimness of the room and the dark fabric of his trousers. She licked her lips in anticipation and encouragement, the flick of her tongue saying *Go on, don't make me wait too long.* A hint of mischief flashed in his eyes as if he knew precisely what he was doing and what she thought about it.

'Good things come, Josefina…' His voice was a raw chuckle.

'To those who wait?' she concluded for him, her own voice husky. She liked this seductive glimpse of Owen Gann as a lover, a man who could tease, who could tempt a woman to abject distraction with a look, with a single line. She watched, hungrily, as he slid those trousers over lean hips and muscled thighs, revealing himself inch by erotic inch. Her own desire ratcheted, a desire to look, to lick, to possess and be possessed by the powerful promise of the body on display. He kicked his trousers aside and she burned with greedy need. He was blond, golden, smooth, so unlike the men of southern Europe. She was hungry for contact, her body starving to assuage the loneliness unleashed inside her. If she could touch him, lie with him, let him fill her, somehow it would drive away the loss that swamped her—it would appease his devils, too. She wanted that, for both of them.

Josefina rose and went to him, plucking at the decorative ribbon at the bodice of her gown as she approached, her voice a whisper of want. 'Undress me, touch me, Owen.' She wanted those big, deft hands on her skin.

He did not disappoint. He made short work of the gown's buttons, his mouth pressing kisses against the column of her neck, her undergarments followed, his hands as quick on lacing as they'd been on buttons, skimming bare skin in tantalising touches until she was left in her chemise. She stepped away then and turned back to face him. She would be the author of this final reveal herself. 'Watch me, Owen.' She gave the low, throaty command as she took the hem of the chemise and pulled it over her head. The fluid movement brought her breasts into high relief and she heard Owen's breath hitch. Then she stood before him gloriously nude, her own desire heightened by his.

She closed the distance between them and placed the flat of her hands on his chest. 'Good lord, you are like marble,' she breathed in erotic appreciation.

'That I am. I'm marble everywhere,' Owen growled, dancing her back towards the bed. She went willingly, feeling the mattress give under his weight as he followed her down, his mouth finding hers in a hot kiss that tasted of brandy and promise and craving. 'I want, I need, Josefina.' There was desperation in his hungry plea that matched her own.

Her arms were about his neck, pulling him close against her, her body thrilling to the strength, the proximity of his. '*I* want, *I* need, Owen. Come and feast with me.'

'Josefina, are you sure?' Owen's sense of decency asserted itself even now amid unbridled passion. It was sweet of him to think she had a reputation to protect and that he should be the one to do it even at such a moment.

She smiled. 'Yes, I choose for myself, Owen, and I choose you.' Wanderers had the freedom to not worry about such things. She kissed him on the mouth in assurance. Desire was driving her hard now—had any feast ever been so needed? His mouth moved down the length of her, from throat column to breasts, sucking, licking its way down to her navel, his hands bracketing her hips, holding her steady as he went lower still, his tongue finding the discreet cove between her folds.

He licked at her, his big shoulders heaving beneath her hands as she clutched at him, desperate to anchor herself against the pleasure that shook her. Yet, this exquisite pleasure was not enough. 'Come inside, Owen,' she begged, breathless but not sated.

The words had barely left her before he moved between her legs, his big body levered over her, his phallus at the crux of her thighs, eager and hard against her entrance, finding her more than ready. The damp evidence of that readiness nearly undid him, proof that her want was as great as his. A guttural exhalation took him and all restraint fled.

They fell to the feast together. This was what he wanted, what his body needed, this joining, her arms about his neck, her legs wrapped tight about his hips as he plunged deep into her depths. She met him there in the deep. Passion did not frighten her. She welcomed it and him with a recklessness his body answered to. Her body arched into him, head thrown back, throat exposed, and he took it, his mouth ravenous for the taste of her. Her nails raked his back, his teeth bit into her skin, until it wasn't clear who was driving whom, their pleasures interdependent and inseparable.

He thrust hard again and deeper still, letting her recklessness enfold them both until he felt her clench about him, felt his own body gather for a final effort and they fell together from impossible heights, a free fall into pleasure's abyss. By the heavens, had anything ever been so satisfying? Had anything ever filled him with such completion he wanted to do nothing but lie here with her and let it wash over them? 'I've made love with a sensual angel.' He sighed contentedly, feeling her nestle against him in the crook of his arm.

She gave a throaty, drowsy laugh. 'No, just a woman, a mere mortal, although for a few moments we might have touched the heavens.'

'Hmm.' Owen pondered the thought, a hand playing idly through her hair, sifting the silky dark strands. He was learning her, her body and her mind, piece by piece tonight, and the process was intoxicating and addicting.

He wanted to know all of her. 'You're a woman from Venice. A woman who has traversed the Continent. My oysters have travelled further than I have.' He laughed. 'I suppose I envy you that. What's your favourite place? The most interesting place you've been?'

She gave a thoughtful sigh. He could almost hear her sorting through her memories. 'If I had to choose a city, I'd choose Marseilles. It's a confluence of culture and trade, like Venice. But it's older, so much older. People from all over the Mediterranean have done business there since the days before Christ. You can hear languages spoken from Turkish and Arabic to Greek and French and Italian. Russian, too. And some languages I don't even have names for. In some ways all that culture reminded me of Venice, at least what Venice must have been at its height. But Marseilles still bustles. The streets are narrow, the buildings are weathered but there are treasures inside them. There's a church, the Church of St Laurent of Marseilles, on top of a hill and it commands a view of the old port. I sat up there for afternoons on end, painting and imagining the city in ancient times when the Greeks controlled it.'

He could imagine it, too. Old streets, bustling with modern life. He could smell the fishy wharves and hear the cries of fishmongers. It came to life through her words as Venice had come to life tonight in her song. 'But if you didn't choose a city?' Owen prompted. 'What would you choose then?'

'Anything in the Alps,' she answered without hesitation. 'I spent time at a castle with a lake on one side of it and a mountain on the other. I was there in the spring, of course, otherwise it wouldn't have been accessible. It was beautiful, rugged majesty cloaked in wildflowers and the bluest skies above it. I painted a few landscapes for the Count who lived there.'

Jealousy pricked. Owen didn't want to think about the Count. He opted to talk about the art instead. 'You're a very talented artist if Counts are giving you commissions. Does Artemisia know?' He was thinking about his friend's wager now and about the hidden trove of talents Josefina possessed.

'No.' She traced a design around his aureole and his flat nipple pimpled into erectness. 'It doesn't signify. I am just a street artist here, an itinerant traveller who will move on to fulfil other dreams in May.'

He stilled her hand, aware that perhaps she was deliberately distracting him. Not yet. He wanted clarity for a moment more. 'But you're not really a street artist. Your father was an artist, you lived well in Venice, well enough to acquire a genteel education that left you fluent in English and music along with painting.'

Josefina raised up on one elbow and smiled, her hair falling over her shoulder. 'I have what one might call a wide-ranging, haphazard education acquired from whatever tutors were on hand and my father when he could spare the time. My mathematics are atrocious, by the way. My father's patrons weren't interested in numbers and science.' He felt her eyes linger on him. 'What are you worried about, Owen?'

He might as well be honest with her. 'Deception.

Artemisia's wager is about turning a street artist into something finer, but you're already quite fine.'

She chuckled. 'I was chosen at random for better or worse, with whatever bad habits and whatever training I might already have acquired. That was the point of the wager, I believe. To take a diamond in the rough and transform it.'

'But you're already transformed,' Owen argued, only to be met with her laughter in the dark as she reached for him.

'Hardly. I am learning plenty from Artemisia. She's a genius and portraiture is not where I excel.' She kissed him softly. 'You'd be surprised by the amount of talent in the pool of street artists—and the stories, too. My background isn't so unusual.' Her hand found him beneath the covers. 'Speaking of transformations, however, this one seems to be coming along nicely.' Indeed it was. When her hand encircled his shaft and began to stroke, he was far more interested in what was happening here and now between them than anything that had gone before.

They made love twice more that night, each time bringing a slightly different variation to their pace and appreciation as they learned one another's bodies. If it had been up to him, Owen would have never got out of bed. He would have traded all his worldly positions to hold on to those precious minutes when there was nothing but peace and pleasure and possibility. After all, he could make another fortune. But this, he thought drowsily as dawn encroached, was more precious than pearls: Josefina asleep in his arms, her dark hair draped across his chest, her naked breast pressed to him, his body and his mind replete. He did not know if he could make this night happen again.

He didn't want to wake up, not fully. He wanted to linger here in this world of impossible fantasy. But the morning had other ideas. The house would soon begin to stir. The cook in the kitchen, the maid to lay fires, Pease to oversee the post-mortem clean-up from the dinner party. Owen's eyes forced themselves open and he groaned against reality.

Had the dinner party only been last night? It seemed a lifetime had passed since then. When he thought of last night, dinner didn't come to mind. He thought instead of the first desperate, thundering coupling, of his body pouring its need into hers, of her body offering rough succour in return, of Josefina's hot words, *Come inside, Owen.* God, yes. His body stirred even now at the echo of that memory. Then he thought of the playfulness that engendered the time after that, and the tenderness of the time after that.

He had not planned for this to happen. He'd not invited her for a drink on the widow's walk with the intention of bedding her any more than he'd intended on inviting her to the dinner party when he'd left the house yesterday with nothing but business on his mind. But there she was, on the shore, the wind pulling her hair loose and her hand pulling him down memory lane, her smile beguiling stories from him. He hadn't wanted to leave her, so he'd invited her to the party and it still hadn't been enough. Like recognised like, two hungry souls in the night had come together. Quite explosively. Quite repeatedly.

Artemisia was going to kill him for this. She'd trusted him with her protégée and he'd seduced her. By no stretch of the imagination did 'I'll be along shortly' cover coming home the next morning after the sun was up. There was nothing for it. Owen shook Josefina awake gently. 'Wake up, love, I have to take you home.' He gave another groan and swung himself out of bed. There was going to be hell to pay. He'd best get on with it. But even that realisation wasn't enough to extinguish a little flame that had begun to burn inside him, something warm that he hadn't felt for a long time.

Chapter Eleven

She'd not been that reckless for a long while. Josefina didn't allow herself to examine exactly *how* reckless she'd been until she was in the privacy of her little studio late the next morning. What she examined made her cheeks flame. She'd not gone to the dinner party with any intention of revealing so much of herself to Owen or of going to bed with him—the host. Not just the host, she'd gone to bed *with the subject of her upcoming portrait*.

It was hardly professional and it ought to be cringeworthy. Recklessness was usually followed with regret and she could not summon any. This was perhaps more shocking than the impetuosity of the act itself. She'd *enjoyed* the night with Owen, more than enjoyed. The word seemed too tepid to describe how she felt about the encounter. It was far *more* than an encounter. *Allora*—not even that word was right. What a dry, objective word, *encounter*.

She sighed and absently laid out her brushes. Her

English was failing her this morning. *Colpo di fulmine.* There, that was better. The thunderbolt. Love falling on someone suddenly, intensely. Only last night hadn't been about love. She would not pretend it had been. It had been about need, want and loneliness overcome. She wanted another. That was yet an additional layer of shock. The spontaneous needy act had created not the desire to regret it, but the desire to repeat it. Owen had been a thorough lover and a thoughtful one who had seen to her pleasure even as he'd claimed his own.

Such attentiveness amid the wild throes of passions begged the question: Why hadn't he been snatched up? She spread out her sketches, laying them side by side on a long table as her mind sorted through the question. A man who was as thorough in bed as he was with his ledgers was a rare find. In her experience, the better the lover, the worse his finances. Not that it had ever mattered. She was gone before such things as finances became relevant. Oh, she liked this sketch, Owen at the shore in his workman's clothes. The eyes were better. She picked it up for closer scrutiny, but it was thoughts of last night that were examined: his insistent mouth on her, everywhere, the strength of the arms that had carried her downstairs to the bedroom, the exquisite body displayed in lamplight, the power of him as he'd thrust into her.

Sweet heavens, she couldn't help but smile at herself. Her body was rousing just from the memory of him. Owen Gann in the grip of his passion was a spectacular sight to behold. He'd given his all, he'd been entirely vulnerable in the last moments of his pleasure, entirely on display. Perhaps that was the reason, she mused, that he was so alone, by choice. A man who made love like that wouldn't put it on display for just anyone to see.

He let you see it. The warning whispered on the fringes of memory. Danger lurked there. What would such a man want in return for his vulnerability? She ought to take warning from it. Perhaps she would, later. For now, she just wanted to savour it while she could. She did not kid herself; the savouring wouldn't last. There would be a price for last night, for letting the hours fly past, for letting Owen walk her home in dawn's early light and kiss her goodbye before she sneaked into the dormitory to tidy herself up before going downstairs for breakfast with the girls as if nothing had happened.

'What happened last night?' Artemisia's voice cut across her thoughts in slicing tones. Josefina nearly dropped the sketch in startlement—not because she was surprised to see Artemisia, her arrival had only been a matter of time, but because her thoughts had been that far away, lost in the remembered raptures of last night's passion and her own reaction to it.

Josefina hugged the sketch to her in a reflexive gesture of protection, of him, of her, of what they'd shared. 'That's private. It's no one's business but mine.'

Artemisia speared her with a sharp look. 'So, you slept with him.' It was not a question.

'I did not say that,' Josefina snapped.

'You didn't have to.' Artemisia moved through the

studio, stopping to casually study drafts of work Josefina had spread throughout the room. 'If you hadn't, you wouldn't be worried about what was private and what wasn't.' She looked up with a shake of her head. 'I don't know what to do with you, Josefina. On the one hand, you're a very talented artist. I like this landscape, by the way. You've captured the beauty and the isolation of Seasalter perfectly. It takes a sophisticated eye to see beyond the mud and the marshes. On the other hand, you're going to drive yourself to ruin with your recklessness.'

'I'm not reckless.' Josefina felt obliged to make the demur. Artemisia raised a dark eyebrow in disbelief.

'I know what you are. You're sneaking out to meet with O'Malley's smuggling gang and now you've taken a shine to Seasalter's leading citizen. You crave adventure.' Artemisia gave a half-laugh. 'I know because I was like that. But it wasn't adventure I craved. It was something far deeper. I spent a lot of years not realising that and I made mistakes because of it.' Artemisia's tone softened, as did her gaze. 'I would warn you off those mistakes so you don't need to make them for yourself.'

She could handle an angry Artemisia. An empathic Artemisia was more difficult. Josefina was wary. 'You're not mad?'

Artemisia frowned and took a seat. Josefina winced. Taking a seat presaged at longer conversation. She'd hoped they'd almost been done. 'I am mad. Your recklessness could reflect poorly on the school. When you go out with the smugglers you set a poor example. The other girls look up to you. They find your lifestyle glamorous—a single girl tramping about Europe with her paints.' Artemisia gave her a knowing smile. 'You and I know differently. It's not glamorous. It's hard. The inns are poor quality, the food worse, the guarantee of work non-existent and there's the inherent risks of being a woman alone. But they are young and impressionable. They're still holding on to fairy tales and we need to be careful with that. So, yes, when you jeopardise what I am trying to build here, I am angry. When you stay out all night with a man and sneak back in with your stockings in one hand at dawn, I am angry. What if one of the girls had seen you instead of Mrs Harris on her way up to the house to start the fires?' Mrs Harris was the redoubtable housekeeper at the farmhouse which served as the St Heliers' residence.

'I'll be more careful—' Josefina didn't complete her sentence, realising the trap she'd laid for herself.

'There'll be a next time, then?' Artemisia didn't miss the implication. Of course there would be. The smugglers were counting on her and she wanted another night with Owen. The women's eyes met and an awkward silence followed. Artemisia gave a sigh, making a decision with herself. 'Do you need a preservative?'

Josefina eased. Artemisia understood the limits of her control. 'No, I can take care of that.'

Artemisia rose and smoothed her skirts. 'Good, because Owen is not the sort of man who would ever let the mother of his child leave him.' She paused and Josefina felt the weight of her gaze settle firmly on her. 'Unless…that's what you're angling for? A rich, lonely man would look like an easy solution to a girl who's tired of running.'

Josefina bristled at the insinuation. 'That is not what I am angling for. I am gone in May.'

Artemisia nodded. 'Then I hope you'll stay safe long enough to make your getaway. We need to discuss sketches, but not today. We'll do it tomorrow when tempers aren't so hot.'

Josefina gritted her teeth and bit back a growl in the empty studio after Artemisia left. The English were so blasted composed even when they were seething. She'd much rather have had a full-blown argument with Artemisia complete with raised voices and loud epithets like any good Venetian instead of Artemisia coolly asking bold, blunt questions and establishing inconvenient truths like the risk to the school. She'd not thought of that, only of the danger to herself. On the road, there was just herself to consider. One more reason to make sure she was gone in May. Putting down roots meant being responsible for others, letting those others know her and making herself open to the possibility of hurt and disappointment that came from long-term attachments. Losing her father was all the loss she wanted to withstand. When spring came, she would move on, pursuing dreams, keeping promises, staying one step ahead of the hurt. This reminder, coming in the wake of a soft night in a man's arms when her guard was down as a result, was exactly what she needed to steel her resolve.

Artemisia with her resolve in full force was, in a word, intimidating to most men. Owen did not consider himself one of them. However, he could easily believe everything that had ever been said of her as she paced his study. 'Did she seduce you?'

Ah, so Artemisia knew. Owen chuckled. 'Is that what she told you?' He'd have preferred to have his interlude kept private, but he also knew how impossible such a wish was in a small village. It didn't get any smaller than Seasalter. Still, he'd rather enjoyed the laconic nature of today. He'd let his mind leisurely replay the night before as he'd looked over the contracts for the boats.

'No, she said nothing. I guessed.' Artemisia huffed. 'She was quite keen to not kiss and tell, if you must know.'

That was gratifying. He liked the idea that Josefina had been protective of what had passed between them. There was something sacred about the night despite its unplanned nature. 'She did not seduce me, to set the record straight. Do you think I'm such a stick-in-the-mud I can't manage a bit of romance on my own?' He flashed his old friend a smile and then sobered. 'No one else knows, do they?' He did not want it dissected as cheap gossip. It would do little to him, but it would besmirch Josefina's reputation and that could not be what Artemisia wanted for her school. Was that why she was here? To protect her school?

'No, and I want to keep it that way.' Artemisia's fury abated. 'Owen, the school doesn't need a scandal. But it isn't just the school I've come about.'

'Then take a seat and tell me about it before you wear a hole in my carpet.' Owen gestured to the spare chair. She was pacing before the fireplace incessantly. This agitation was about more than a truant student. Artemisia was no prude and he was a grown man capable of managing his own affairs discreetly. 'If you're worried I'll hurt her, you needn't. We'll be careful, in all ways. No one will know and I won't leave her with a child.' He paused, wondering if that was a promise he could keep. They hadn't been that careful last night, but going forward, he'd see to it. 'If there was a child, you know I would do the right thing.' Marriage. To Josefina. To have last night, every night, to wake up to a family, the empty halls of this house filled with running feet and raised voices. Josefina would not have a quiet home.

'Get your head out of the clouds, Owen,' Artemisia snapped. 'She's not looking for that.' Owen gave her a quelling look. Friend or not, she had no right to charge in here and shatter his daydreams. She bit her lip, taking his look to heart. 'I'm sorry. I'm out of sorts today. I know you wouldn't hurt her. It's not her I'm worried about. It's us.' She pulled a letter from her pocket. 'Addy's written. Sir Aldred Gray has been asking questions about Josefina. Hazard says Gray's hired a Bow

Street Runner.' Hazard would know. Before marrying Addy, he'd been a Runner himself. His connections were likely very well informed.

Owen read the short note, his mouth pursed in a grim line. 'He means to discredit her, to paint her as a loose woman if she wins and by extension to cast aspersions on the school. If she loses, it's all matter of fact that, of course, you can't turn a sow's ear into a silk purse. Neither way is incredibly flattering to you or the school.'

'My deduction exactly.' Artemisia sighed. 'I'm starting to think my wager with him was foolhardy.'

'It's not the first time you've done something rash.' Owen handed the letter back to her. 'You'll sort it out.'

'Usually the truth is on my side, though, while I'm doing the sorting.' Artemisia shook her head. 'Not this time. I don't know anything about her. Sir Aldred Gray could make up whatever he liked and who would gainsay him?' She sighed. 'What a mess. I *assumed* he would play fair. I *assumed* she was just a starving artist, that she would be so thrilled to be here with a roof over her head that she wouldn't engage in anything illicit. I was wrong on both accounts. I made a classic mistake. I'm only just now starting to ask questions I should have asked weeks ago. Who is she, where did she come from, why is she here and not there? Who are her people? Everyone has a story, I just assumed I knew hers.' Artemisia sighed. 'Then last night, I had to rethink that. I couldn't ignore the evidence before me. She plays the pianoforte. She was more than up to sitting at a formal table. I can't protect her if I don't know.' Ah, so he wasn't the only one trying to put pieces together.

'Have you asked her?' Owen played with the paperweight, feeling uncomfortable with where this was going. He *could* enlighten Artemisia, but the things Josefina had told him in the confidence of the post-coital bed weren't for general consumption. They were private, personal, things just between them.

'Yes, she's been very closed. She doesn't talk about her life before. She's from Venice.' Artemisia gave a half-smile. 'I learned that last night. It was something of a surprise when she sang.'

Owen shifted in his seat. This was a deuced awkward position to be in. He knew some of the answers Artemisia was looking for, but obviously Josefina had withheld that information except from him. It didn't matter the reasons. He was hardly going to sell her secrets. But at the same time, he could not let his friend worry more than she already was.

'She's good. She's had prior training, that much is evident. Addy chose a highly qualified candidate for our wager,' Artemisia mused out loud, slanting an enquiring gaze at him as she fished for information.

'Perhaps her family were artists, like the Stansfields.' Owen could give Artemisia that much without feeling as if he were betraying Josefina's confidences.

'Were?' Artemisia asked. 'Do you think they're all gone?'

Owen evaded the question by calling for Artemisia's coat. 'I don't know much at all,' he said, helping Artemisia into her outerwear and escorting her to the door. He knew only that he wanted to see Josefina again, wanted to burn again, wanted to feel that for a brief time there was a place for him again.

While he was musing over the last of the paperwork, wondering how he might arrange seeing her, she came to him armed only with her sketchpad and satchel for subterfuge. 'Miss Ricci, to see you, sir,' Pease announced, with mild distaste over the spontaneous visit. Unscheduled arrivals meant disruption to Pease's carefully cultivated routine. Owen, who usually disliked disruption as much as Pease, simply didn't care. He wanted only to drink her in, the sight of her enough to set his body stirring with memories of the night and hopes for what might yet come.

'What are you doing here?' Owen rose from behind the desk. He took her satchel and helped her out of her coat, taking any excuse to touch her, to breathe her in.

'I need a few more sketches. I can just sit and watch you work. I'll be quiet.' She'd not been quiet last night, nor still. There was a small chunk out of the wall behind the headboard this morning in testimony.

'I don't like you quiet, Josefina,' he murmured at her ear, 'or still.' Did he imagine it or did her pulse jump at the base of her throat? 'Is that all you came for? Sketches?'

'No, not all.' It was her turn to flirt as she took up her station in a chair beside the fire. 'I came to see what else you can make with oysters.' She licked at her bottom lip, a quick, coy flicking motion that drew the eye to her mouth. 'Or are you just a one-trick wonder?'

Chapter Twelve

Owen leaned back in his chair, hands behind his head, and favoured her with a devilish smile, one that she was coming to believe was just for her alone, then he began. 'There's fried oysters, pan oysters, baked, broiled or smoked oysters. Roasted oysters. Steamed oysters. Stewed oysters: cream stew, plain stew, dry stew, box stew on toast with cream sauce. Are you hungry yet? If not, there's more. There's devilled oysters, glazed oysters on toast, scalloped, sauce coated, there's fancy fry, there's croustade of oysters.'

'Stop!' Josefina laughed, throwing up her hands in mock surrender. She liked him this way, his stern demeanour set aside. 'All right, I'm convinced, oysters aren't a one-trick wonder—for now.' She gave him a teasing smile and rose from her chair to approach the desk. She rested her hip on the edge. 'What of yourself? Are your skills limited to…oyster stew?' His eyes lingered on her face in a long stare that suggested he understood her innuendo. But he did not take the bait.

'I can cook a variety of oyster dishes. I'll do a croustade for you sometime.' Sometime. Would that be before May? Before she had to leave? To move on and keep promises?

'It sounds complicated. I like things simple and straightforward. Box stew on toast sounds more like me,' Josefina pressed. She'd come for more than oysters and sketches. She'd come to see if the passion between them could live now that the edge of loneliness was gone or to determine if the edge had been sufficiently blunted. She wanted more of last night, but perhaps more didn't exist. Perhaps it was just a single, brilliant flame, meant to burn only once like a falling star.

Owen rose from the desk and moved towards the bookshelves and the door, away from her. Josefina resisted the urge to follow him. She needed to be patient and let her words do the work for her. He knew very well what she was talking about. He wanted to make things between them complicated like a croustade, when they needn't be. She needed to show him how simple it was. At the door, he stopped and pulled it shut, the lock snicking into place. 'Josefina, we should talk.'

Oh, this sounded dangerous and disappointing. 'I disagree.' Josefina was quick to head the conversation off that path. They ought to do something, but talking wasn't it. 'I didn't come for conversation, Owen. I came for you.' She sat on the desk, legs crossed, willing him to come to her. She was not going to cross the room to him and beg. He was going to own what he wanted and come to her. She held his gaze with her own, steady and strong, letting her need reflect in her eyes. 'I don't want for ever, Owen. I want a few nights, a few months. I want your mouth on me, I want your hands on me, your kisses at my neck, I want you inside me, filling me until I can think about nothing else, until I can do nothing else but scream your name when the pleasure takes me. I want you, Owen, just you.'

Everything he'd ever wanted was sitting on his desk in a workaday blue wool skirt and a high-collared white blouse, the standard uniform of the art school, wanton words falling from red lips. *I want you, Owen, just you.* The words had him hard with yearning. Josefina couldn't possibly know how those words were a balm to a wounded soul, to a man who'd given his heart to a woman who'd stomped on it and treated his very touch with contempt. Alyse Newton had acted as if the very nearness of him dirtied her. It had been a long while before he'd been able to not take her rejection personally, to believe that he could be enough for a woman, to realise the problem was with her, not with him. But the incident had certainly made him wary of trying again. Holed up in Seasalter, he'd found there was very little temptation to gainsay that wariness. It had been a comfortable isolation, until now.

Temptation leaned back on her hands and licked her lips with her wicked tongue. 'Well? Owen, will you have me?'

It was a rhetorical question at best, which she likely well knew. Josefina was confident with a capital *C*. Did he want her? Yes, he'd thought of little else today, which explained the stack of work still on his desk. Would he have her? He answered with his body. The throaty words had him crossing the room, his mind in sudden agreement with his body. She was right. It didn't need to be complicated. A few nights, a few months to hold the long lonely winter at bay and the memories to keep afterwards.

'Do I want you?' He gave an incredulous growl. 'I want you like I want to breathe.' Her legs parted as he approached and he moved within the vee of her skirts. He could feel the heat of her, smell the early scent of rising arousal. His mouth bent to hers and he was lost to reason, lost to restraint, the embers of last night easily prodded to flames. Her arms were about his neck, her mouth open beneath his, her tongue tangling with his, proof that her want had not been words alone. She moved against him, her hand on the length of his cock where it jutted up hard against his trousers, and Owen was nearly undone.

Recklessness was contagious and heady. He pushed back her skirts, his hands on warm bare skin high at her thighs. Her hips pressed into him as her hand stroked him through the barrier of his clothing, her mouth at his ear now, whispering decadent prompts. 'I want you inside me again, Owen.' He wouldn't last long at this rate. This was nothing like last night's slow, deliberate lovemaking. This was a fast-moving storm. There was no time for beds and disrobing. There was time only to appease the aches of their bodies, brought to a fine point after a day of denial.

'Free me.' His request was guttural and hoarse. Josefina's hands worked open his fall, her hand closing around his hot, aroused flesh at last. If he'd entertained any thoughts of relief at being freed from the confines of his trousers, his body to be soothed by her touch, they were short-lived. Her touch only inflamed him further. She brought him to her core, nudging his head against the dampness of her entrance. He bit at her neck. 'I know where it goes, my dear.' He'd demonstrated that quite aptly last night.

He thrust into her hard, honouring her request and his overwhelming need. He was thankful for the foresight of the locked door. He couldn't have stopped and given a pretence of normality if his life depended on it. Pease would have had to just stand there and wait until he was finished. Impatience and want were driving them both frantically now, the peak rising fast before them. This would be over in a matter of moments, their bodies already gathering to summit that peak. Josefina's head was thrown back, her legs clenching tightly around his waist, cleaving to him like a drowning man to driftwood. He thrust once, twice more, felt her shudder, heard her cry out as his own pleasure let down and he pulled away, releasing against her thigh with a thundering pulse.

Josefina breathed a sigh of relieved contentment at his ear, as if a great weight had been lifted from her. He wrapped his arms tight around her, holding her close.

This. Whatever this was, he wanted it for now and always. His body hummed the incoherent, indefinable thought in the wake of his own contentment. He could stand here joined with her for evermore. It was an impossible thought, but one he didn't feel inclined to argue with at the moment, not with her dark head resting on his shoulders, not with perfection so near to hand.

She sighed against him. 'The night didn't lie.'

'No, I suppose it didn't.' Owen stepped away reluctantly and righted himself. Then he lifted her in his arms and carried her to the divan set before the fire. He sat and gathered her to him, liking the way she snuggled into him as if she'd always belonged there, as if their bodies had always known how to fit together, how to be together.

'So, this is the room where you work your magic?' She peered up at him, her eyes still misty with the haze of happy completion, her voice soft.

'Yes. I've shown it to you before.' But not like this. The kind of magic he associated with this room might be drastically altered by what had just transpired. He wasn't sure he'd ever be able to work from behind that desk again without seeing her sitting on his polished surface, her legs and lips inviting him to indulge right there among the ledgers. And indulge he had, *they had*, madly, deeply, ferociously right there on his desktop. He had not been alone in that and the realisation filled him with a sense of awed hindsight. Reckless Josefina Ricci had got into more than his trousers. She'd gotten beneath his skin and into his mind.

She'd become…*important*…to him in a shockingly short span of time. He no longer reviled her recklessness, but revelled in it. How had that happened? Why had he *allowed* it to happen, he who kept himself carefully guarded? Who'd learned painful lessons well. And why *now* should an itinerant artist tempt him to match her in recklessness when he was on the brink of achieving his ambitions, when business was requiring all his attentions, financially and otherwise. It was not the most ideal of times to find those attentions dragged away from his ledgers.

'Tell me about the deal you are masterminding. I've realised I don't know a thing about it, only that it involves ships.' Josefina snuggled in more comfortably, content to let him talk.

Owen chuckled into her hair, breathing in the scent of it. 'You weren't so interested in economics the last time we discussed it. I believe you found me rather boring.'

'Not forthcoming. Those are two different things,' Josefina corrected, sitting up. 'Besides, you were being stiff and obtuse on purpose.' She leaned in to give him a quick peck on the cheek, her eyes dancing merrily. 'I know you better now.' She snuggled back down. 'Tell me about your latest venture.'

Knew him better? The idea that someone might seek to know him filled him with warmth. How long had it been since anyone had sought to understand him? His father hadn't understood his dreams. His mother had smiled patiently at them, but she hadn't believed in them no matter how much she believed in him. Simon understood, but in a world of nearly a billion souls, one person who believed in him seemed a measly number. Perhaps it was the idea of adding a second person to that short list that brought the warmth. 'Well, if you really want to know, I'll indulge you,' Owen said drily.

'Indulge me, please.' She wiggled against him, making him think of other indulgences he might enjoy.

'It's the final piece in a vertical building scheme of mine. Several years ago, I realised I could be more efficient and make more profit if I wasn't reliant on other people to fulfil parts of my supply chain. I started with the oystermen. Instead of relying on oystermen to sell to me, I went to them. I offered them a regular salary so they weren't reliant on the poundage they brought in. This was good for business; I had a consistent supply without overharvesting for short term gain and it was beneficial for them. They didn't have to settle for whatever the other buyers were willing to pay by weight, especially in years when the harvest was lean. They had a guaranteed wage from me. Next, I bought boats for rowing out to the hoys and I bought hoys to sail out to the beds. Then I bought the factory at Seasalter, then another at Whitstable and another at Faversham. After that, I bought a line of transport drays that could take barrels of oysters up the road to London to sell in the markets instead of paying other teamsters to haul for me.'

'And now, you are buying a fleet of ships to send

your oysters to the Continent and beyond?' Josefina surmised.

'Yes. The royal courts of Europe love oysters from the Kentish coast.'

'Such acquisition is expensive.'

'Yes.' Owen sighed. 'This last has me stretched at the moment, but it's always that way in the beginning of a big new step. I'm not worried.' At least he wouldn't be once the first batch to the Hapsburg court was sent off in a few months. By July, money would be flowing again. Until then, though, he tried not to worry overmuch.

The room had grown dark, a reminder of how much time had passed since she'd walked through his door, satchel in hand. 'Are you hungry? I am sure it's well past supper.' It was an effort for Owen to rouse himself from the divan. 'We can raid the kitchen. The cook always leaves something from lunch behind.'

The kitchen was warm and Owen made a quick assembly of bread and cheese to slide into the oven. 'No oysters tonight.' He grinned over his shoulder, aware that she was watching his every move.

'How is it that you haven't been snatched up by a woman who recognises the rare treat of a man who cooks?' Josefina leaned on the worktable, her gaze intent on him. His body liked her scrutiny.

'Not every woman finds cooking a desirable quality in a husband.' He tried to make light of it as he laid out plates and set out a bottle of wine.

'Ah, I see. My mistake.' Josefina fell quiet. She took the bottle and struggled to work the cork free, her brow knit, her mouth a tight line of concentration. 'You are looking for a wife of high birth. A final piece to your vertical empire perhaps?'

'I *was* looking,' Owen corrected, refusing to be offended by her implication. He took the bottle from her and gently wrestled the cork free. He poured, the sound of wine filling the glasses seeming abnormally loud in the space left by her silence. 'I decided I wanted more from a marriage than a mere acquisition.' He paused. Best to be honest. 'Which worked out for the best since it seemed titled women were averse to an oysterman.' He reached for the tray of bread and cheese from the oven and deposited it on the table between them. 'I didn't want a wife who was repulsed by her husband's money-making tendencies.'

'I'm sure that wasn't the case,' Josefina said, but he cut her off with a shake of his head.

'I assure you it was. My heart was in it, but hers was not. I am thankful I discovered that before it was too late.' He flashed her a smile. 'Too many complications, as you like to say.'

'Well, I'm sorry. It couldn't have been easy if your heart was engaged.' She took a slow sip of her wine, her eyes holding his over the rim of the goblet. A sharp stab of want pierced him. Good lord, she could burn him to cinders or rouse him to flames with a single look.

'Now you have my secret. Turnabout is fair play. Have you ever been in love?' Owen leaned across the table, closing the distance between them. He hoped not. It was an irrational realisation and a selfish one that rather surprised him. Why did he care? She'd had lovers, that was one thing. But to be *in* love, that was another, a more sacred place.

She shook her head and he let out a breath he hadn't realised he was holding. 'No, not in love. Flirtations certainly, men I've felt great respect and admiration for, but not love, not like you mean it when my heart was engaged.'

'Is that why you left Venice? A man loved you, but you didn't love him? I remember you said you didn't have a reason to stay that was palatable to you.'

'No, he didn't love me. He loved what I could do for him.' She gave him a slow smile. 'Perhaps, like you, I, too, felt that marriage should be something that involved the heart. When that was not on offer, I made other decisions.'

Darkness settled, offset only by the lamp on the table. He watched as she finished her bread and cheese, washing it down with a final swallow of wine before she answered. She ate deliberately and slowly, gathering her thoughts. He'd hit upon a delicate matter, then. 'There was a man, a friend of my father's. He offered to marry me. But as I said, he did not love me, not like that. He wanted me in his bed, he expected children, he expected a lot of things—let's just leave it at that—and in exchange I'd have the protection of his wealth, his name, his social standing. A lot of women would have thought it a good trade. But I expected more and he would not give it.'

'More?' Owen had forgotten his own bread, mesmerised with her tale here in the dark, lamplight flickering over her face, the flames highlighting her features, the fine cheekbones, the dark eyes, the elegant length of her nose. 'Like love?' What more would there be?

'Not love. I wasn't in love with him.' She favoured him with a slow smile. 'I wanted a place in his workshop, I wanted him to support me as a wife *and* an artist in my own right.' She reached for her glass, only to find it empty.

Owen poured, cautious of his rising feelings. He should not exult in the fact that the man didn't offer her a love match or that she'd not wanted one. 'What happened?'

'My father died and this man became more insistent, thinking I was vulnerable. But my father's death changed everything for me, my priorities, my possibilities.' She took a swallow of wine and explained, 'When my father knew he was dying, he asked me to promise him that I would not tie myself to patrons, to people who would steal my dreams in pursuit of theirs. My father spent his life wanting to travel, wanting to paint the wonders of the world, but he hadn't the freedom to do it. I promised him I would go in his stead. After such a promise, I could hardly limit myself to working in a workshop, let alone being a wife. But this man felt otherwise, that my father's request was unreasonable and that I should give up the quest. He pressed me for an answer the morning of the funeral.' The way she said 'pressed' made Owen's anger rise. This man had not pressed her with words alone. Josefina's voice was low, matter of fact, in the quiet of the kitchen. 'I knew he would not relent until he had what he wanted. There would be no reasoning with him. I promised him an answer after the funeral.'

'And what was that?' Owen could guess. She was here, after all.

'I never went back,' Josefina whispered quietly. 'After the funeral, I simply walked away from the grave, down the road, and kept on walking.'

He could imagine it. Josefina, straight-shouldered, turning her back on everything and everyone, walking down the road and disappearing without a backward glance. The temerity of it almost made him smile until he realised one day she'd do the same to him—walk away without a backward glance. She *would* leave. She'd said as much and she'd said why. She was off to see the world. Her father's predicament resonated too well with him. He, too, had spent his own life building safety, security for those around him at the expense of his own freedom.

The wick burnt low on the lamp and their meal was long done. 'Shall I walk you home?' Owen offered, although letting her go was the last thing he wanted to do. What he wanted was…

She gave him a coy smile and he felt his body tighten

in anticipation of a wish about to be granted. 'No, but you may walk me upstairs and in the morning I'll make you Turkish coffee.'

Chapter Thirteen

She made him coffee the next morning and the morning after that and the one after that until their days fell into a rhythm of discretion: long nights in Owen's bed, followed by early morning walks back to the school, hands interlocked; days spent in her studio painting until she could sneak off again to Owen, to passion.

Not only passion. To say this affair was based solely on lust was to demean it, to not understand it. It was fast becoming something more than what it had begun as. It was hard to describe, not even *colpo di fulmine* would suffice. Whatever 'this' was, it far exceeded the thunderclap of sudden, overwhelming desire. This was deep and abiding, something that transcended physical need, a fulfilment of a different sort.

To be with Owen, to lay in bed with him and talk of anything and everything, was like finding sanctuary. With him, she could talk of her father, of her life in Venice, of her art—things she'd not talked of with another since she'd left home for fear of giving in to grief and for fear of leaving too many breadcrumbs behind if anyone was looking for her. It was as if she could set aside fear in Owen's bed.

In the days leading up to the Oyster Ball, Josefina was happy, content, in a way she had not felt in a long while, or perhaps ever, and it worried her. Happiness, contentment, was changing her. It dulled the edge of her recklessness. She no longer felt the keen need to slice through life, taking herself and others by surprise, always seeking the next thrill. Some might call this new order peace.

Josefina snuggled against Owen's warm body in the early morning hours, testing to see if he was awake. His hand tightened reflexively at her hip in answer. If this was peace, it was imperfect, her new contentment tinged with a guilt that hadn't plagued her old reckless self. She was riddled with regret, a relatively new experience.

She was regretting the promise she'd made to Padraig about using Owen's cellar, regretting involving Owen unknowingly in the smuggler's plans, regretting that she could not change the trajectory of Padraig's plans now with the cargo planning to drop at Shucker's Cove tonight, regretting that she could not tell Owen, for his own safety. There were too many moving parts to this plan to call it off now and they were all counting on the money. With the money from tonight's drop, her travel plans in May would be secure. She would be able to afford passage to the Americas, afford rent on a small house where she could paint once she arrived in the Caribbean. All she could do now was to dance Owen's feet off tonight at the Oyster Ball, keep him oblivious and keep him safe. It would all be fine. It would go off without any trouble.

She'd been repeating that litany for days now and sometimes she managed to convince herself it *would* be fine. It was *always* fine. Padraig hadn't been caught *ever*. Worry couldn't change anything now. The Josefina who'd come to Seasalter in January would have thought nothing about tonight's upcoming escapades. But the Josefina she was becoming saw the lark in an entirely different light. It did not sit comfortably—what was she to do with this new Josefina?

There was an hour or so left before she had to go back and she didn't want to spend it alone with her thoughts. If this new peace of hers was tinged with the guilt of a secret, it was also tinged with complication, something she was reminded of every morning when she left Owen. He walked as far as he could with her, but the final length was always a distance she had to walk on her own. It was an apt metaphor that lived in her mind each morning. One day in spring, she'd walk away from him for the last time. He would have come as far as he could on her journey and she would be alone, again.

The thought made her restless. 'Owen,' she whispered his name, wishing him awake.

Maybe this was why she made a point of blowing through places like a storm, never staying anywhere too long. Staying was dangerous. Staying risked missing some place or someone. Staying risked being found, in case anyone was looking. Staying risked forgetting her promises, forgetting the dreams she'd shouldered on her father's behalf. Staying risked her freedom. There were so many reasons to go, to keep moving, and only one reason to stay—this warm, virile man beside her, who worshipped her body with a reverence that astonished her, who'd revealed himself layer by careful layer, showing her the poor boy who'd grown up on the beaches, who'd taken on the work of a smuggler at fifteen and the work of a man at sixteen, who'd grown an empire from the simplest of beginnings armed only with a quick mind, who made love with the same single-minded intensity he devoted to his business.

'Josefina?' Owen's voice was gravelly with morning's drowsy rasp.

She turned into him, her head on his shoulder. 'You're awake.' She ran a hand down his chest. She never tired of touching him, of feeling his muscles ripple beneath her fingertips.

'Yes, you minx. Don't act surprised,' Owen chuckled. 'You woke me. Don't think I didn't notice your wiggles and whispers.'

'I haven't the faintest idea of what you're talking about.' She laughed, her fingertip drawing an idle circle around the aureole of his flat nipple, raising gooseflesh in its wake.

His arm tightened about her, pulling her close. She felt safe, wrapped in the cocoon of blankets and his body. Would that she could stay here for ever. *For ever.* The words were as dangerous as the idea of staying. This wasn't supposed to be about for ever. For ever implied expectations, and she remembered very clearly that night on the widow's walk when she'd insisted there was nothing to lose, nothing to expect beyond the moment. Had that only been a short two weeks ago? It seemed a lifetime ago, they'd been different people then. She didn't like it. She *couldn't* like it.

'You're thinking this morning, Josefina. Did you wake me to share your thoughts? Have you some grand scheme?' He chuckled, lazy and carefree before the day settled its burdens on him.

'I woke you because I didn't want to think.' She rolled on top of him, straddling him between her thighs. His hands framed her hips and desperation seized her: desperation to have him inside her, to fill her, to thrust her worries away, to distract her from the thoughts haunting her mind. She levered up over him and slid down his length. He was more than willing, but he was less than convinced. Even as she made quick, frantic work of finding pleasure, she was aware of his eyes on her, his gaze not quite as lost to passion as their bodies.

Afterwards, he gathered her to him and let her float in the slice of oblivion she'd found before he whispered, 'Are your demons back in their cages?'

She sighed. 'Chained, at least.' She hadn't been subtle at all, another regret to add to her list. 'I'm sorry.' It was poorly done of her. She'd used him selfishly this morning for pleasure, for release, as a place to run and hide.

'Tell me?' he prompted. He wouldn't thank her for it, but perhaps it was what both of them needed—a dose of reality, a reminder that they were just playing.

'I was thinking this can't last.' It wasn't speculation, it was simply fact. She levered herself up enough to watch his face. What would he say to that? Owen the protector, Owen the fixer who tried to make life better, safer for his people even when they didn't know it. Would he do the same for her? Offer her platitudes about how things could change, how they could decide to redefine their association when the time came? What would she say if he did? It would all be just an extension of the current fantasy. There could be no real redefinition. She could not stay.

She waited for the platitudes, but they didn't come. Owen said simply, 'We never thought it could last, Josefina. That doesn't mean it will be easy when you go. I, for one, prefer not to think about it yet.' He paused and gave her a considering look. 'Are *you* thinking about it? Do you *want* to leave?' She thought she heard a note of panic in his voice, a note quickly subdued. Perhaps she'd imagined it. Owen Gann never panicked. He was the embodiment of stability to her storm.

'I am *not* thinking about it,' she said resolutely, settling down into the crook of his arm. She envied him his control, his ability to tamp down worry. He took life's bumps in his stride, consuming them with his power; he'd risen above poverty and rejection. He'd rise above her, too, when she left. She needn't worry about him. That should be relieving. She didn't want to hurt him. And yet, part of her wanted to be remembered, wanted to leave her mark because she knew already that he would leave his on her.

The room was getting brighter. She found the willpower to roll away and swing her legs over the side of the bed. She needed to get dressed and he did, too. This was a big day. He would be busy with final preparations for the Oyster Ball tonight. She had her own arrangements to make.

Owen reached for her. 'Don't go yet.'

She moved beyond the temptation of his arm. 'I have to. Artemisia might turn a blind eye to my leaving, but she expects me back. It's part of our tacit bargain. She doesn't complain and I don't disappoint her.' Artemisia hadn't broached the topic of Owen with her since that first day. Josefina had been grateful for her discretion and she'd done her best to repay Artemisia with discretion of her own. 'You have the Oyster Ball to oversee.' She slipped into her clothes and put her hair into a hasty braid. Owen moved about the room, putting on his own clothes. She helped him with his cravat, giving it a final pat.

'Speaking of the ball…' Owen captured her hands before she could step away. 'Shall we pick a gown for tonight from the wardrobe in the guest room?' He was feeling playful this morning, a bright juxtaposition to the gloom that haunted her. 'There's a red gown that would be beautiful on you. You can take it with you. There's slippers, too.'

'I thought I would just wear the gown from the dinner with the bankers.' Josefina hesitated, her earlier guilt pinching at her. She was not entitled to more from this man. He'd put his heart on offer to a woman before to great disappointment. She did not want it to get that far again. Bodies on offer were one thing. Hearts were another.

He dropped her hands and moved to his bureau with a glint of mischief in his eyes—there were many such glints these days as his walls came down. She also noticed he'd ignored her polite protest about the dress. He pulled open a drawer and withdrew a velvet bag. 'There are these, too. I've been meaning to show them to you, but I haven't found the right moment.'

Josefina moved closer to him with a smile. 'And dawn is the right time?' she teased.

'It seems so.' Owen laughed and opened the little drawstring sack. He poured its contents into his hand and held them up for her to see. 'The Gann pearls, the ones I was telling you about.' He studied them with a wry grin. 'Not much to look at, as I mentioned.' It was true. The strand was not perfectly matched like the one she'd left behind in Venice, the first piece of jewellery her father had bought her when she'd turned eighteen.

'It has character, though, a collection of generations, history on a string,' Josefina said softly. She touched a pearl at the top of the string. 'Tell me about them. Which one is this?'

'That's the primary pearl, we call it. The first one, found by my great-grandfather. In fact, these seven are all primaries. He found them over twenty years of working the beds. No one has ever found as many pearls as he did.' Owen nodded to the next set. 'Those were found by my grandfather, these by my father, and these last three were found by me.' He paused. 'There were four, but I sold one for a doctor and medicines for my mother.' The remark sobered the joy of the morning. He'd smuggled and sold a family heirloom for his mother. There was no length this man would not go to for those who held his heart. Josefina curled her hand over his.

'I should have insisted we sell the pearl sooner. I should have pushed to have sold them all. We waited too long. She argued she'd get well, that it was just a cough, that we needn't spend money on her. By the time we did, it was too late. That's when everything changed for me. Money would have protected her if we'd had it sooner. Watching her waste away unnecessarily, I vowed I'd never let those I loved go without again.' Owen gave her a rueful smile. 'Enough of that, though. I didn't show these to you to be morbid. I wanted to ask, will you wear them tonight?'

Josefina's smile faded and she took an involuntary step back. Men bearing jewellery were to be avoided. Men bearing family jewels especially. She'd left the Swiss Count the night he'd presented her with an emerald tiara that had belonged to his grandmother. 'I couldn't, Owen. It wouldn't be right.' Hadn't they both just agreed this was never meant to last? And now here he was, pushing pearls on her as if this was more than a secret *affaire*. It wouldn't be secret much longer if she showed up in his pearls.

'What wouldn't be right about it?' Owen was already moving behind her, placing the pearls about her neck and fastening the clasp, his hands sending a warm trill shooting through her where they rested on her shoulders.

Her hand couldn't help itself from touching the pearls at her neck. They were warm and smooth beneath her fingers, like the man himself. 'These should be worn by…' She couldn't finish the sentence. It was too dangerous. *By someone you love. By your wife.* She didn't want to put impossible ideas in his head. She could be neither of those things to him. She didn't want him to love her, not enough to hurt, and she certainly couldn't marry him. She cleared her throat and tried again. 'They should be worn by someone who isn't me.' It was the best she could do.

'Nonsense, it's not as if they're diamonds.' Owen remained stubborn, refusing to remove them. 'It's just for the night. Consider them on loan, like the dress and the slippers.' He smiled broadly. 'The next time I see you, you'll be my lady in red, wearing the Gann pearls.'

The earlier pinch of guilt became a gouge. Here she was, helping smugglers sneak illegal goods into his home, and he was heaping her with 'riches,' a gown, slippers, all to make her the belle of the ball, *his* ball. She would be on his arm tonight, everyone would see her with him. 'Are you sure? People will speculate about us.'

Owen tucked her arm through his as they left the room. 'People have been speculating about me for years.' He paused, considering. 'Do *you* mind?'

'No.' Josefina let him usher her into the guest room and fill her arms with the red gown and all its accessories. The dress was a bright ruby shade. No one would overlook her in it. That was all to the good. If anything went wrong tonight, everyone would know Owen had no part in it. No one would dare accuse him of having been anywhere but on the dance floor with his lady in red. It was a significant consolation to hold on to and she clung to it gladly as something to offset her guilt and restore her peace. Everything would be fine tonight. Nothing would go wrong.

Something had been wrong with Josefina that morning. The thought niggled at Owen, refusing to let go throughout the day despite the busy agenda of overseeing refreshment tables and the unloading of food. She'd been distracted and desperate, that desperation evident in her lovemaking. Not that he hadn't enjoyed her desperate ride astride him in the dawn. There was something intoxicating about frantic lovemaking and the reckless speed of it. He'd willingly given her whatever succour she could find from his body. But this morning, he thought it hadn't quite been enough. Her demons still rattled their cages, still claimed her attentions. Whatever they might be.

'Bring the barrels of ale over here,' Owen instructed as men began to unload beverages. He wandered over to the chairs being set out for the older folks who preferred talking to dancing and then up to the dais being erected for the musicians, trying not to give in to the temptation of thinking through those demons. He failed to keep his thoughts away from them. The list of options was short: their relationship or leaving their relationship. What else might be on her mind? Perhaps he was missing something because their relationship was on *his* mind, occupying more mental space than even the vertical acquisition.

'Brother!' Simon called to him, waving from the factory door. Simon strode forward. 'Your head's in the clouds. I've called to you three times now.' Simon looked around. 'But it seems you have things well in hand as usual: chairs, tables, beverages, musicians.' He grinned in high spirits and clapped him on the shoulder. 'Elianora and I are looking forward to it. Her father is going to stay with the baby.' Simon paused. 'May I venture to guess what you were thinking about so intently you didn't hear me come in? Perhaps dancing with the delectable Miss Ricci?'

Owen smiled. There was no sense in hiding it from his brother. 'Perhaps I am.'

'My brother in love is a happy sight to see.' Simon's grin widened but Owen's vanished. Simon's gaze questioned his. 'Don't like the *L* word, dear brother?'

'I think that overstates the situation. We have become…friends. She is painting my portrait, we are spending time together as I show her around Seasalter, giving her a sense of my background. But that should not be misconstrued as something more.' He was rambling now, perhaps making the argument more for himself than for his brother.

Simon sobered. 'I didn't mean to bring up a touchy subject.'

Owen made a gesture to suggest it was of no import. But it was. He felt a fraud to disavow the relationship, as if it did Josefina a disservice and himself. He was *lying* to his brother. In the name of discretion and honour, of course, he reminded himself. To tell the truth was to be indiscreet, to risk rumour about Artemisia's school, to risk Josefina's honour and his own. He would be expected to do the right thing by her.

Simon looked uncomfortable despite his absolution and Owen relented. He directed Simon to a quiet corner, his voice hushed among the hubbub of workers. 'It's complicated because it's not complicated. She's here until May and that's it.' He was less sanguine about that then he'd made out to be with Josefina. She would leave sooner than May, that was merely the date of the show in London. Artemisia would want to go up earlier in April and open the town house and take care of a hundred details.

'That's it? You'll let her walk away?' Simon pressed in quiet tones.

'What else can I do?'

'Give her a reason to stay, for starters,' Simon argued. 'What's she in a hurry to get to, after all?'

It was a good question. In all the conversations they'd had, where she went next hadn't come up. Not surprisingly so. After all, to talk about where she went next meant talking about a future they didn't share. He was in no hurry to have that conversation. Josefina had changed his world in a very short time. She'd brought companionship, passion and a new delight to every day that had been missing. He could share with her. She was not put off by his humble beginnings. She embraced him as he was. Perhaps that was because their association wasn't permanent. But for now, he didn't want to question it. He wanted to enjoy it. He'd spent years looking ahead, looking down the road and for once, he just wanted to live in the moment.

Simon looked as if he wanted to pose another question. Owen shook his head, warding it off. 'Say nothing more, please.' Although the damage might already be done. His mind was beginning to spin with intriguing possibilities. What if things could be different? What if there was a future where he and Josefina could be together? Would he want it? Would he fight for it? How might he win her over? These were dangerous thoughts. He pushed them aside. 'I just want to enjoy tonight, Simon. I don't want to look beyond it, not yet.'

Chapter Fourteen

He could not look beyond her. Josefina was radiant and he simply could not tear his gaze away from the moment she entered to the moment she reached his side, weaving her way through the crowd, a bright scarlet thread amid a sea of more sensible blues, greys and greens. Even when she stood before him, he could not look away, his eyes lingering at the pearls at her neck. *His*, they seemed to say. She was his.

'You've outdone yourself, my dear.' He was glad he'd dressed the part as host more formally, choosing dark evening wear that would pass muster in London. The guests expected it of him, and tonight Josefina's appearance demanded it, her inky dark hair piled in ringlets and threaded with a ribbon, gold earbobs dancing at her ears, her gown pressed to perfection. Even if it was from a collection at least ten years old, the cut was excellent and the fabric expensive. It deserved, *she* deserved, to be partnered with its equal. She held up the hem of her skirts to show off the matching scarlet slippers with a mischievous smile.

'You look quite fine yourself, sir.' She made a little curtsy, her cheeks high with colour. 'What a party this is! Look at all of the food, I hardly know what to do first: eat, drink or dance.'

He offered her his arm. 'Let's dance and work up an appetite.'

She slid her arm through his and flashed him a naughty smile. 'What sort of appetite would that be, Mr Gann?'

Owen laughed. 'A hearty one, *signorina*.' He led her to the dance floor and found them a place in a set for the scotch reel, a lively circle country dance. He closed his hand around hers as the music began and she smiled at him. Not a bedroom smile, but a smile of simple joy. She *wanted* to be here with him. The thought warmed him as the music began. There was a rightness to being here with her like this, in his factory, among his people, in the place he was raised. The dance was fast, a series of half-steps and heel clicks as the circle went left and then right, couples moving to form a star and then re-forming the circle and passing partners.

He acknowledged his new partner, but his eyes were riveted on Josefina across the circle from him. She sparkled, dazzling her partner with her smile, her laugh. She was grace itself as she went through the steps, her skirts swishing, her slippers flashing on her feet. How many nights could be like this? Dancing with Josefina, watching her with his people? What a hostess she'd make, bringing life and excitement everywhere she went.

Just a hostess? His conscience laughed at him. *You are not so selfless*, it said. *This is not just about serving your people. She'd serve you well, too. You want her by your side, regardless.*

He did want her by his side. He hadn't even realised how dead he'd been inside until she'd shown him with her flashing eyes and her arguments what it meant to be alive, to move away from his lonely isolation. The dance ended, but they stayed on the floor, moving into a speedy country galop of a dance that left them laughing and winded, but still they danced on, neither of them interested in leaving the dance floor, or interested in relinquishing each other. He relished his hand at her waist, the nearness of her body as they moved around the dance floor, her face turned up to his, her eyes alight. Good lord, he would give the world to hold on for ever to the feelings she stirred in him, for holding *her* for ever. What would he give for *this*?

Elation buoyed him across the floor, speeding their steps. Thank goodness this wasn't London. Such freedom would not be possible there. But, oh, how she'd shine in town, gracing the ballrooms with that smile, in fashionable gowns, pearls about her neck—matched pearls, perhaps, a better quality than his own string. He could afford the best.

'You are floating somewhere, Owen. Care to take me along?' Josefina laughed up at him.

'I'm just happy.' And that was more than enough.

The music stopped, the musicians taking a mid-evening break. 'Let's get something to eat, I am told the oysters are spectacular.' Owen winked at her, ushering her through the crowd. They filled their plates at the tables laid out buffet-style and filled mugs with foaming ale from the barrels. Owen found them a quiet place beneath the stairs. It was tempting to go upstairs to his offices, but he'd not be able to manage it without everyone noticing.

'Do you really think oysters are an aphrodisiac?' Josefina slurped an oyster off the half-shell with easy dexterity.

Owen laughed. 'I think they could be. A scientist friend of mine told me there was a lot of zinc in oysters and zinc inspires one's libido. So, perhaps there's some legitimacy to the idea. But I think one can make an aphrodisiac out of anything.' He tapped his head with a finger. 'It's all in one's mind. Though, it's good for business. Men are impressed with its…um…certain properties.' He leaned close, breathing her in. 'You in a red dress, though, are all the aphrodisiac I need.' He caught her lips and stole a kiss, tasting the sweet ale on her tongue. She moved into him, all soft, warm, willing woman. Her arms twined about his neck and he wanted to be anywhere but here, preferably in his bed, with her. Owen whispered between heated kisses, 'I wish all these people were gone. I wish we were home.'

'I don't.' Josefina slipped a hand between their bodies, finding his member fighting a rather public display

of arousal. 'Intimacy in a crowd can be rather erotic.'
She kissed him full on the mouth.

'Josefina, have a care. I might feel like marble, but
I assure you I am merely a man,' he breathed against
her, his member firm beneath her hand, beneath his
trousers. 'I'll have to go back out there. I can't possibly do that in this condition you have me in.' At least
his trousers were dark, but his evening coat was cut
rather unhelpfully in that regard, sitting square and
short at his waist. So much for being fashionable. He
was missing the folds of his greatcoat.

She licked her lips, leaving them red and glistening
in the dimness of the stairwell as she whispered her
temptation. 'I can take care of that, if you're up for it.'
The minx was daring him. His body wanted to take
that dare, but his mind knew better. What sort of host
took his pleasure in a dark corner while his guests par-
tied? He'd been a poor enough host already, devoting
himself singularly to just one guest. Although, after
enough ale and full bellies, his guests were likely not
to notice.

'Am I up for it?' Owen gave a hoarse chuckle. 'What
do you think?' He'd never done anything so outrageous
in a public venue and the thought was rather intoxicating. 'You're rubbing off on me, Josefina. I'm becoming reckless.'

'I like it, Owen. All work and no play makes for a
dull man. Shall I take you with my hand right here or
do you want to step outside?'

Outside would be safer, but in for a penny, in for a

pound. 'Here, Josefina. Right here.' He kissed her then, drinking all of her as she opened the fall of his trousers and slipped her hand inside, circling his swollen member. He didn't last long, he hadn't been meant to. By the time she'd got her hand on him, the anticipation of the act and very thought of where it was taking place had already done much of the work, his arousal rock hard and complete, needing only the lightest of coaxings towards release.

'Better?' She flirted up at him, taking his offered handkerchief. She was right, stolen intimacy in public carried an eroticism of its own that lived beyond the act. When they went back out there and joined the others, whenever their eyes met the rest of the evening, they would think of this, of these decadent moments apart from the crowd.

'Yes, thank you.' He smiled, trying to match her playfulness and falling short. He could not forget the desperation she'd awakened with this morning, how she'd sought oblivion with his body, her thoughts worrying over the future, not unlike his own thoughts perhaps. Had she, too, played the 'what if' game?

Josefina moved as if to return to the party. He put a hand on her wrist, gently stalling. 'Wait, I want to ask you something.' He'd not planned to do it this way, but the moment seemed right and momentum was on his side. He drew her to him, into the vee of his thighs, his hands gripping hers. 'It's about what you said this morning.' He gave her a moment to think back to that conversation, his gaze intent on hers. 'Josefina, what if you stayed? What if you didn't leave in May?'

She worried her lower lip with her teeth. He'd caught her by surprise, something he didn't think happened often, not when it came to men. 'What are you saying, Owen?'

'What if you didn't leave in May? What if you never left? What if you stayed with me, here?'

Her finger was soft against his lips. 'That's not the plan. I don't need you to play the gallant, Owen. We said no expectations.'

He moved her finger aside in a gentle gesture. 'Plans change and an absence of expectations doesn't rule out surprises, only anticipated prospects.' He needed to be careful here; there was a thin line between persuading and begging. He would not beg. She would not respect a beggar, a man with no self-respect. 'Tell me you don't want to stay. Tell me you don't want more of this.'

'It's not about want, Owen. Of course I *want* more of this. But I *need* to go. I have promises to keep.'

Owen took a deep breath, steadying himself, and she stepped back, a bad omen, surely. 'We should not discuss such things tonight. This evening is for fun and revelry. I dare say we're not in our best minds. We should dance and feast and enjoy each other's company to the full, not make plans for an uncertain future.'

He reached for her hand. She hadn't stepped so far from him that he couldn't touch her. He raised it to his lips, unwilling to leave the discussion with nothing. He needed a token of her commitment to allay the knot of panic that had tied itself in his stomach, his intuition screaming that amid all that was right, something was wrong. He didn't know what, only that the wrongness was there, a nugget hidden among the hoard of his happiness. He turned her hand over, palm up and kissed it. 'You're right. Tonight is not the night. We have time. Tell me you'll think about it, though. Promise me that much at least.'

She gave him a soft smile and the words he needed. 'I will, but you need to do something for me.'

'Anything.' The ill-fated words of Richard III played through his head, *my kingdom for a horse*. He'd give it all for her. Economically, it was a poor trade, but his heart wasn't buying it at all. Perhaps Simon was right and he was on the brink of falling in love.

His conscience laughed. *On the brink, my boy? Oh, heavens, no, you've already jumped into the abyss.*

And he was still falling. If there was a bottom he hadn't found it.

She flashed him a smile. 'I want to dance and dance until the sun comes up and my slippers are worn through.' Ah, *that* he could manage.

He did manage it: circle dances, reels, dashing polkas. The headiness of the evening returned, unmarred by his error beneath the stairs. He had misjudged the situation. He had pushed for too much against his own good sense. He should have stuck to what he'd told Simon this afternoon: he was looking to enjoy the evening and not beyond it. Besides, he knew how the evening would end—with Josefina in his bed. That was enough for now and for the weeks to come.

Half-past eleven there was a commotion at the factory door. His instincts had him leaving the dance floor and crossing the wide room before Simon could signal him. Josefina trailed behind him. 'What is it? What's going on?'

'I don't know.' He turned to her, his hands on her shoulders, feeling the slickness of silk beneath his fingers. 'Stay here, my dear. I'll be back in a moment. It seems some business has arisen. It will be a minute, nothing more. I can't imagine anything serious on party night.' At the door, he recognised Lieutenant Hawthorne. 'Lieutenant, how can I help you?' He ushered the man outdoors into the dark where they might have privacy. 'Has anyone given you some ale? Food? There's plenty.' He felt for the man, having drawn the short straw on party night.

The Lieutenant didn't smile. 'I've not come for entertainment, Mr Gann. I will need to pull you away from the party, in fact. There was a cargo unloaded this evening on the cove not far from your home.' The Lieutenant waited, watching him. The Lieutenant expected a reaction, Owen realised. The cargo was supposed to mean something to him.

'I am surprised to hear that, Lieutenant.' All revelry fled, his mind shifting gears into twin modes of protection and predation. Whatever the Lieutenant was hunting for he would not find it here. The Lieutenant might, however, find that he was not the hunter any longer, that he was on foreign ground.

'Are you?' The Lieutenant had become grim. Owen racked his mind for any mention of a drop tonight. There'd been none. There wasn't likely to be any more until spring, in fact. There had been talk, though, a couple of weeks ago, about a large cargo of French brandy, but no place to land it and store it until it could go up to London. Talk of it had disappeared. Had it resurfaced and he'd missed it somehow? He'd been wrapped up in his vertical venture and in Josefina, his mind elsewhere these past weeks—it was entirely possible, but that assumed arrangements had been made, that the earlier obstacles had been overcome. If so, he should have been on his roof tonight. He would have seen Lieutenant Hawthorne's men.

'Perhaps you will also be "surprised" to know that Padraig O'Malley and five other men are under our supervision at present and that twenty barrels of brandy are currently in your cellar.'

Owen didn't even need to feign surprise. That was positively shocking and impossible. 'I've been here all night. Everyone will tell you that. Padraig O'Malley has been here, as well.' Only not all night. He began to sort through the evening in his mind, stealthily, not to give any hint of doubt to the Lieutenant. Padraig had been at the party. But for how long? Up until he and Josefina had stepped behind the stairs. Owen wasn't sure he could recall seeing the man after he and Josefina had returned. Even more interesting, the man hadn't sought to dance with her. Odd, given that Owen knew Padraig and Josefina had danced often at the Crown. Of course, that was before her relationship with him. Still, at an informal party, one might have thought Padraig would seek one dance at least, or perhaps not. Owen had not thought overmuch about it until now.

'I will need you to come with me to Baldock House and sort this out.'

'I'll be right with you, let me leave word with my brother.' Owen turned to go inside, and a flash of red glinted on his periphery. Josefina in the dark.

'No.' Lieutenant Hawthorne's tone was authoritative and definitive. 'I don't think you understand, Mr Gann. Your home is holding illegal goods and you are potentially moments away from being arrested on the grounds of dealing in contraband. You are in no position to negotiate.'

That was a mistake. One was always in a position to negotiate. Some positions were just better than others. Owen drew himself up to his full height and breadth. 'And you forget, Lieutenant Hawthorne, that you most recently dined at my table as my guest.'

Lieutenant Hawthorne stiffened at the reminder of hospitality and the idea that his behaviour at present was in violation of that hospitality. 'That, sir, was when I thought you were an honest man.' Hawthorne had gumption, Owen would give him that and he would remember it. This would not be the only negotiation tonight. There were men counting on him to untangle this mess.

Owen hazarded a quick look to the left where he'd seen the flash of red gown. Their gazes met in a swift moment, her eyes wide with concern. He wanted to go to her, assure her all would be well, but there was no time. Hawthorne was insistent. He gave thanks that Josefina hadn't been among the smugglers tonight or she would have been taken, too, the very nightmare he'd warned her about. That was a stroke of luck, at least.

Was it? Luck? A happy coincidence? His conscience teased with cynical disregard for his feelings.

Perhaps she'd been playing her part? His heart gave a cry in the dark, *for how long?* Had it been a part she'd played behind the stairs so Padraig could sneak out? Had she been playing that part all night? For weeks?

And then he knew, this was the nugget. This was what was wrong. He and Josefina. Oh, God. He wanted to collapse, wanted to slink away and sort through it, understand it, but he couldn't even think about it now because five men needed him to save them from the hangman. After one final look, he turned to follow the Lieutenant.

Chapter Fifteen

She had to save him. Josefina stepped back into the shadows, bracing herself against the wall for support as she watched Owen follow Lieutenant Hawthorne into the night, into disaster. Her mind was a frantic mess. This wasn't how it was supposed to be. Owen was innocent. Being with her tonight was supposed to have deflected any guilt away from him should things go awry and keep him in the dark if they went right. Just the opposite had happened. Padraig and the men had been caught at the house and, by extension, their presence at the house itself had made Owen guilty. Oh, what a mess this was and it was all her fault. There was no escaping her part in this and Owen had known it.

That last gaze, when their eyes had met before he turned away, had made her nauseous. He knew; he knew that she'd known about the drop, that perhaps she'd known they were using his house, and the speculation that this evening had been planned. It had bordered on condemnation. It wouldn't take long for that condemnation to become full blown. His mind was fast—he would soon figure out what had happened and what she'd done. He would doubt her, doubt them, and then he would hate her. Perhaps even see her as a woman worse than the one who'd rejected him those years ago.

The enormity of what that meant sent her sliding down the length of the wall, the cold of it seeping through the back of her gown and into her skin, stealing all the warmth from the night, a night that had, up to that point, been quite warm. A moan escaped her, the realisation providing as much physical anguish as mental. She covered her mouth with her hands, lest someone hear her. It was all gone. Everything was gone: the warm nights in his bed, the worship in his eyes when he looked at her, the reverence of his hands on her body, the way he listened to her, the way he talked to her, spilling tales of his boyhood over the kitchen counter as he cooked for her.

She rocked herself in the dark, her arms wrapped around her waist, trying to subdue the pain, trying to keep the hurt in. In her recklessness, in her desire to belong, she'd endangered a good man. More than that, she'd endangered a man who *loved* her. She saw that now even if that word hadn't been used. He'd asked her to stay, tonight. He didn't want her to leave. He'd given her part of himself—the stories of his childhood, the tragedies of that childhood as well, the heartbreak of early adulthood, the hard realisations that no matter how much money he made, he'd always belong to a place between two worlds.

A man did not make himself vulnerable on a whim, not to any woman, not if he'd been burned by love before. What had it taken for him to open himself so completely to her? Look what she'd done with it. She'd betrayed him. Would he believe she'd betrayed him in all ways, that everything between them had been tied up in this one betrayal? Would he think tonight, those vital moments behind the stairs, had been nothing more than a distraction? Would he think her a trollop, a woman who had used her body in exchange for smuggler's money? That all of this had been her earning her pay, her cut of tonight's ambitious drop?

The factory door opened, a shaft of light piercing the darkness, the raucous sounds of the party filling the silent night. She wanted it gone, she wanted no reminders of the joy she'd felt only minutes ago. A shadow stepped across the light. 'Josefina, what are you doing out here? Where's Owen?'

Simon! Josefina swiped at her cheeks and scrambled to her feet, events falling from her lips in a mad, incoherent rush. 'Lieutenant Hawthorne was here—there was a smuggling run tonight and he caught Padraig at Owen's house, hiding the barrels in the basement. The Lieutenant made Owen go with him.' She gripped Simon's arm. 'He thinks Owen is guilty, that Owen had something to do with it. Owen doesn't, though. He was here all night.'

'Being here doesn't mean he hadn't had a hand in

organising it.' Simon's face wore a grim expression. 'It will be hard to prove that he hasn't masterminded this.'

Terror gripped her. That thought had not crossed her mind in all the planning. 'He is innocent, Simon. He didn't plan this. He didn't even know Padraig was going to store the barrels there.'

'I'll go at once. Perhaps you might go in and tell Lady St Helier? It wouldn't hurt to have a viscount on Owen's side.' Then he relaxed and he forced a smile. 'Don't worry, Josefina, I am sure by the time I get there Owen will have it all smoothed over.' But Simon set off into the dark after his brother with great speed, a sign that he, too, was worried. Smuggling was a grave offence, in all ways.

Josefina went back inside and found Artemisia and Darius. She pulled them aside and delivered the news, but speculation was already running through the crowd. People had begun slipping off to their homes, or gathering together in tight knots. Everyone had seen Lieutenant Hawthorne at the door, even though Owen had tried to escort him outside quickly before panic could set in. Redcoats weren't welcome around here. They meant only one thing—trouble. In these parts, trouble was smuggling.

The party was effectively over. Owen hadn't been the only one involved in tonight's cargo. Josefina looked about the emptying room; Charlie's wife, white-faced and stoic, as she comforted Ned's pregnant bride; Thomas's wife slipping out the door alone, no doubt going home to make the house safe, to prepare for whatever came next. For the first time since Lieutenant Hawthorne had taken Owen, Josefina found the strength to move beyond her own fear. What would happen to these women's men? Men who were husbands and fathers? Would Owen be able to save them? She knew he would try. He would not let his men, his workers, go to the gallows.

Artemisia was asking her questions in low, rapid tones. 'What happened?'

'I don't know. Someone must have told Hawthorne about the drop. Somehow he found out. He's got everyone at Baldock House. Even Owen.' Tears were starting again. She turned her gaze to the Viscount. 'Please say you'll go. You cannot let them blame Owen. He didn't know anything.'

Artemisia pursed her lips. 'Don't be naive, Josefina. The barrels are in his basement. He likely knew everything. How else would O'Malley have got in? I have no quarrel with smuggling. It's how things are done here. However, I didn't know Owen still dabbled in it. I thought he'd left it years ago. That's fine. It's his choice, after all. But we can't make ridiculous arguments of innocence with the Lieutenant. He won't believe them and we'll look foolish.'

'The cellar door is an outside door and it's unlocked.' Josefina's voice was a whisper as the folly of what she'd done overwhelmed her. What had she been thinking to risk Owen like this? Owen had warned her, hadn't he? That day in the parlour? But she'd not taken his words to heart. Then, he'd been nothing but a stuffy man without an adventurous bone in his body. How wrong she'd been and now he was going to hang for her if she didn't set the record straight.

Artemisia shook her head, unconvinced. 'Further proof that Owen is part of this. Doors aren't just left unlocked. No doubt Owen and Padraig arranged it between them. How else would Padraig have known the door was open?'

Josefina met Artemisia's gaze, steady and even. 'The reason Padraig knew the door was open is because I was the one who arranged for him to use the cellars. Owen knows nothing about it.' She swallowed hard, trying not to think of the consequences of her confession, only of what must be done. 'I will tell the Lieutenant. Owen *is* innocent.'

'You will do no such thing!' Artemisia snapped sotto voce, flashing a speaking look at Darius, who gave a curt nod and headed towards the door. Artemisia's grip on her arm hurt. 'Do you want to be hung? Transported? To admit to such a thing is to condemn them all.'

'I would do it to save him,' Josefina whispered fiercely. She would sell them all to Lieutenant Hawthorne if it made a difference. They'd all made terms with the risks of their endeavours. Owen had not. Owen had not asked for any of this.

'It won't come to that,' Artemisia said staunchly and Josefina desperately wanted to believe her. She looked longingly towards the door. She should be out there, at Baldock House, arguing with the Lieutenant. She wanted to see Owen, wanted to explain everything to him, to assure him. Of what? That she loved him, too? Did she love him? She feared she did, but she'd not acted like a very good lover. Lovers didn't betray one another. He would be hard pressed to find her protestations believable.

'Absolutely not.' Artemisia read her mind. 'The best thing you can do now is to come home with me and wait.'

'I want to do something,' Josefina argued.

'You will be. No sneaking out, no going over to Baldock House. You are to stay as far away from that mess as possible. For Owen's sake, for your own sake and for the school's sake, I need you to follow directions this once.' She looped her arm through Josefina's. 'Let's go home. There's nothing more we can do now except hope that St Helier can work some magic.' The room for doubt in Artemisia's words caused her to worry anew.

'Simon says Owen will have it sorted out,' Josefina offered, but Artemisia's gaze was dubious.

'Smuggling is serious, it's not easily sorted, Josefina. So few are actually caught, the Crown is dedicated to making a very good example of those they do catch as a reminder of just how grave an offence it is to steal from the King.' That was when it truly dawned on her how much trouble Owen was in. He could hang. Not just hang. He could die. Because of her. A grave offence indeed.

'Smuggling is a grave offence, Mr Gann.' Lieutenant Hawthorne had the audacity to sit behind *his* desk.

The man had wasted no time commandeering the office at Baldock House as his own. Two eager young Corporals stood at attention at the door while Hawthorne's men had established a perimeter guard about the house. The place was like an armed camp and, in Owen's opinion, a bit over the top for the situation. Then again, Hawthorne was likely bucking for promotion, a hard task in peacetime. Owen was not sympathetic. The Lieutenant had locked him in the cellar with the others until the Lieutenant was ready to 'interview the prisoners,' as he put it.

'As is an obstruction of justice.' Owen strolled to the sideboard, *his sideboard*, and poured himself a drink just to prove he was still in charge of his domain, no matter who sat behind the desk. He did not offer Hawthorne one. He'd offered the man enough of his hospitality. 'I would be careful how you proceed, Lieutenant. You cannot go about throwing citizens into cellars without a warrant. Neither can you go about assuming people are guilty until proven innocent. I believe it works the other way around.' He took a swallow of the brandy, letting it burn down his throat in a slow, fiery river.

'The barrels are in your cellar,' the Lieutenant reminded him coolly. 'I am not sure how much more proof I need to demonstrate.' That was, of course, something of a surprise and a stumbling block. Certainly, Padraig knew what the barrels were doing there, but Padraig had said nothing down in the cellar. Perhaps he'd been worried about being overheard or self-incriminating. Whatever the reason, the big Irishman had barely spared him a glance, which spoke of layers of guilt Owen wasn't ready to contemplate. First things first. That meant getting these charges removed and getting these men home to worried families.

'A man cannot have liquor in his cellar? Where else would he keep it?' Owen queried. He set down his glass and strode to a drawered cabinet where he kept his cheques. Casually, he opened the drawer and took out his chequebook.

The Lieutenant gave a tired sigh. 'You and I both know the liquor is illegal.'

'It's illegal to drink brandy?'

'It's illegal to have brandy that has not cleared customs. You are being tedious, Mr Gann. You and I both know there is a tax on brandy. Not paying that import tax is akin to stealing from the Crown.'

Owen approached the desk, his gaze hard as steel. 'Get yourself a drink, Lieutenant. I need to sit down and you're in my chair. It's difficult to conduct business standing up.' The Lieutenant met his gaze for an uncomfortable moment. Owen did not flinch. This was his house, dammit, and these were his men in the cellar. He was not going to let a promotion-hungry lieutenant ruin their lives. Lieutenant Hawthorne's Adam's apple bobbed and then he rose. 'Thank you.' Owen slid into his chair and took out a fountain pen. He dipped it and began to write. 'There you are, Lieutenant.' He pushed the cheque across the desk.

'What is this?' Hawthorne's eyes narrowed and then

widened at the amount. It was a rather staggering sum, one that would deplete his ready resources for a time. 'Is this a bribe, sir? Because I assure you that a King's Officer does *not* take bribes as a substitute for justice.'

'Hardly a bribe.' Owen managed to look coolly offended. Under other circumstances, he would have liked to have debated the Lieutenant's assertion. 'I am making the brandy legal. As you are aware, I was not at home when it arrived. I had no chance to pay. Given the chance, as is clearly evidenced by this cheque, I am more than willing to pay the taxes on it and, in fact, had always intended to do so.'

Hawthorne would not touch the cheque. 'There is no customs house in Seasalter. *Legal* brandy comes to London. It does not come here. Seasalter is a hotbed of smuggling activity.'

'Says who?' Owen stared him down. 'I know of no smugglers. No one has been caught, to my knowledge. So how would you know if there was any smuggling happening here?' He furrowed his brow in puzzlement. 'I'm afraid I don't follow your logic.'

'There was a French ship last month,' Hawthorne sputtered. Owen hid a smile.

'The war is over. The French are allowed to sail these waters. I heard about that ship. I believe it was empty, nothing of note was found aboard. I'm not sure what that proves, Lieutenant.'

'That we caught it after it unloaded its cargo. Right here.'

'But no cargo was found,' Owen persisted. 'An

empty ship off the coast of Seasalter, a fishing village with no harbour, I might add, does not make a strong correlation, let alone offer proof of anything.' Hawthorne's frustration was evident. There was a moment in every negotiation when it became important to claim what you wanted and that moment had arrived. Owen smiled empathetically. 'I appreciate your commitment, Lieutenant. Truly. But this is not your night. Surely even you can hear how ridiculous your claims are as you talk through the situation right now. I shudder to think of how much weaker a professional barrister would make those claims sound in front of a judge and a packed courtroom.' He paused to let that last piece sink in. A man hoping for promotion could hardly risk being the centrepiece to a farce.

He let Hawthorne imagine it—*a man tried to pay his legitimate taxes on brandy and you refused his money.* It wouldn't sound like smuggling as much as stupidity on Hawthorne's part, especially when the man in question was Owen Gann, a man with plenty of money who didn't need to skirt taxes.

Hawthorne took a nervous swallow of his drink. Owen pressed his advantage. 'Now, I am sure you are disappointed. It is hard to get advancement during peacetime, nearly as hard as your impossible assignment of catching smugglers. Take the cheque, see to it that my honest money for honest brandy goes into the King's coffers.' Or not. Owen didn't particularly care if Hawthorne pocketed the sum. Either way, the man wouldn't be able to inform on him. If he kept the money and tried to convict Owen, Owen would have the cheque number and the draw on his bank to show he'd paid the taxes.

'This isn't right, Gann, and you know it,' Hawthorne huffed, but he took the cheque.

Owen shrugged. 'No, Lieutenant, I don't know it. What I do know, though, is that innocent men are locked in my cellar for a non-existent crime. I'll go let them out and send them home. Meanwhile, I'll expect your men gone within the next quarter-hour. There's no reason for them to stay and I'm sure they'll welcome their own beds. It's been a long night.' It would be longer still for Owen. There was more to be done, more to be reckoned with. Confronting Lieutenant Hawthorne had been the first of many confrontations. There was still Padraig to deal with, and Josefina. He would save her for last because she would take all the strength he had left.

Chapter Sixteen

Owen faced Padraig man to man after he'd sent the others home. 'I would like my cellar back as soon as you can move the brandy.' He'd like a lot more than his cellar back; he'd like his heart back, his self-respect back. His money back. Josefina back. But all of those things were beyond his reach. He had to settle for what he *could* have back. In the immediacy, that meant a dark, empty space he never used. The money would come later. He could always make more. His self-respect might take a bit longer, but he'd put that back together once before, too. He could certainly do it again. As for Josefina, that was likely unsalvageable, nor should he tempt himself in that direction again even if it was, not when he knew such disastrous truths.

To his credit, Padraig didn't make excuses. 'We can have it distilled and ready to move out in two days.' Owen nodded. They could take as long as they liked, technically. After all, the brandy was legal now, paid for twice over. But the sooner any sign of his folly was removed from his house, the better.

Regret was written plainly on Padraig's face. 'It wasn't supposed to turn out this way.'

'What went wrong?' Owen asked directly.

'Hawthorne knew.' Padraig shrugged. 'I don't know how, but I will find out. If it was a leak, if someone here betrayed us, I will put a stop to it,' he said grimly. 'Thank you for what you did tonight. We can never repay you.' Owen knew he meant it quite literally. The sum had been exorbitant. An oysterman would never see that much money in his entire life.

Owen clapped the man on the shoulder. 'I can't lose my best harvesters, not with the season about to peak. Now that the liquor is legal, you boys can cut it at leisure in the cellar and sell it without worry.'

'That's very generous.' Padraig hesitated. 'I'm sorry about her, too, Gann. I should not have let her do it.' Ah. Bitter confirmation of his suspicions. Another nail in the coffin of his hopes. He could not ignore the truth now. She had offered up Baldock House without his knowledge, behind his back. He could not pretend otherwise, not with Padraig's confirmation. He'd made it easy for her. He hadn't even tried to resist her.

Owen gave a short nod. 'Well, if you hadn't used my cellars you couldn't have taken the delivery.' It was best to think about the practicalities and not the motives behind them. The best way to get through a crisis was to simply put one foot in front of the other, to do the next thing, to not look too far afield. If he gave himself permission to think about her, he would break and that was not something he could allow yet.

'She's a lot of woman to handle,' Padraig commiserated, not taking the hint Owen would like to leave the subject of Josefina alone. She wasn't meant to be handled. That was any man's first mistake, Owen thought. Josefina was meant to be *enjoyed*. Preferably from afar, like a brilliant lightning storm at sea. He should have followed his own advice in that regard. He never should have walked her home that night in January when he'd spied her on the beach. He never should have agreed to sit for the portrait. Josefina was something a man might look at but did not touch except at risk to himself.

He gave Padraig another short nod and excused himself. There was still more work to be done before his night was over. There was Simon to see, instructions to leave, trunks to pack—he could not stay here. There was Josefina to deal with. He did try to talk himself out of the latter. Why not just get in his coach and leave? He did not owe her a goodbye. He owed her nothing after tonight. That was the coward's way out. He was no coward. He would face her, he wanted her to know that he knew what she'd done, to him and to them. She'd broken his heart and taken his trust. Those were no small things to do to a man. Then, when he was in his coach on the way to London, he would let himself grieve for all that could have been.

He came to her well after sunrise, unkempt, still dressed in his evening clothes, his cravat undone, his shirt open at the neck, stubble on his cheek, his blond hair falling forward on to his face so that he had to push it back every few minutes. Perhaps he should have changed and shaved, but his horses were as fresh as his pain and he wanted to be gone, on to the next thing that needed tackling to keep the pain at bay. If he could stay busy enough, perhaps he might avoid grieving altogether.

She was at the farmhouse with Darius and Artemisia, all of whom had kept vigil throughout the night. The night had not been kind to her. She was pale and drawn, dark circles beneath her eyes, an old shawl wrapped about her shoulders. Her hair was down and she still wore the red dress. The two of them had turned into pumpkins, she with her wilted gown and old shawl, he with his dishevelled clothes. Gone was the girl who'd dazzled him hours ago, yet his eyes were drawn to her. He had no attention for Artemisia and Darius.

At the sight of him, she was on her feet, a cry of relief on her lips. 'Owen!' She crossed the parlour at a run, dodging furniture edges in her haste. She flung her arms about him and pressed close, her lips spilling questions and information all at once. 'You're safe, Hawthorne's let you go? I was so worried. I saw him take you away. I sent Simon and Darius after you, but they were turned back. Hawthorne had guards all about the place and I feared the worst.' It took her a moment to realise he had not hugged her back, had not wrapped his arms about her, but had stood there aloof while she'd showered him with affection. He did not want her to guess how hard it was not to give in, not to hold her close and breathe her in as if nothing had changed. He supposed he could. He could pretend he didn't know, that Padraig had kept her secret. But what point was there in rebuilding a relationship on a lie?

She quieted, her eyes stilling on his as she stepped back and smoothed her rumpled skirts. 'Owen, I am so sorry. I didn't mean to hurt you. What I did was wrong, so wrong.' Her dark eyes filled with tears that tore at his heart, but he strengthened his resolve. If he allowed himself to be won over by a few tears, he would never get his self-respect back.

'Hurt me? By that, are you referring to breaking my heart or nearly breaking my neck? There are, after all, only so many ways to hurt a man. I have saved my neck for the time being.' But his heart was clearly still hers and might always be. He'd have to find a way to go on without it, then, because there was no question of putting himself through this again. He was aware of Darius and Artemisia discreetly leaving the room. He waited to hear the soft snick of the door shutting behind them.

'You could have got me killed.' He let the quiet words fill the room, more potent for the muted volume of his voice than if he'd yelled them. He wanted to yell, though, wanted to throw something, several somethings for the satisfaction of watching them shatter like his heart. But that would accomplish nothing.

'Your absence, your ignorance of the plan, was supposed to keep you safe.' She reached for him again, wanting to put her hands on his shoulders, wanting to reason with him through her touch. He stepped away.

'Quite the opposite occurred. Fortunately, I was able to pay the taxes due on the brandy and legitimise it. Everyone is safe and the smugglers still have a product to sell.' He laid out the facts with the objective efficiency of a barrister. It was easier to talk to her that way. 'Padraig explained everything.'

A little smile of relief—of hope?—hovered on her lips. Did she view this as some sort of absolution? 'Then the worst is over.' Her smile widened. 'No harm done in the final analysis.'

He cut her off almost savagely. 'No harm done? You lied to me. You made me believe you—' *love you*—no, he wouldn't say the words '—you *cared* for me. I told you things, showed you things that I've not ever shared with another person and all the while you were stealing from me: my home, my heart. You are reckless, Josefina, with yourself and with others. You were reckless with me.'

She shook her head, pleading, 'I made a mistake, Owen. I should have told you. I should have asked you to help. I was trying to keep you safe.' He'd never been more unsafe in his life than when he'd been with her. He'd been exposed, vulnerable, and that had been used against him.

'How much of it was a lie, Josefina?' He ground out the words. 'All of it? When we were behind the staircase last night was that just a ploy, a cover so Padraig and the others could slip out of the party unnoticed?'

When he replayed those moments, he felt the complete fool, a love-sick schoolboy led by the ear, overwhelmed by the elation of intimacy that had surged through him, the recklessness. He'd begged her to stay; he'd nearly proposed. And she'd refused. He understood why now.

Josefina blanched at the accusation, her face white with shock and fury. Ah, so she had followed those words to their logical implication. 'If you are suggesting I slept with you only for the purpose of helping the smugglers, then I am not the only one in this room who needs to apologise.' He'd hurt her. His heart kicked. What a beastly thing to do, to *say*, and yet sometimes beastly things were true. She hadn't denied his claims.

She put her hand in her pocket and pulled out a familiar velvet bag to hand to him. 'These are yours, of course.' He took the pearls and stuffed them into his pocket. It would be ages before he would be able to look at them again without seeing her in them, the way they'd lain around her neck, the way they'd seemed to belong on her. She gave a toss of her head, a gesture he'd seen her make countless times. 'I am disappointed in you, Owen Gann.'

That made two of them. Disappointment wasn't in short supply this morning. He was disappointed in her, in himself. 'Perhaps I should not have come.'

She nodded. 'Perhaps you should not have.' She was all coolness now, ice protecting her flame. Somewhere in the past few moments she'd moved beyond the girl pleading for reconciliation in a rumpled red dress.

Owen took a final look at her. Less than a day ago

he'd been in love with her, had wanted to marry her. Those were dangerous feelings, feelings that still lingered, mingled now with the devastation of betrayal, leaving him confused. How could he still want a woman who'd betrayed him? Those were feelings that could ruin a man, if he let them. It was right to leave. His feelings would go away over time, and over distance. If he stayed, he'd be tempted to give in. He could not afford another disaster. 'Goodbye, Josefina.'

He turned on his heel and exited the room, his body aware that she'd taken one last step towards him and stopped, perhaps by her pride. He shut the door behind him. Halfway down the hall, a strangled cry reached him, followed by the sound of china shattering against a wall. That was the difference between them, wasn't it? How had he ever thought such opposites could fit together?

Josefina was on the floor, scrabbling for pieces of the broken shepherdess when Artemisia found her. The figurine had shattered quite thoroughly into shards too tiny for repair, but she had to try. If she could piece the shepherdess together perhaps she could piece her heart, her world, Owen back together. Her hands trembled as she fitted three pieces of the shepherdess's skirt together, a sharp edge pricking the pad of her finger.

'My dear girl, what have you done?' Artemisia was on the floor beside her, taking the pieces from her.

'I broke your figurine.' She sucked on her finger, the tears she'd held back in front of Owen beginning to fall. He was right. She was reckless. With other people and their things. She'd broken Artemisia's figurine and she'd broken Owen's heart. She'd not meant to do either any more than she'd meant to break her own.

Artemisia took her good hand in her own. 'It seems you've broken more than that. Care to tell me about it?'

She shook her head, but the words tumbled out anyway. 'He loved me. He wanted me to stay.' That had been the worst of the visit, listening to Owen lay himself bare, confess to his feelings. Another man, a lesser sort of man would have made a show of bravado, insisting that she meant nothing to him to save his own pride. But Owen had said she'd stolen his heart, that she'd made him believe she cared for him. She turned a tear-stained face to Artemisia. 'He *loved* me.' He'd not said the word per se. A man like Owen would not use that word easily, not when he'd already lost in love once.

Oh, God. How he must be suffering. She rocked a little, choking back sobs, for her, for him. He'd trusted her enough to try again. Artemisia's arm was about her. 'Is there no way back for you and Owen?' she asked softly.

'How could there be? He thinks I betrayed him.' Which she had. She could not pretend it was all a misunderstanding. She had betrayed him. It was the motive behind it that was the sticking point. She could barely bring herself to say the words. 'He thinks all that was between us was a lie, that I slept with him for the sake of the smugglers' cache. I didn't, Artemisia. I swear it.' She was suddenly frantic to be believed, by someone, anyone. 'I did it because I wanted to, because I wanted him.' Like she'd wanted no other and now he was broken. Owen would repair himself. He was a strong man in all ways. She envied him that. Perhaps this morning, he'd already been trying to heal himself.

'Shh, hush, my dear girl, you remind me so much of myself.' Artemisia held her, a soft hand in her hair, soothing. 'It always hurts like this at the beginning.'

'What will I do?'

'You will finish your painting and in the spring we will go to London as we planned. After that, you will carry on, just as *you* planned. Losing one's self in one's work does wonders to ease the pain. Distance and time will do the rest.' She hoped Artemisia was right, although she noted Artemisia hadn't said it would cure the pain, only ease it.

Chapter Seventeen

Owen arrived in London just in time. He'd been in residence at his town house for three days before the first letter came. Mr Matthews had written to say there'd been a change of plans. He was no longer able to recommend that his bank invest in the proposed shipping venture. He was very sorry, of course, and wished him the best of luck. Letters from the other investors arrived in short order. By the end of the week, they had all withdrawn with polite, vague apologies citing a change in plans, except for the last one, which helpfully suggested that unsavoury rumours surrounding his reputation had arisen. It confirmed for Owen what he'd feared: that Lieutenant Hawthorne had discovered there was more than one way to hang a man. Owen crumpled the letter in his hand, letting reality sink in. He was going to lose the fleet, the apex of his vertical empire, the final piece in his ability to control all aspects of his industry, three years of work ruined. Along with everything else he'd lost in the last few days, he was going to lose that, too, at least a part of it. Unless…

Unless he lost himself in his business instead. It had worked once before. When Alyse had left him, he'd buried himself in building the business to unprecedented heights. Business had saved him, but he hadn't loved Alyse, he saw that now. Against the backdrop of the passion he'd shared with Josefina, his feelings for Alyse showed for what they'd been: lukewarm at best. He'd liked the idea of what she represented, the placeholder she filled. He'd wanted the entrée she could provide him.

It would have been a poor reason to wed, in his estimation. She'd done him a favour in jilting him, although it had taken years to realise it and longer to believe it. Perhaps in time, he would see Josefina's betrayal as a favour as well, perhaps he would be thankful he'd seen what her wildness could lead to before he'd done anything foolish like marrying her. Right now, it was hard to believe that would be the case with Josefina. But he could try. He couldn't save what had existed between he and Josefina, because it had never been real, just an illusion of something wonderful, but he could save his business.

Losing one's self in work did wonders for the pain. Goodness knew there was plenty of it—pain and work. Neither ever went away entirely, but the one numbed the other. There were enquiries to make about Hawthorne, about what Hawthorne had done with the cheque; there were oysters to send, beautifully displayed on perfectly shucked half-shells on ice in elegantly carved gift boxes, accompanied by expensive champagne, to the bankers and private investors who'd once sat at his table and toasted the shipping venture.

He would deal with Hawthorne and he would win the investors back. These were things he knew how to handle, men he knew how to handle. He had a plan for them. He could meet them on the battlefield of the boardroom. But love's battlefield? There was no one to fight there but himself and he wasn't sure he wanted to win. Winning meant forgetting her, forgetting how he'd felt. He'd felt *good, free, cherished*.

Late at night, once the letters were written, the correspondence read, and he was alone in his bed, it was easy to convince himself it would be better to keep the pain if it meant keeping the memory of her, of how they'd been together, for as long as he could stand it. It gave him an excuse to remember the feel of her touch on his body, the smell of summer roses on her skin, the press of her mouth on his, her laughter, the toss of her head, the red of her lips, the way she moved through the world as if it was hers for the taking, all ardour and audacity. He would fall asleep with those memories, dream them into existence and wake up hard, paying the price.

It didn't stop there. Throughout the day, he'd catch himself staring off into space, beyond ledgers and letters, imagining her at her easel. She would be painting, painting him. There was a bittersweet quality to the knowledge of that. She'd be faced with him every day. Was she still in tears as he'd left her or had she, like him, harnessed her emotions into something more productive? Was she watching the calendar pages turn? Counting the days to the show, the days until she was free of England? Did she think leaving England would free her from him or was she already free? Had she already forgiven herself? Already forgotten him? After all, she'd had what she wanted from him—access to his house for the smugglers.

His heart refused to accept that. *Unless, unless*, it would pound out, unless their time together had been more than that. What if it had? It didn't really matter. Betrayal or not, she was leaving in May. It would only have prolonged the agony of losing her. Yet his heart would not accept that either, the same way his mind would not accept no as an answer from his investors.

His mind was right. Owen sat back in the chair behind his desk, allowing himself a smug smile of victory, the recent letter open on his desk. He'd been correct in not taking no for an answer, in persisting with gifts of oysters and champagne. The board at the bank was willing to meet with him. Tomorrow at noon. He'd been right about Hawthorne, too, the bastard.

Owen reached for the second letter from his bank, confirming that Hawthorne had cashed the cheque. It had not gone to the King's coffers, but Hawthorne's own personal accounts. That was fine. Either way, the money had accomplished what Owen needed it to. He was free, his men were free. The gallows were thwarted and Owen had leverage. Now that Hawthorne had pocketed the money, he'd have to retract the rumours. Hawthorne had no proof and, if he persisted otherwise, Owen would threaten to expose what he'd done with the cheque.

But Hawthorne would be on the watch in the future. Shucker's Cove was no longer a hidden entity. O'Malley would need to lay low for a while, and, when he did resume smuggling activity, he'd need to be extra-vigilant. Owen wouldn't be there to watch from the widow's walk at Baldock House, not for a long while. It would be some time before he could walk the halls of his house with any peace, let alone his roof. Oh, Lord, his *roof.* Just thinking of those nights up there was enough to render him hard—the first night he'd carried her downstairs and made love to her in his bed, and the night they couldn't wait.

Focus, man. You have a presentation to make, a fleet to win. Your heart has already sailed.

Owen entered the boardroom at noon sharp, dressed soberly like the cohort assembled before him. 'Thank you for meeting, gentlemen.' They'd left the chair at the foot of the table open for him and he took it, looking each of them in the eye, letting them see his appreciation and his confidence that he fully expected this to end well. 'I want to begin by speaking frankly and addressing some unfounded rumours that I believe may have led to your reconsideration.' He laid out his case, firmly and directly, making no attempt to shield Lieutenant Hawthorne from actions that had been proven in hindsight to be precipitous and unnecessarily damning. He kept it simple. 'There was no illegal brandy brought in by me, as Lieutenant Hawthorne led you to believe. I understand your unwillingness to want to associate with free trading—however, I assure you, as I assured you upon your visit to Seasalter, that I am not involved. I assure you as well, that the proposal, as presented to you, still stands to make a profit. That hasn't changed, which is why your investment should not change.' He watched a look ripple around the table, passing from man to man.

'Would you excuse us, Mr Gann? I think we'd like to converse among ourselves.' Mr Matthews was all pleasantness. Owen stepped out of the room and waited. He didn't have to wait long, which had to be a good sign. He tugged once at his cuffs and stepped back inside. A folded sheet of paper sat at his place at the table. Another good sign. For the first time in weeks, something was finally going his way.

Mr Matthews nodded towards the paper. 'We are pleased to make you an offer, Mr Gann. We hope you are amenable to continuing our association.' He understood there would be no negotiation. The sum on the sheet would not be a starting place but a final offer, an only offer.

Owen smiled, politely, and picked up the paper. He unfolded it and stared, masking his disappointment. This was a compromise and it simply wouldn't do, as perhaps they'd been well aware. However, it did allow them to save face for allowing rumours to cause them to retract their original offer. No one could say they hadn't tried to participate in the venture. Owen folded the sheet calmly and put it back on the table. 'Gentlemen, it simply isn't enough. I thank you for your time. Good day.'

He was preternaturally calm as he exited the building into bright April sunshine. Spring was out today in London. He waved off his carriage, choosing to walk the distance home, buying himself time to think, time to grieve. He'd lost the fleet. Not him, actually, but Josefina. Her recklessness had cost him the fleet, the dream. He waited for sadness over the loss to fill him. He waited for resentment. He wanted to be angry with her. Perhaps anger would free him from her lingering spell.

Anger didn't come, sadness didn't come. Tenacity came, the determination to survive against the odds came, the same determination that had got him through the loss of a father and a mother, and through the raising of a younger brother, through the early beginnings of founding his company. He could not have a fleet, he needed help for that. But he could have one ship. He could do that on his own. A new dream formed. It was a start. It would keep him busy, perhaps busy enough to ignore that it was April, that she would be in town soon. London was big, the Season crowded and bustling. He needn't see her. Not unless he wanted to, which Owen feared would very much be the case. He would need to steel his resolve one more time. He just had to get through another month and she would be beyond him, out there, somewhere unknown in the wide, wild world. But not here. Surely, the distance would solve what burying himself in his work could not subdue.

Josefina could not subdue the nervous flutter in her stomach as she dressed for the evening, her first evening out in London under Artemisia and Darius's aegis. A maid tightened her corset and tied her petticoat tapes before slipping a sapphire-blue gown over her head. Josefina loved the way the expensive fabric felt sliding over her skin like a lover's hand, decadent and sure. Under other circumstances, she'd revel in the fine evening that laid before her, the opera and then a rout at the Duke of Boscastle's afterwards—the Duke was an art friend of Darius's. It would be an introduction of her to London society and to those who were interested in the Royal Academy as well as those who were carefully following the progress of Artemisia's wager with Gray. Some would argue that securing Boscastle's support was a victory all its own, regardless of how the wager turned out. Yes, indeed, under other circumstances, this would be an exciting evening, a milestone in which she would celebrate having stepped out on her own as an artist.

But under *these* circumstances, she felt more nerves than excitement. Not over dancing, not over meeting noblemen—she'd attended balls and masques with her father through his patrons and she'd dazzled plenty of noblemen in Venice. No, most of her nerves centred around one question: Would Owen be there? And then all the questions that followed that one: What would it be like to see him again? Would he acknowledge her? Had he forgiven her?

'Sit down, miss, and let me put up your hair.' The maid had finished with the dress. It was the shade of Owen's eyes when they burned bright with passion. She might have chosen a different colour. She could do with fewer reminders, but Artemisia had insisted. Her wardrobe had been carefully curated and created with an eye to how the St Heliers wanted to present her to society—not as a poor woman rescued from the streets, nor as a debutante feigning a certain innocence, but as a sophisticated young woman. Artemisia felt such an image would help others take her work more seriously. 'You want to look as sophisticated as your painting,' Artemisia had said.

The result had been a whirlwind of shopping that had occupied her first weeks in town. Artemisia had seen her supplied with everything a young woman about town would need to participate in the Season. She'd protested, of course. She didn't need that much. She wasn't even going to be here for the whole Season, just until the show on the first of May. Artemisia's argument had simply been, 'You never know what might happen.'

But she did know. Josefina stifled a sigh as she sat still for the maid. She studied her reflection in the mirror while the maid worked, pinning up tresses and curling locks. She could stay. Even if she didn't win the competition between Gray and Artemisia, she would win recognition. Her work was good. She would get commissions if she wanted them. Artemisia would see to it, as she would likely see to a spot at the school. With her sister leaving shortly for Florence, Artemisia was in need of an instructor. *She could stay.* The three words formed a dangerous litany.

For what? Seasalter was dead to her. When she'd left for London, she'd said goodbye to the little place. She wouldn't be going back. She would go to London and keep on going. Seasalter without Owen held too much pain. March had been proof of that. She'd spent it in her studio painting Owen, faced with his image daily, and his ghost haunted her rambles when she went out. She couldn't get away from him. He was there when she looked out over the water or walked the shoreline or wound her way through the little streets of village huts.

Everywhere she looked, there was a story, a remembrance of something they'd done, of something he had said. Her feet had a habit of turning towards Baldock House, shuttered, pristine and utterly empty now. She'd not understood the last day she'd seen him that he'd meant to leave town. It had taken a week before she realised he was physically gone. Darius had finally told her over supper. He'd gone to London to try to save the business. The news had stolen her appetite. She'd cost him even that, his beloved vertical acquisition. Chances of forgiveness seemed slim. If she stayed, she'd have to face him, or worry about facing him, day after day.

Staying would be painful. Staying would be another betrayal. This time of her father. She'd promised him on his deathbed to be his dream. Staying would contradict that promise entirely, it would commit her to a life of relying on patrons. She would be tied to London, tied to society. She'd left Venice to avoid any scenario that tied her to another, that fettered her freedom. Patrons and marriage weren't that different in that regard.

There was a knock on her door and Artemisia slipped in, gowned in an exquisite coral silk. 'Are you ready? You look stunning. Darius has the carriage ready downstairs. We need to pick up Addy and Hazard at half past and we want everyone to get a good look at you in our box before the opera starts. Don't forget your gloves.' She paused. 'What is it? Aren't you excited?'

Josefina stood up and smoothed her sapphire skirts. 'Just nervous.' She hesitated and then opted for boldness. 'Will Owen be there?' It sounded like both a plea and a prayer. What would she say to him?

Artemisia shook her head, the pearl earbobs dancing. 'I don't know, honestly. He could be. London is a big town, but the upper circles are smaller than one might think.' Artemisia reached for her hand. 'It is inevitable that you will encounter him, it's just a matter of when and where. But you needn't worry. Whether he is or isn't there this evening, tonight is the first night of the next chapter of your life. You will meet people who will create opportunities for you.' She smiled. 'It's nice to have choices, Josefina, even if you think you don't want them. Not every woman gets such a luxury. Enjoy the moment.'

Josefina wished it was that easy, but all she could think of throughout the evening, watching Artemisia with Darius and Addy with her husband, Hazard, was that she'd enjoy the moment so much more if Owen was with her. There were times when she caught herself looking for him in the crowd, at the theatre and later at Boscastle's. Other times when she felt as if his eyes were on her. Once, she even turned around, expecting to see him. But it was only her imagination. Owen was gone from her.

Chapter Eighteen

He was *here*. She'd not imagined his presence after all. Josefina's gaze snagged on a pair of broad shoulders and a blond head that towered above the rest of Boscastle's guests. She'd know that build anywhere. She'd spent hours at her easel, figuring out how to show it to advantage, and hours in bed, tracing that body with her fingers until it was intimately imprinted on her mind. She didn't need to see his face to know it was him. Artemisia discreetly stepped on her toe, dragging her attention back to the conversation. One ignored the Duke of Boscastle at one's own peril.

Josefina made a point to nod and smile. She liked the Duke and his son, Inigo, both of them friends of Darius and supporters of the arts. Boscastle had mentioned he had several of Artemisia's pieces. She made sure to follow the general gist of the conversation, but her mind insisted on being allowed to disengage long enough to follow its own train of thought. How long had Owen been there? Had he been here all night? Had he seen her? Surely, if she'd felt his gaze, he must have. If he turned, he would see her now, dressed in fashionable silks, talking to a duke, his handsome heir to her right and Viscount St Helier on her left. Quite a different setting than Seasalter. No more borrowed ten-year-old dresses and smugglers for company.

They were both far from home. Even Owen looked different beneath the chandeliers of Boscastle's ballroom, although she'd seen him in evening clothes before. Tonight, he was more polished. There was an urbanity to him she'd not seen before. There was a mask, as well. This was a different version of Owen and an incomplete one. London was not allowed to see the man who shucked oysters with a knife at lightning speed, or the man who walked among the oystermen as if he were one of them. They saw only the successful businessman with a fortune that exceeded many of their own and they were jealous of it. A woman in his group leaned forward and tapped his arm with a fan. She was pretty in a worldly way, with her knowing eyes and teasing mouth. Whatever look he gave her, seemed only to spur her on.

'That's Lady Stanley... Alyse Newton as she was known before her marriage,' Artemisia whispered. 'Apparently she finds Owen more attractive now that's she married to someone else.' The edge to Artemisia's tone was unmistakable. This was the woman who'd thrown him over for a man with a title. Josefina disliked her instantly and she disliked the idea of Owen spending time with her, even in a group under bright lights.

She watched as Owen's head made a short nod and his broad shoulders set to turn. She froze with the knowledge that within moments he couldn't help but see her. This was not to be feared. This was her chance to apologise again, to convince him she'd not used him, that what they'd had was real.

She stepped backwards, out of the circle of conversation, and met Owen's gaze. She skirted the circle in a bold approach, making it clear that she intended to meet him. Her palms were sweaty inside her gloves. She didn't want to do this. But she had to. If she ran now, she'd be in hiding the whole time she was in London. Worse, she'd know herself for a coward. She'd made this mess, she could very well brazen it out. 'Owen, it's good to see you.' She didn't hold out her hands, didn't want to see if he'd deign to touch her. The last time they'd met, he had not.

He made her a small bow, his own address more formal. '*Signorina*, are you enjoying the evening? Did you find the opera on par with Venetian standards?' Ah, so he had been there. Perhaps her thoughts had not been so fanciful after all.

'I enjoyed it very much.' She stepped closer, her skirts brushing the leg of his trousers. She didn't want to talk about the opera or the evening. She wanted to talk about him. 'How are you? Are you well? I heard—'

Owen interrupted, his hand at her elbow, nothing more than a gentleman's guiding touch and yet it sent lightning through her. Her body knew this touch, craved it. 'Not here, *signorina*,' he chastised. 'Perhaps

I might escort you outside for a bit of air?' It was a reminder that she'd been indiscreet, about to ask him personal questions where anyone could overhear.

She let him escort her outside to join other strolling couples. Boscastle's town house boasted a rare-sized garden for the city, complete with gravelled pathways and a fountain at its centre. For an event held before the official start of the Season next week, the event couldn't be described as a crush, but the garden traffic was significant. Still, there were fewer ears to overhear out here than indoors.

They strolled in silence to the fountain at the garden's centre. Perhaps he, too, was marshalling his thoughts, organising himself for the encounter, getting used to being with her again just as she was doing the same for him. 'Are you well, Owen?' she repeated her question. 'I heard you lost the business deal.'

'I did.' He was all flat neutrality, his answer devoid of description.

'What happened?' She wanted details. She wanted him to look at her when he spoke instead of watching the fountain.

'Nothing that matters. The bankers were unwilling to stand by their original sum, so I left their offer on the table.'

'And gave up the fleet? But that was your dream.' She didn't understand. The fleet had been everything for him, the culmination of years of work. This disaster, too, could be laid at her feet.

'I have a different dream now. I will start with one

ship and build from there.' He was succinct and stoic, the way he'd been the first time she'd come to Baldock House. All business and no fire. But she knew better now. She knew there was more to him than this.

'I am sorry, Owen. That's my fault, too.' She'd cost him everything with her foolishness. 'I wish I could take it back, I wish it was all a misunderstanding that I could explain away.' But it wasn't. What it was was an undoable action that would exist between them for ever. There was no clearing it up, there was no need to. They were both very clear on what had transpired and why.

'I wish that, too,' was all Owen said.

She grabbed his arm, desperate to touch him, to reach him. He was so far from her, treating her with the same aloofness as he'd treated Lady Stanley. 'Will you look at me? I have something to say to you and I want to see your face.'

He faced her, his expression cool. How she wanted to see him smile again, to see his blue eyes dance. But she would take this small victory. 'I *am* sorry, Owen. Do you believe me?'

'Yes, I believe you are sorry for the smugglers getting caught.'

'For *all* of it, Owen. I am sorry you were implicated. I am sorry the men were caught. I am sorry you lost your business deal because of it. But most of all, I am sorry that you had reason to doubt the sincerity of my feelings for you, which were entirely separate from anything to do with the smuggling arrangements. Owen, I love you.' She could not make it any plainer than that. She clutched at his arm and let everything she felt shine in her eyes. He could not doubt the physical proof of her words now, not with her vulnerability so blatantly on display.

He gently removed her hand from his sleeve. 'I suppose it doesn't matter now. We were never destined to last anyway. That piece was a bit of whimsy on my part. I have only myself to blame for it.' He turned then, his hand dropping to the small of her back as he made to escort her back indoors, a clear sign the interview was over.

'But I am here, Owen,' she protested, taking an unwilling step back towards the ballroom to keep up with him. 'Don't you understand what I am saying?'

He halted and faced her. 'I understand, *signorina*. You want things to be as they were before and then you will leave in May. You are an enchanting creature, but even so, I am in no hurry to have my heart broken again.' How did he manage to look so strong while making himself so vulnerable all at the same time? How could she respond? That it would be different this time? That she would stay? Both would be a lie. She had promises to keep. She *would* leave. She had to.

'But do you forgive me? Do you believe me?' She wanted that much at least and she wasn't too proud to beg for it. His words from that fateful morning still haunted her. *You were reckless with me.* That was the greater sin. He might forgive her for all else, but not that. Owen who was never reckless with people, Owen who had given his life in service to those he loved—his mother, his brother, his people in Seasalter.

For the first time that evening, she saw his gaze soften, but it did not mean victory. 'You can't help it, can you, Josefina? Living out loud, showing every feeling the moment you have them? It's who you are. It's what makes you unique.' His hand skimmed her cheek, an echo of past intimacies. 'As for forgiveness, I've come to terms with what happened. I just don't think I can live with you. I see that now. You're a flame, Josefina. You are meant to consume everything in your path. I can't afford to be consumed and I can't afford to lose you. I lost my mother, I lost my father, I nearly lost Simon. I know what it does to me and I cannot go through that again. I cannot let you consume me and then lose you. I would lose the most important part of myself.'

She held his hand, trapping it against her cheek. 'Do you believe I love you? That I am not like that woman you were speaking with? Artemisia told me who she was.'

'I believe you love many things, Josefina, but you are nothing like her. Do not worry on that score.' He was drifting away from her without taking a single step. His blue eyes were shuttering, becoming polite and aloof. She was losing him. If he wouldn't believe her words, she had to find another way to reach him, to convince him.

'Come to the show and see the portrait.' She held his gaze, willing her stare to root him to the ground, to keep him with her awhile longer. If he could see the portrait, he would know she spoke the truth about her feelings. Even if he would never come back to her, the truth would help him heal. He would know her love had been real even if realised too late.

'Goodnight, *signorina*. I thank you for the stroll.' He left her there, on the pathway. She watched his broad back make its way inside until she lost sight of him. Then she imagined another crack in her heart.

The evening was lost, after that. Owen took his leave of his host and headed out into the night, thankful to escape with his dignity intact. Facing Josefina had been as dreadful and as necessary as he'd imagined it to be. Seeing her at a distance at the opera in that sapphire gown had been a stab to his heart as her beauty swamped him again as if for the first time. It was always like that with her. He'd once thought such a sensation would wear off after a time. But he knew now that wasn't true. She would always swamp his senses.

Perhaps it was best she was leaving. Otherwise, he'd never get over her or past her. She'd always be there in Seasalter and in London. Tonight had proved the large scope of London had not protected him against her. She'd managed to find him anyway, or was it the other way around and he'd found her? It had not taken much investigating to divine Artemisia's plans for launching her. The society columns had been touting the St Heliers' early return to the city since the first of April and speculating that the reasons for it were connected to the Italian protégée Lady St Helier had in tow.

Had he subconsciously wanted to see her? Had he wanted to test his resolve? If so, he'd discovered his resolve wasn't nearly as strong as he'd hoped or needed it to be. She was fetching in her contrition and sapphire. Beautiful and sincere, he had no doubt of that. She was genuinely sorry. She'd said more than that, his conscience prompted, forcing him to acknowledge the rest of her admissions. *I love you.* The words had shaken him. It had taken every ounce of his newfound resolve to brush over them, to remind her they didn't, and couldn't, matter because she was leaving. The only thing that shook him more was the raw pain on her face when he denied her the things she wanted from him. It was for both of their sakes. Did she have any idea how close he'd come to gathering her in his arms, to offering the absolution of a kiss, to exchange her pain for his? Happiness for another month was a tempting offer and he'd nearly taken it. It had been right to walk away. Best for both of them, but especially for him. Only, she'd had the last word anyway and she hadn't let him leave completely.

Come see the portrait. Maybe he would, because misery loved company and he'd been the one to make them both miserable tonight. The only thing stopping him from taking the happiness on offer was himself. What a masterful intrigue she'd set up. If he was miserable, he had only himself to blame. She was offering to wipe the slate clean. Of course, that was definitely in her interest.

She nearly sent you to the hangman.

Apparently his conscience was of two minds where Josefina was concerned. Even if he forgave her, he'd be a fool to forget. Josefina would always be wild, always be reckless. He couldn't change that and in truth he didn't want to.

But can you live with it? He'd nearly died for it. *And now? Are you living now without it? Is this living?*

Maybe the answer didn't matter. Maybe it was all a careful man could have.

Chapter Nineteen

They were being careful with her, all of them—Artemisia, Darius and Addy—handling her with the same expert skill she applied to packing her canvases. Josefina wrapped the latest stack of canvases in sailcloth and tucked them securely into her new supply trunk where it stood open against the wall of her bedchamber.

It had taken her a couple of days to realise their strategy of busyness and constant companionship. She was always on the move, always with them, never alone in the days leading up to the exhibitions. Mornings were spent shopping with Addy, gathering supplies for both of their trips. Addy and Hazard would leave at the end of May for Florence. She, of course, would leave far sooner than that. She could leave next week. *Next week*. Soon. Just seven more days and she could leave England behind. Just when the weather was starting to get nice, alas.

Josefina began folding clothes she would not wear again before she left. The pile of clothing on the bed brought a wry smile to her. She'd come with three gowns and her brushes, but she was leaving with three trunks full of clothes and paint supplies. Artemisia and Darius had been generous; the town wardrobe would go with her and they'd opened an account for her to purchase paints and canvases and brushes and an exquisite folding travelling easel to take with her.

There was a knock on her door and Artemisia entered. Her eyes swept the room and she sighed. 'Packing is going well, I see. We have maids to help if you need them.'

Josefina shook her head. 'No, I want to pack on my own. It helps me to know where everything is and I can establish an inventory.' It also filled the time, it kept her hands busy and it was the only part of the day when she was on her own, allowed a chance to sift through her thoughts. She knew Artemisia meant well. Perhaps Artemisia even guessed what had happened in the Boscastle garden with Owen and this was her way of easing the pain.

Artemisia drew an envelope from her pocket and handed it over. 'I have your passage. Darius arranged everything.'

Josefina opened the envelope and peeked inside. 'A first-class cabin? That's not necessary.' How would she pay them back for that? It was more than she'd budgeted for. She'd been very clear that third class was fine. 'I can't afford it,' she said bluntly.

Artemisia shook her head. 'It's our gift to you.

There's no need to pay us back. There's something else in there, as well.'

Josefina saw it now. 'A second ticket?' For a wild moment she thought it was for Owen, that somehow he'd decided to come along.

'Yes, Darius has found a companion for you, a cousin of his who is a young widow looking for a new start. We think the two of you would suit admirably. He's sent for her. She'll be here at week's end.'

'I'm not to be alone on my adventures either?' Josefina raised an eyebrow. She laughed when Artemisia feigned confusion. 'I know what you've been up to, keeping me busy with shopping in the mornings and outings to the British Museum, the Tower and everywhere a lady ought to go, working on the exhibition in the afternoons and evenings out to grand parties. I haven't had a moment to myself since the opera. I don't think it's been by accident.'

'No, because the last time you were alone, you went into a garden and got your heart broken.' Artemisia strolled about the room, studying the half-packed trunks.

So, Artemisia did know. 'Not on purpose. I went into the garden hoping to apologise, hoping to be forgiven, hoping that there might still be a chance of salvaging my heart.'

Artemisia flung her a rueful look. 'How did that work out?'

'You know how that worked out. It's why you've spoiled me with travelling trunks, supply budgets, first-class tickets and constant company.' Josefina turned her attention back to folding clothes.

'Does it really matter, though? What if he had changed his mind? Would you have stayed or would you have simply hurt him again in a few weeks?' It sounded quite cruel when Artemisia put it that way.

'It's not just that. I need him to know that my feelings for him are real. What we shared was not a ruse.' She gathered up the stack of clothing and strode to a trunk. 'Being someone else's pawn and realising it post facto is an unpleasant feeling, especially when one thinks otherwise and engages otherwise based on those assumptions. I would have honesty between us if nothing else.' Even if nothing could come of it, especially when Owen had been hurt in love before. He deserved more than that.

'You don't have to go,' Artemisia said softly. 'You know you can come back to Seasalter with us, make a life at the school. I need an instructor with Addy leaving. Or, perhaps you could stay in town with my father in Bloomsbury or at Addy's house. It will be empty while they're in Florence. You can recruit for the school, take commissions of your own. Perhaps you and Owen can find your way back from this? It's only been a couple of months, Josefina. These things take time.'

'No. I have plans. I've already stayed longer than I thought I would,' Josefina said firmly. She could not allow herself to be swayed, to be tempted to something that would only bring her pain in the long term.

'Then I shall be deprived of both my "sisters" all at

once.' Artemisia gave a rueful smile and Josefina felt her heart twist at her words. She'd found so much more in Seasalter than just a place to shelter for the winter. Artemisia had made her a part of a family, part of a group and a community. Artemisia had treated her as a sister, a comrade in art. She *could* have a life in Seasalter. But it would be a painful one. Owen would be there and it would mean breaking her promise to her father. She wasn't sure how to reconcile those sacrifices with the rewards of staying. It was far easier to pack, to stay busy, to not look around or look ahead, just to put one foot in front of the other until she was on board the ship and London was fading from sight.

'She's leaving in three days. I thought you'd like to know.' St Helier's voice cut through the haze of Owen's thoughts. He lowered the newspaper, the words having faded minutes ago, a half-hour ago, he wasn't sure. How long had he been staring at the same news story? He'd like to blame it on the soporific effect of the quiet atmosphere of the club in the afternoon. The Beefsteak Club would be deserted until four.

St Helier sat down in the chair across from him and signalled for a drink, a sure sign he meant to stay awhile. 'I see you've come to interrupt my peace.' Owen set aside the newspaper and fixed St Helier with a strong look.

'I thought I might find you here.'

'Here' being the Old Lyceum Theatre, the club's home on the Wellington Street.

'Hiding.'

The last was said with no small bit of accusation.

'I am not hiding,' Owen answered. He had, however, been counting on the likes of St Helier to not venture beyond the comforts of St James's. 'I am in my element—one might wonder why you are not in yours?'

St Helier took his drink from the waiter and answered him in all seriousness. 'Because when I see a friend hurting, I cannot sit by and watch them suffer alone.'

He did not pretend to not understand the reference. He steeled himself to blandly say her name, to withstand the onslaught of emotions and images that came with it. 'Josefina will be fine. She'll recover.'

'Not her, you. *You* are the friend to whom I refer. I saw your face when you came in from the garden at Boscastle's and you left shortly afterwards. You haven't been to any parties since. That was a week ago.' He paused and took a swallow. 'I think you're afraid to see her again.'

Owen tossed back the rest of his drink and signalled for another. It was going to be a two-brandy afternoon. 'If I had not been a rich man with a fast mind, I would have hung for her carelessness.' That was an inescapable fact. Whenever he felt weak, whenever he was tempted to forgive her, tempted to see her and let his feelings run their course, he simply had to remember that.

He was not ready for Darius's response. 'Josefina will always be wild. If I may be so bold, I think it's

what you love about her, what we all love about her.'
Owen had not been expecting that. He'd been expecting
minimising, some empty words about how she'd made
a mistake, how it had all worked out in the end—easy
words to say when it was someone else's bank account
on the line, someone else's reputation to be rebuilt. But
Darius had not argued with him. Darius had agreed
with him and that made the response more difficult.

'Yes, I suppose it is.' He gave a short laugh. 'I remember the first time I saw her, at your wife's welcome-back-from-the-holiday soirée. I danced with her
and the moment I touched her I knew what she was—a
flame, bright and vibrant, and that she'd burn a man
alive.'

Darius gave him a commiserating look. 'You are not
the first man to become an Icarus.' He leaned forward.
'I felt that way the night Artemisia burst into my bath
and called me to account. I knew what she was and I
still could not pull my hand away from the flame. It's
not a reason to retreat, man, it's a reason to press on.'

'Easy for you to say—hindsight is on your side and
your wife didn't almost kill you.' Owen took his glass
from the waiter and let Darius digest *that*.

Darius was not daunted. 'No, but standing up for her
did endanger my relationship with my father.' It was a
relationship that was still strained, Owen knew. 'It did
cost me certain acquaintances within the art community and it did risk my reputation as a critic. I've had to
build all that back,' Darius reminded him. 'Artemisia
and I have each other and the life we want, the life

we are actively seeking. However, it's not a fairy tale. We fight for it every day.' He paused. 'And just when I think we've gained back ground, she goes and does something like this deuced wager with Aldred Gray.'

Owen heard the frustration in his friend's voice and the lesson, too. He'd not thought of their marriage that way before. It did indeed look like a perfect love story on the outside. Darius continued, bringing the lesson full circle. 'I will never change Artemisia. She will be saying outlandish things to the Academy and making outrageous wagers for the rest of her life. I want her to. I don't want to change her. Years from now, when I inherit, she will be the most notorious Countess of Bourne to ever grace the Rutherford family tree. I wouldn't want it or her any other way.'

He didn't want Josefina any other way either. He wasn't looking to change her. He'd told her as much in the garden. But neither could he change himself. It wasn't in him. His people needed his protection, everything he'd built had been for his family, for his people. He could not walk away from that and become a different man. 'Josefina and I, we don't fit well together,' Owen told Darius. 'I think we're often attracted to opposites because they possess skills, talents, values, beliefs that are different than ours. It's an intoxicating novelty and after a bit the novelty wears off. It's not sustainable.'

Darius thought for a moment. 'Are you sure that's all she is to you? An intoxicating novelty?'

'It's all she can be, Darius. I envy her freedom to

come and go as she pleases. But that can't be me.' These days, he envied the fact that she'd be able to sail away and leave England behind, leaving memory markers behind that he would have to face every day. His house, the beach, the rowboat, the art school. Everywhere he looked he'd see the echo of her. How would he ever be able to forget? Whereas forgetting would come easy to her. She would be in new places with new people, and eventually with a new lover. She wasn't made to be alone and when that happened she would forget him.

Darius finished his drink and rose. 'I appreciate your time. I'll let you get back to the news and your financial pages. I hope we'll see you at the exhibitions, both of them. Our show opens tomorrow, a day in advance of Somerset House. You can come as our guest. You needn't feel as if you're coming for her if that mitigates any sense of temptation on your part.' It did indeed. What a fine barrister the Viscount would have made, Owen thought. He knew just how to get into a man's head and convince him the action he wanted him to take was the right one. But he would see her, no matter who he came for. He could not be in the same room and not be drawn to her, not seek her out.

He reached for his newspaper, but Darius didn't leave. 'Is there something else?'

'Yes. I've always thought you were a fighter. I think she'd stay if you gave her a reason,' Darius offered baldly. 'Goodness knows, we've tried to give her reasons: a post at the school, taking over Addy's position in town. But she resists. We have nothing she wants, nothing we could offer to offset her leaving, at least. But you do.' Darius sat back down, levering himself on the edge of his seat. He leaned forward, his voice low as the club began to fill with late afternoon arrivals. 'She came to you and she confessed her feelings. She loves you, Owen. It's up to you. If you want her, a life with her, all you have to do is claim it. Give her a reason to stay.'

Owen grinned at the other man. 'You make it sound so easy.'

'It can be that simple. Once I decided it was, it made all the difference.' Darius rose again. 'We'll see you tomorrow, I hope.'

A gauntlet could not have been thrown down more effectively. Going tomorrow would be a declaration. He fiddled with his glass, holding the tumbler up to the light of the club's long windows. He watched the sunlight dance in the facets of the glass and let his thoughts play through. How could a man love something or someone who wasn't good for him? Was that true? Did he feel Josefina wasn't *good* for him?

She made you feel alive, his conscience prompted. *You were happy, you were free and you didn't even have to leave Seasalter. She challenged you. She awakened you.*

She'd not changed him. She'd accepted him as he was, a lonely, admittedly cold man who rambled around a big house on his own, living vicariously through his brother's happiness. Then she'd breezed into his life, blowing away the cobwebs of the past. He wanted to feel that way again, wanted to feel that way always. She had accepted him at face value. To have her, he needed to return the courtesy. Darius's words echoed. *Josefina will always be wild.* Yes, he thought. And thank God for that. He didn't want her any other way. It was a frightening decision to make. What if he couldn't convince her to stay? What if he'd decided to claim her and it was too late, despite Darius's opinion that she was waiting for him? What if he lost her again? The answer sprang easy and full grown. If she wouldn't come with him, he would go with her. He chuckled to himself. Darius was right. It could be that simple. He rose, his brandy unfinished. He had a lot to do before the exhibition. If he was lucky, tomorrow just might be a new beginning.

Chapter Twenty

The day had finally arrived, the day upon which the last five months had been fixed. In many ways, it was the beginning of the end. Josefina sat ramrod-straight in Darius's town coach, her gaze locked on the passing street scene outside the carriage window, seeing but not truly ingesting the activity. She had too much on her mind. The first of the two exhibitions was today. It was, in fact, already underway. Darius had arranged for her to arrive late. 'A good artist is never on time,' he'd told her with a laugh.

This first show was private, by invitation of the Viscount St Helier only, held at St Helier's exhibition hall on the Strand, a property Darius had rented and then bought after Artemisia's ground-breaking exhibition. It would be followed by a reception and preview at Somerset House for the Royal Academy's official opening tomorrow. The reception was important. Tonight, the artists and their guests would see which works had been awarded prizes. Artemisia's wager with Sir

Aldred Gray would be settled. Then Josefina had the official exhibition tomorrow when her portrait of Owen would be on display for all the *ton* to see, hopefully with a blue ribbon beside it. After that, she would be free to go. She let that sink in. *This time tomorrow, she'd be free to go.*

The coach began to slow, joining a queue that wound towards the exhibition hall, but her heart began to race. What a crush Darius had managed to orchestrate. All these coaches to see her work! Not just hers, she reminded herself. In addition to the portrait for the Academy's show, she'd done a series of paintings of Seasalter and the oystermen that would be on display here, but her series would hardly fill the big hall. Darius was acting as an agent for five other independent artists, as well. It would be good to have company, good to not be singled out. But that didn't stop her artist's nerves from surging to the fore as the coach came to a stop and the coachman helped her out. Would Darius's guests like her work? Would Artemisia be proud of her? Would she be glad she'd made the rather significant investment of taking her on? Josefina feared she'd been more trouble than Artemisia had bargained on.

Papa, would you be proud?

She gave a quick glance to the sky as her feet touched the ground. Was it true that the ones we loved looked down on us from above? What did he see when he looked down? His daughter was a featured artist at a London exhibition. She was exhibiting at the Royal Academy and she'd done it on her own merits. She'd not begged favours from his friends or been cosseted in someone's workshop because of her father's name. Surely, he would have celebrated this moment with her. But this was not the dream he'd had and it was not the promise she'd made.

But I am leaving soon, Papa. I'll be off to the Americas. I'll swim in the warm waters of the Caribbean and paint the green-hilled islands that rise out of the sea.

At the entrance to the hall, Josefina drew a breath and straightened her shoulders. This might not be the promise she'd made, but this was a moment to savour. She'd done good work on her oystermen series. A waiter passed with a tray of champagne flutes, bubbling, fizzing and sweating with their golden liquid. She felt just like that—bubbling with excitement while her palms sweated inside her gloves and her stomach fizzed with nerves. She took a glass for courage and stepped inside.

It was a spectacular space, a wide room that had once been used in Tudor days as a counting house. Now that space was open, a wall of windows interspersed with French doors that led out on to a narrow balcony that ran the length of the building overlooking the Thames below. Perfect light, she thought, for accounting clerks or aspiring artists. She took a sip of the cold champagne, letting it trickle down her throat, as she looked about the crowded hall. She spotted her series immediately at the far end. The five pictures had been hung together to tell their story. Darius and Artemisia were there already and a group was gathered about them. Darius caught sight of her and beckoned her over.

'Here she is, my wife's protégée, Miss Ricci,' he introduced her. She knew Boscastle and his son, but the others were new to her. One gentleman, a Lord Monteith, was already insisting that he have the painting of St Alphege's.

The place where Owen had learned to read and write. She pushed the thought away. She would not think of him today, she would not let regrets cloud this moment. 'Of course, we have great hopes for her portrait on display at the Royal Academy,' Darius was saying.

After that, Darius and Artemisia circulated her from group to group, introducing her to their guests. There was another glass of champagne in her hands and Artemisia whispered, 'It's going well, you're a natural, my dear. Are you sure you haven't done this before?' Artemisia was teasing, but Josefina gave a bland smile in response. How many events like this had she attended with her father? With his friends? Supporting their exhibitions, chatting up potential patrons and collectors. Perhaps she should have told Artemisia more about her background, but she hadn't and now she was leaving. It hardly seemed worthwhile. It was notable, however, that Owen had kept her secrets, despite what she'd embroiled him in. He'd not claimed revenge. She was failing in her charge not to think of him, it seemed. No matter how hard she pushed the thoughts away, they came back. He was determined to haunt her. She could practically feel his eyes on her. She froze. Perhaps there was a reason for that. She turned slowly. He was here.

She was surrounded by admirers, by earls and heirs and the *ton*'s glittering assemblage when Owen arrived. Some of his earlier confidence ebbed. Perhaps she would not have time for him. Perhaps she wouldn't even notice he was there, the oysterman among the lords. Perhaps he should wait another day to make his case. *You don't have another day,* his thoughts pointed out. Tomorrow at the Royal Academy would be even more impossible and then it would be too late.

She was stunning to watch and the urge to hide among the crowd, sipping champagne, was tempting. She was dressed in a deep emerald silk that could pass from this reception to the evening reception at Somerset House, a paisley shawl artfully draped through her arms and drifting at her waist, her inky hair piled high in ringlets, showing off the long curve of her neck and the sweep of her jaw. When she laughed, her gold earbobs danced. Every man in the group about her was enthralled. Owen couldn't blame them. He was enthralled at a distance. *She loves me.* His gut tightened at the prospect, with nerves and the excitement such a thought engendered. That such a flame loved him was a heady concept indeed.

Should he approach? Should he steal her away from the group? Owen played a game with himself. If she saw him before the waiter came by with more champagne, he would go to her. If not, he would wait. He was nearly done with his glass when he saw her back stiffen just a fraction, her body become alert, aware. She turned, a question in her eyes. That was his cue.

She met him halfway. He took her elbow and steered her towards the freedom of the French doors and the long, narrow balcony beyond. 'I didn't think you'd come,' she said when they were alone. The balcony was too narrow for strolling, being more for decoration than actual use. But a private conversation could be had while those inside looked on. 'Have you seen the Seasalter series yet?'

'No, I've only seen you,' Owen admitted honestly, letting her see in his gaze that he meant it. 'I came to apologise, Josefina. I conducted myself poorly the last time we met. When a woman tells a man she loves him, she deserves better from him than a cold shoulder.' He would start with the apology and move on from there.

'I understand,' she said, but he didn't want easy absolution. He wanted to explain.

'I was protecting myself. I was hurt and I was afraid I'd be hurt again. As a result, I was unappreciative of the honour your feelings did me. Most of all, though, I was dishonest.' Somehow their hands had found their way to each other. He was gripping them now, encased in their gloves, and they gave him strength to persevere. How had he lasted these months without touching her?

'You are the most honest man I know, Owen Gann.' She gave him a soft smile.

'Not that day I wasn't. When you told me you loved me, I should have said that you made me feel alive, that you'd brought joy back into my life, that I was happy when I was with you, that my life was vibrant again, that it had meaning again. But I was afraid to love you and so I said other things instead.'

She was silent for a long while, her dark eyes suspiciously shiny. Her voice was shaky when she spoke. 'Thank you, Owen. For believing me, for believing that my love for you is real. Thank you for sharing your own heart with me, trusting me with it when perhaps I don't deserve a second chance.' She licked her bottom lip in that little gesture of hers. 'But now, Owen? Are you still afraid to love me?'

'No,' he whispered, just for her, even though there was no one else to hear. He wanted to sweep her in his arms and kiss her. But that was out of the question with two hundred of Darius's guests just beyond the glass. He bent his head to hers, foreheads touching. 'I was wrong to run away from us. I want a life with you. I did not come here today only to apologise, but to propose. I want to marry you, Josefina. Do you want to marry me?'

He heard her make a little gasp. The question had surprised her, shocked her. In a good or bad way? He couldn't tell. 'Owen, it's not that simple.'

'Yes, it is. A friend helped me see that. I was making it too complicated.' Owen smiled and she smiled in return, but not with her eyes. They were holding something back. Something inside him recoiled in worry. Was she going to refuse? Was she going to hurt him again after all the courage it had taken to get to this point? 'When two people love each other, Josefina,' he said, 'they should be together.'

'Yes, they should. But I don't know how that works for us. I love you, Owen, but I made a promise to my father, right before he died, that I would do what he couldn't. That I would live free, free to travel the world and see the things he could not see, to paint them. That I wouldn't tie myself to patrons, or to be at another man's beck and call, that I would paint for myself. I can't stay.'

The knot in his stomach eased. He'd known she'd say that and he was ready. 'I know. That's why I will go with you.'

She was speechless. Her brow furrowed as she processed the possibility of that. It was a delight to watch her thoughts, her emotions cross her face. 'But how? You can't walk away from the factory, the oystermen, the smugglers—they're all counting on you. Who will watch out for them?'

'I've made arrangements. I've been up half the night writing instructions. O'Malley can manage the factory. Simon can handle the business correspondence and the shipping. I can have my important mail forwarded to ports of call.'

'I can't believe you would do that for me.' She was glassy-eyed with emotion. She smiled and stole a kiss, regardless of who would see. 'You're an incredible man. I think no woman has ever been loved better. Now, come see the Seasalter series and then I hope you don't have any plans, because I'm not letting you out of my sight. We have the Academy reception after this and a very important portrait to unveil.'

We. That sounded wonderful. And if she hadn't given him a direct answer, he had her smile, her dewy eyes, and her arm possessively threaded through his as collateral. There was no mistaking she was a woman in love and all was right with the world at last.

That rightness was furthered as they stood before the series of pictures she'd painted. Seeing the paintings was like watching his life unfold in retrospect. 'I called the series, "An Oysterman's Life,"' she whispered to him. There was St Alphege's on the little hill that overlooked the marsh. The huddle of huts, the weathered two-storey structure of the Crown. The one he liked best was the one of the oystermen pulling their rowboats in from the water. 'I think I see Charlie and Padraig,' he joked.

'You do. I used their faces,' she confessed with a laugh.

He leaned in to study the fifth picture, a landscape that featured the marshes, the pebbly beach and a deliberately fuzzy structure in the distance that managed to look pristine and organised, at odds with its unorganised natural surroundings. 'What is this?' Owen asked, squinting a bit to make it out.

'Don't you recognise your own home? That's Baldock House,' she teased, but only a bit.

'Why is it fuzzy?'

'Because it's the oysterman's dream, isn't it?' She stepped closer to him. He could smell roses on her, sweet and welcoming. 'You aspired to Baldock House, thinking it would mark something, prove something.'

He nodded. 'But it didn't make me happy. I understood that almost as soon as I bought it. It didn't bring me the joy I thought it would. It didn't bring my mother back.' Baldock House had been a disappointment from the start except for the widow's walk, where he could use the house to do some good. 'I was merely a man living in another's man house.' He studied the painting with fresh eyes. This painting was about one man's journey of self-discovery. 'I can't decide if I like it. It makes me uncomfortable.'

The painting was a potent lesson, not just to himself, who knew the lesson of this painting personally, but it would teach that lesson to any man. Be careful what you wish for. True happiness did not lie in material things. Once attained, the marker moved. It was a warning, as well. A man could spend his life chasing the wrong things.

'It's a beautiful series, Josefina,' he complimented, meaning it. 'You've captured my home, my life, all of it, so perfectly. I might have to buy the whole set.'

She laughed up at him. 'You can't. Lord Montieth has already bought the church.'

'Well, I know the artist. Perhaps we can work something out.' He gave an exaggerated sigh and they both laughed, drawing stares from those around them. This was how it would be from now on. The two of them, laughing together, happiness welling up inside of him because this woman loved him.

Chapter Twenty-One

It was wrong to mislead him. Guilt tugged at Josefina even as she embraced the rightness of the moment, the rightness of being with Owen, of having him at her side while they made the short journey to Somerset House in the spring twilight, the feel of his hand at her back, ushering her through the reception hall, all of it felt so incredibly right. But it was wrong. It was selfish to claim this man, to take him from all he knew and all those who relied on him. He was going to give it all up for her, to come with her.

That revelation still stunned her. She'd thought her latest confession as to why she couldn't stay would hurt him. Instead, he'd been ready for it. He'd not hesitated. He'd been so sure of himself. *I will go with you.* She envied that about him—his surety, his confidence in knowing what he wanted and what he was doing. Owen never hesitated, never put a foot wrong. Once he was decided on a course of action, he saw it through.

That was why she had to stop him from this course

of action. Most of all, she wanted him to decide he couldn't come. She did not want to decide it for him. But she needed him to see that he could not leave, that he would hate himself for it in the end, for leaving his people, leaving his own dreams. She'd shown him the Seasalter series in the hopes that he would start to think not about her, but about what coming with her would cost him. She'd already been the object of his scorn once, she did not want to be the object of it again. She didn't want those blue eyes to look on her with the polite disregard he'd displayed in Boscastle's garden. Owen believed that when two people loved each other they should be together, but when two people loved each other, they also had to put the other first. It made for an imperfect happiness otherwise.

Owen took two glasses of champagne from a waiter as they stepped into the hall. 'Just in case you need some more, besides, it looks good for appearances.' He chuckled. 'I can't remember the last time I've had so much champagne before nine o'clock in the evening and it's only six now.' He smiled. 'Are you nervous?'

'A little,' Josefina admitted. 'I don't want Artemisia to be disappointed. Aldred Gray is such a toad, not winning a prize would be like losing to him directly. My pride is at stake.' She'd tried to tell herself all week that winning didn't matter. It didn't change anything. Winning didn't influence whether she stayed or left. She would go regardless. And yet, she *wanted* to win, for Artemisia, for herself. She didn't need to win first prize, just second or third would do. It would be enough to secure the wager for Artemisia and to prove to herself that she'd been right to leave Venice, to not tie herself to a workshop. She liked to think of it as a little encouragement for the road.

She took a sip of the champagne. 'It's silly to be nervous. It's already been decided. Someone in this room already knows. Being nervous can't change anything.' She favoured Owen with a smile. 'I'm glad you're here with me. It does help.'

Artemisia and Darius joined them. 'Shall we go in? They've opened the main gallery now.' Artemisia was bristling with excitement. It helped as well to know that she was not the only one rippling with anticipation.

Josefina straightened her shoulders. 'Yes, let's get it over with.'

Artemisia laughed. 'That's not quite the attitude we're looking for, my dear. I'd say, "Let's get on with it. I have a feeling I'm going to enjoy this moment all night."'

Inside, the long gallery was already crowded with artists and their personal guests, everyone jostling for position to view this year's work and this year's prizes. Artemisia glanced at the programme in her hand. 'The portraits are at the far end this year.' She shot a look over her shoulder at Owen. 'Are you ready for some fame? Everyone always wants to meet the models who sit for great work.'

Josefina let her own gaze slide in Owen's direction. How would he feel about that? Being an artist's model? This rich, self-sufficient businessman? Would he like the painting? He hadn't seen the work. She was suddenly nervous for a different reason. Would he like the way she'd depicted him? Would he be embarrassed to be the centre of so much attention? But Owen's expression gave nothing away except perhaps that he was pleased to be at her side.

They navigated the length of the hall, Artemisia's arm slipping through hers as they approached the portraits, her voice low at her ear as the two of them stepped apart from their men to see the portraits together. 'Oh, my dear girl, look what you've done.'

It took a moment for everything to register. Josefina found the portrait, her gaze resting on the blue eyes that peered back at her from the canvas, before her gaze moved to the top left corner, where the long, silky rosette was pinned. In blue, to match the painting, had been her overly alert mind's first reaction. Her second reaction was, blue, because she'd won. She'd not only taken a prize, she'd won the category.

'You won.' Artemisia's voice carried the faintest tremor of overwhelmed excitement. 'I can't believe it.' They were surrounded then, by their family and friends: Darius, Addy and Hazard, Boscastle and his son. They hugged her in turn and then she was in Owen's arms, letting the moment make her incautious. She kissed him full on the mouth in her excitement, not caring who saw. What did it matter? This was the man she loved. Why should she not show the world?

'You did it, I am so proud of you,' he whispered at her ear.

'Do you like it?' She looked up into his face, searching for a response, but there was no time. They had to celebrate. They were besieged with well-wishers and congratulations, everyone eager to meet her, to meet Owen, the model, to shake Artemisia's hand and to congratulate Darius. There was more champagne. There were toasts. People wanted to discuss the painting, to talk about her palette of blues, the shading she'd done on the turquoise curtains to hint at shadows, to commend the skill it had taken to depict a meaningful scene beyond the window behind Owen in the portrait. She was swept up in the glamour and the fame of the moment. She'd attended nights like this in Venice, but always for someone else. But tonight it was for her. She was the one in a silk gown, champagne in her hand, the toast of the hour.

It was some time before the crowd thinned and the reception began to move towards its denouement. Owen had stayed close, but not too close. He'd been happy to let her bask alone in her success. Now that the crowd had dispersed, he was beside her once more. 'Owen Gann, Oyster King of Kent,' he read the caption beneath the portrait out loud. 'That's hardly a scintillating title.'

'But very apt.' Josefina smiled up at him. 'It's who you are, Owen. It's who you're meant to be.'

'You painted me in the office at Baldock House, after all. I thought you were rankly against that.' The office. The desk where they had made love was positioned between him and the window in the background. He still couldn't work at it without thinking of her.

'I was, but I changed my mind.' She cast him a coy glance and he knew she shared his thoughts about the office. She gave a toss of her head, teasing him, 'I needed the window.'

'And I need you.' Owen settled himself behind her, wrapping his arms about her waist and pulling her close, taking advantage of the emerging privacy of the emptying gallery. 'Does this portrait have a story like the Seasalter series?' She felt his breath feather her ear, felt his thumbs gently press into her hips where they rested amid the folds of her skirt. She wanted nothing more than to be alone with him, to make love with him in his big bed and to wake up beside him. Her body was thrumming with the knowledge of those truths.

'Every portrait has a story,' she murmured.

'Tell me this one. Tell me about the man in the picture.'

'You might not like it,' she cautioned.

'Tell me anyway,' Owen said in all seriousness. 'After all, what does Plato say about the unexamined life?'

She gave a soft laugh and leaned against the power of him. 'Well, just remember you asked.'

'Why the office? Why the window?' Owen prompted.

'Kings live in castles and their subjects live beyond the palace walls, free to go about their lives in ways kings can't. I wanted the window to show the separation between you and the world you watch over. You told me once that you lived between worlds, belonging to both and neither. I wanted to depict that, not just for you, but for other businessmen. This is often the dilemma for rich merchants. The *ton* needs their money, but they are reluctant to marry their heirs to merchants' daughters.' The turquoise curtains had been both a sign of luxury and limits, the gilded cage of a king. Freedom lay beyond the window.

'So it's a study in leadership?' Owen asked. 'The price of responsibility?'

'And more. That's just the story of the setting. Then there's the story of the man. This is a self-made king. All around him are the trappings of his kingdom, but he wears no trappings.' She directed him to the hands she'd spent hours painting. 'He wears no signet ring, nothing that announces his position but his own efforts. These are the hands of a worker.'

'Oh, my word, you've captured the little scar on my pinkie, the one I gave myself shucking oysters years ago.' She heard the awe in his voice and it filled her with pleasure that he should appreciate the effort. 'And my tenacity as well, in the grip I have on the back of the chair.' His voice was softer now. She knew he'd noticed the pearls clutched in that grip, the pearls of working men acquired over generations of effort, another nod to tenacity and his origins.

'Yes.' Only the rounded top of the chair was visible at the bottom of the portrait. His hands rested on it, but not merely rested. Gripped. His hands gripped the ornate back of the chair as if they were anchoring him to the life of privilege that surrounded him. By doing so, there was a sharp contrast between the luxurious chair and the rough hands with their scar and pearls.

'Am I a benevolent king?' Owen asked.

'What do you think? Look at the eyes, Owen. Do you see your soul in them?' After the hands, the eyes had been the most difficult for her to do. She'd wanted to convey his vulnerability, his compassion along with his strength and determination. Here was a man who used his power for good, his gaze said. Here was a man who, without hesitation, had spent his personal money to save the smugglers, who had personally rowed out to the oyster beds after a storm to assess the damage because his crew needed him to.

'It's well done, Josefina. I do not know if I've ever been seen so completely before. It is humbling to be laid so bare.'

She looked about, realising only they remained. Artemisia and Darius, Addy and Hazard were waiting patiently at the other end of the gallery at the door, no doubt to give them privacy. 'I suppose we should go.' Although she would not have minded standing here in his arms all night looking at paintings. She would not have minded if time had chosen that moment to stand still.

'May I call on you in the morning before the exhibition opens tomorrow afternoon? We can settle our arrangements then.' She nodded. Tomorrow would be soon enough to let him down. Let them both have sweet dreams tonight.

'Sir Aldred did not come?' Josefina asked Artemisia as they joined them at the door.

'No, perhaps he knew the results and is waiting to show his face at the official opening tomorrow.' Artemisia gave a nonchalant shrug. 'Oh, well, my gloating will have to wait another day.'

There was a commotion outside in the dark beyond Artemisia's shoulder. A carriage pulled up to the kerb. Josefina squinted, trying to make out the figures getting out, two men. She frowned. 'Or maybe Sir Aldred is just arriving very late.'

Artemisia and the others turned as Sir Aldred Gray approached. The other man hung back in the darkness. 'You've left it rather late,' Darius drawled. 'The reception is over, but my wife is happy to accept your congratulations.'

Sir Aldred hmphed. 'You must excuse my tardiness. I was delayed by business, business concerning our wager, actually.' He speared Artemisia with a piercing look. 'Your protégée won and you think this proves something, that you can teach a measly street artist and a woman to boot with no real training to paint like a master. You think such evidence will enhance the standing of your precious school.' The words were spoken with such hatred and force that Darius took an involuntary step in front of his wife. Josefina felt Owen's grip at her waist tighten. Any charge against Artemisia was a charge against her, as well.

Sir Aldred's cool gaze turned her direction. 'I have someone with me who is eager to meet you, *signorina.*

He's travelled all the way from Venice, at my request, and only just arrived.' Josefina's racing mind froze, a thousand possibilities holding her rooted to the ground when she ought to run.

'What is the meaning of this?' Owen enquired, cold steel in his voice. He, too, had stepped forward in the face of Sir Aldred's vitriol.

The man dissembled. 'Nothing but a chance to re-unite old friends who are far from home. *Signorina*, I have someone I'd like you to meet.' He gestured for the man at the coach to come forward. 'Allow me to present Signor Bartolli. I believe you know him.'

'Does she know me?' The big man's chuckle chilled Josefina's blood. This was proof she'd stayed too long in England. Long enough to be found. 'I dare say she knows me—I am her betrothed.'

Chapter Twenty-Two

Owen's first instinct was to protect Josefina. He felt her sway against him, seeking his strength. This man, this Signor Bartolli, frightened her. He drew her to him, keeping her wrapped tight in the shelter of his arm. His second instinct was that this man was a liar. This was the man she'd ran away from, the reason she'd not gone back after her father's funeral, the man who'd propositioned her. He would need very little provocation to plant a punch in the man's face. 'He is not her betrothed.' Owen stared the man down. 'He may know her, but that is a lie.'

Sir Aldred shrugged as if the lie had no bearing on his case. 'That is between them, of course. It's clear, though, that they know one another, which is all that matters to me.' He turned his gaze on Artemisia. 'Did you think I wouldn't find out what you'd done? That you would be able to pass off Felipe Zanetti's daughter as a street artist you've somehow transformed?'

'I know nothing of the sort!' Artemisia's response was swift.

Addy stepped forward. 'How could we have known that? I picked her at random at the market. You were there. I think you both are mistaken. How could we ever have plotted something like that? To plan to encounter you in the market? To set that wager? There is too much of the spontaneous to it.'

Owen waited for Josefina to come to Artemisia's defence, to affirm Addy's argument, to declare who she was. But Josefina said nothing.

'This is not the woman you are looking for. This is Signorina Ricci. The name doesn't even match,' he pointed out.

'Is that what she told you? And you believed her?' Signor Bartolli sneered. 'Are you her lover? Is that why you defend her so earnestly? Well, you're not the first to be besotted with our *signorina*. Ricci was her mother's name.' He dropped the information with a triumphant smirk. 'I not only know her, but I know her far better than you do, it seems.' He held out a hand. 'Josefina, you've had your little adventure. Now it's time to come home, to Venice, to your father's workshop, to me and all you've left behind. You've given us quite the scare disappearing as you did. We'd given you up until a man came around asking questions.'

'Who might that man have been?' Owen ground out, trying to keep his feet firmly on the ever-shifting ground that was Josefina. There was so much to focus on, so much to distract him from his objective—protect

Josefina, first and foremost. All else could be sorted out afterwards. 'Did you send spies?'

'I sent Bow Street. I wanted to know more about the protégée.' Sir Aldred met his gaze with smug victory. 'She's left quite a trail all over the Continent. I wasn't expecting that, but Bow Street didn't fail me.'

'It cost you a lot more to find her than the wager was worth,' Owen noted.

'You don't strike me as a man who would put a limit on the price of his pride, Gann.' Aldred's gaze raked him. 'But I also didn't take you for a man who thought with his cock. She must be quite…convincing.' He laughed as Owen's fist clenched and unclenched with restraint. 'I don't like to lose.' Sir Aldred's gaze swivelled to Artemisia. 'I especially don't like to lose to a woman who cheats.'

Owen felt Josefina stiffen. She stepped away from the protection of his arm. 'That's enough. *Lady* St Helier didn't know who I was. She never knew. I never told her, I never told any of them. If there's a fraud here, it's me and it's him.' She gestured towards Signor Bartolli. 'I *am* Felipe Zanetti's daughter, but this man is not my betrothed. He would like to be. He propositioned me right before my father's funeral and demanded an answer by the end of the day. He made it clear he would not take no for an answer. So, fearing for my safety and my virtue, I left.' She fixed Sir Aldred with a stare worthy of Medusa. 'Are you pleased now? You've found a woman who did not want to be found and you've brought her face to face with a man who is dangerous to her. Well done. Was winning your wager worth *that*?' She turned towards him and Owen could see what the admissions cost her. Her eyes fought against shiny tears. 'Owen, I am so sorry.' Words failed her then. Something wild and desperate lit her gaze as she turned from him. She pushed past Sir Aldred and headed down the stairs of Somerset House to the street, her emerald skirts fading to black in the night.

Owen moved to go after her, but Darius put a hand on his arm. 'Let her go. This has been a shock to her. She won't go far.' Owen hoped Darius was right. His instincts told him otherwise. He excused himself. His mind was reeling with its own questions and, without Josefina beside him, he was acutely reminded that he wasn't family. Artemisia and Addy and their husbands had their own fallout to sift through. It was not appropriate for him to be part of that. His own carriage pulled up to the kerb and he climbed inside, grateful for the dark. 'Drive until I tell you otherwise. I don't care where,' he instructed. He wasn't going home until he had come to terms with what had happened and what he was going to do about it.

He let the questions come. How was it possible that he'd just claimed happiness a few hours ago and it was being tested yet again so soon? Was this happiness real? He didn't even know her real name and he thought he did. That was the real kicker, wasn't it? *He'd thought he knew.* He thought he knew her. Now a man who styled himself her betrothed had shown up, knowing more about her than Owen did.

He wanted to punch Sir Aldred for spying on her, for digging up a past she'd wanted to bury, yet the lie was all hers. *She had good reason for it; she didn't want to be found.* He tried to rationalise the lie. Even as he did it, he recognised it for the slippery slope it was. How many lies, half-truths or belated discoveries would he have to rationalise throughout a lifetime with her? Was this all? Or was there more?

Does it matter? You love her. She understands you better than anyone. You saw that painting, the way she captured the dilemmas you've faced, the choices you've made to be who you are. What fool throws that kind of understanding away? What kind of fool lets that woman run into the night thinking there's no hope? Love is simple. Don't overcomplicate it.

Love was love. He rapped on the carriage and called up to the driver. 'Lambeth Palace, at once.' Never mind it was after nine in the evening, far too late for a social call. The Archbishop would forgive him once he saw the size of the endowment Owen was going to make him once that special licence was in his pocket. And that was just the start of his evening. Josefina had been full of surprises. It was time for a surprise of his own before she could slip away.

Josefina slipped enough coins in her pocket to pay for a hack to the docks and help with her trunk. She was on the run again. She took a last look around the room. The other two trunks stood open. She couldn't take them for the twin sakes of speed and conscience.

She wanted to be gone before Artemisia and Darius came home. She couldn't face them, not after what had happened at Somerset House. Artemisia would be furious, she would hate her now. Josefina had made her look like a fool. Perhaps Artemisia would know how sorry she was when she saw that she'd left the gowns and the trunks. She'd taken only the art supplies and the three gowns she'd come with. Josefina shut the door behind her and headed downstairs, dragging her trunk, thumping on the steps as she went. The staff were abed for the evening. She hoped they wouldn't bother to enquire about the noise.

She breathed easier once she and her trunk were aboard the hack. It was almost a clean getaway. Now she had to hope that her ship would allow her to come aboard early. If not, she would have to find a hotel and then hope no one found her. Only a false name would protect her. It would be a long, anxious two days. How would she face Artemisia and Darius after tonight? All the brilliance of the evening had been stripped away in a single condemning moment.

It wasn't just Artemisia she didn't want to face. It was Bartolli. She needed to hide from him. He would *drag* her back to Venice and he would drag her to the altar, here or there, if he could manage it and he wouldn't be kind about it. And then there was Owen. What must he think of her now? Would he be disgusted? Would he realise what a narrow escape he'd had? He'd been her anchor tonight, his arm about her waist, protecting her despite a mind that must have

been reeling with questions and disbelief. And he'd
been betrayed for his efforts.

The hack was slowing. Josefina looked out the window as the docks came into view, eerie in the settling
fog. Relief warred with sadness. Each necessary step
took her further from Owen, but there was no choice.
She got out and spoke to the guard on duty, smiling
prettily until he went up to speak with the Captain on
her behalf. She sat on her trunk, twisted her hands and
looked about her as she waited for his return. Sweet
heavens, it was taking for ever, and her senses were
on high alert. Docks in the dark were not safe places
for women.

She slipped a hand into her pocket, taking comfort
from the little knife there. She knew how to handle men
who couldn't handle themselves, she reminded herself.
A knee to the balls would drop even the biggest and
her knife could do the rest.

She laughed to herself. She really was getting soft.
This was what life had been like up until January. How
quickly she'd forgotten what it was like to live on the
edge of alertness. It would come back to her.

'Josefina!' A voice cut through the night, a glimmer
of blond hair shining in the dark as Owen descended
from his coach. She hadn't even heard it and, in the
fog, she'd not seen it. She was rusty indeed.

She rose, her pulse racing as he neared. 'What are
you doing here? How did you know?'

'Lucky guess. I'm glad I didn't take Darius's advice and wait until tomorrow. You'd have been gone.'

Maybe. She didn't bother to correct him. He held her gaze for a long moment, his gaze making her want to melt against him. He was strong and certain. Right now, she was none of those things. 'Actually, it wasn't a guess. I know you, Josefina. I knew exactly what you were going to do.' He reached for her hand, his grip warm around the cold chill of her fingers. He knew and he'd come anyway. Josefina felt some of the fear that had frozen her begin to melt. She shouldn't let it. Fear was a great motivator.

'When you left Somerset House you were frightened. That man upset you.' Owen paused, running his hands down the length of her arms in a warming motion and she thawed a bit more. Thin ice was dangerous. 'You're frozen with fear, Josefina, and you are not thinking straight. We make poor decisions when we're scared. He can't hurt you. He has no papers, no agreements, no claim to you other than his word. You've given no consent and no one has consented on your behalf.'

'He will hunt me down.' Her eyes darted around the foggy docks. Even now, he might be on his way. If Owen had found her, perhaps Bartolli could, too.

'Then let's put you out of his reach, let's stop running.' Owen spoke in reasonable measures, his words slow and sure. 'I have been to Lambeth Palace and I have a special licence in my pocket. We can be wed tomorrow if we like.'

'Tomorrow?' She trembled from the cold, from the events of the evening. 'Isn't that a little precipitous?'

Owen shook his head. 'We've already discussed it. I proposed earlier this afternoon. Love is simple, remember? It's just people who complicate it.' He made it sound so logical, it was hard to remember her defence. Why not marry Owen?

Then she remembered. 'You want to protect me, you don't want to marry me.'

'I love you. If protection comes with the territory, then so be it,' Owen corrected. 'If travel comes with it, so be it, as well. I thought we'd settled this.'

The sailor came down the gangplank. 'Miss, Captain says you can come aboard. Shall I take your trunk?' His gaze split between her and Owen, confused.

'No.'

'Yes.' They spoke simultaneously.

'Wait,' Owen instructed and Josefina bristled.

'It's my trunk.'

'We're not done, Josefina,' he said sternly. 'You love me. I love you. There is no reason we can't marry.'

'But there is! I am a disaster, Owen. I ruin things if I stay long enough. Look what I did to you, to Artemisia. And I wasn't even trying. Now you're getting a special licence and planning a wedding in less than a day, and walking away from all the people who are counting on you. For me. You're giving up *everything* for me.' Her voice trembled as she pleaded. She had to make him see. 'You're too good of a man. I need to save you from me.'

'And who will save *you*, Josefina? Let me. Have you ever thought that, maybe, opposites attract because they're meant to save each other? Balance each other out?' He bent his mouth then, capturing her lips with a kiss full of sweetness and sincerity. 'You brought me back to life, Josefina. Do not underestimate the power of that. When I met you, I envied how free you were, how you could go where you wished and it reminded me of how trapped I was by my own making. Now that I am alive again, I don't want the fire to go out. I will want you always. You, just as you are, are incredible. Don't you see? I don't want you to change. I want your fire, your wildness, you just as you are.'

She looked up at him and wet her lips. 'That's just it. I want you the way you are. You're not a man who leaves those he cares for at the drop of a hat. You are not a precipitous man. It's what *I* envy about *you*, love about you, and now being with me is asking you to act against that.' Cross-purposes was making this impossible. Her heart was breaking.

But Owen was intractable tonight. 'Then we must find another solution, one that satisfies us both. Marry me, spend a year with me in Seasalter, *planning* our voyage to your dreams, planning how I can set aside work to travel with you, and then we'll go however far, for however long it takes for you to keep your promise.' He smiled at her and her resistance began to melt. Maybe she needed to take the leap.

'Miss, are you coming?' The sailor was impatient.

Owen held her gaze. 'The world is your oyster, Josefina. I will serve it on a half-shell to you every day for the rest of your life.'

All she had to do was say yes. Maybe love was simple, after all. She smiled at Owen. 'And I will do my best to be your pearl.' And then she frowned. 'But what about Darius and Artemisia?' Love might be simple, but there was still the exhibition, the mess she'd made of Artemisia's wager.

Owen grinned. 'I've been thinking about that, too, and I have an idea how to salvage that. As for what they'll think of you, let them surprise you before you think the worst.'

Chapter Twenty-Three

They did surprise her, as Owen had surprised her. There was no condemnation, no scolding, no stony glares when Owen carried her trunk back into the town house, only relief, exclamations of joy over her return, hugs and warm drinks in the small parlour set aside for intimate family gatherings.

'This is not insurmountable,' Owen said once everyone had settled to their tea or something stronger. Darius and Hazard nodded, their minds already busy at work. 'This is a discovery. Artemisia can claim credit for having found Zanetti's daughter after a bet with Sir Aldred Gray led to selecting an artist at random from the Covent Garden market.'

'I think that's up to Josefina,' Artemisia put in, causing Josefina to look up from her tea. 'Do you want to be found? This would be a very public announcement. Right now, it is just Sir Aldred's word against ours. We can manage him.'

Josefina shook her head. 'I don't want him managed

with a lie.' She would not have these good people do such a thing on her behalf. They had done too much already, most of it unlooked for and undeserved. 'Besides, I am not ashamed to be Felipe Zanetti's daughter. I loved my father. It just became rather inconvenient for...' she groped for the right word '...escaping.'

'Escaping Bartolli?' Artemisia pressed. 'He can be dealt with, as well.'

'Certainly Bartolli, but more than that.' Josefina sighed and furrowed her brow, looking for the words to express it. 'He was the embodiment of all my father wanted me to avoid.' She felt Owen's hand settle over hers, lending validation and support. She did not care that every eye in the room noted it. 'My father was a great landscape artist. He dreamed of sailing the world and painting the great landscapes: the Great Wall of China, the Pyramids, the vast wilderness of America, the green, humpbacked islands of the Caribbean. But he could never go. His wealth, his success, was tied to patrons. He had no freedom to pursue his passion without sacrificing the security of his wealth. I promised I would go for him. It was the last thing he asked of me.' Not just to paint for him, but to live free so that her dreams would not be limited by social strictures.

Addy swiped at her eyes. 'That's a beautiful story, but a hard one, too.' She cast a soft look at her new husband of a few months. 'I used to think that freedom meant being alone, but it doesn't. Freedom can be shared and supported by the people who love you. Your freedom is their freedom. And you are loved here, Josefina. You needn't hide, you needn't choose between your promises, your dreams and the people who love you. I've learned that and Artemisia has learned that.'

Josefina looked around the circle gathered about her and knew it was true. That was the secret that lay beneath every glance these couples exchanged with one another. She'd been blind to it until tonight. It had taken Owen's persistence to allow her to see it for herself. When she met Owen's gaze, his blue eyes twinkled with a teasing *I told you so.* 'Thank you, you've all been so gracious. I am happy to be announced as Felipe Zanetti's daughter, but how will this affect the wager? I don't want Sir Aldred to make things difficult for you.' She wanted to start giving back to these people who had given her so much, who treated her like family.

'We'll let him be part of the victory. I don't think he'll complain much if he can share in the momentary fame,' Darius offered.

'But the school? The wager was supposed to prove that the school provided excellent instruction for women. I'm not sure what's happened proves that.' Simply being who she was would negate the premise of the bet.

Artemisia smiled. 'I think it does other things for the school. After all, if it's good enough for Felipe Zanetti's daughter to paint there incognito and produce a winning portrait for the Academy, it can't be all bad. Families will want their daughters there. I expect enrolment will go sky-high next term.' Josefina didn't miss the veiled invitation. *Stay. Teach.* After the debacle of this evening, she'd not expected that invitation to be extended a second time. Well, maybe she could stay and teach for a while. What had Artemisia said? It's good to have choices even if you don't think you want them? She was starting to see the merits of that.

'What of Signor Bartolli?' Hazard put in. 'We've handled the exhibition and the wager, but those are not the reasons he's here. He expects to go home with a bride.'

Owen's hand squeezed hers as he cleared his throat. 'Josefina and I have taken the liberty of resolving that. We are to be married. I have a special licence, newly minted just this evening and effective as soon as to-morrow morning, although I think we'd prefer to wait and marry in Seasalter.'

'But by wait, we don't mean to wait too long,' Josefina put in. 'Maybe just a week or so, long enough to take care of things here.' Now that she could see the future, a bright, vivid landscape laid out in front of her, she wanted that future to begin now.

There were gasps and exclamations of excitement. People moved from their chairs to congratulate them. 'This calls for champagne.' Darius laughed as he shook Owen's hand. 'Can anyone stomach some more? I'll call for sandwiches, as well.'

'Oh, don't wake the staff,' Josefina protested. No doubt they'd just got settled after the late call for tea. 'We can do it ourselves. Owen is a fabulous cook. We'll raid the larder.'

All six of them trooped down to the kitchen, led by

Josefina, Owen in tow, for the most spontaneous engagement party London had quite possibly ever seen. Artemisia lit the lamps while Hazard stirred up the fire, Darius was sent to the wine cellar for champagne and Owen set to work slicing cheese and bread for toasting while Addy rooted through the kitchen for some of Elianora's cream cakes, shipped weekly to the town house during the Season.

Food assembled and cooked, champagne poured, they gathered around the kitchen worktable for toast. 'To love,' Owen said to the room, but his eyes were on her as they had been all night, 'which makes the impossible probable and has the power to turn tragedy to triumph at a moment's notice.' As they drank, Owen whispered at her ear, 'Don't ever forget it.'

Josefina held on to those words throughout the days that followed: the triple whirlwinds of the exhibition, the prize and *The Times* announcement, penned at dawn by Darius, proclaiming the discovery of Felipe Zanetti's daughter, followed by another announcement posted by the Oyster King of Kent himself, Owen Gann, sharing news of his engagement to Josefina Zanetti. Following that, a first-class ticket leaving immediately from London was delivered to Signor Bartolli's hotel, compliments of Viscount St Helier. Josefina couldn't think of a better use of her ticket. It was an explication of tragedy to triumph in action. What could have ended in disgrace had ended in celebration.

But what she treasured most in those heady, whirlwind days was the quiet time she managed to steal alone with Owen. Today was no exception. 'Where are you taking me?' Josefina asked gamely, settling inside his carriage. It was cloudy outside and she thought it might rain. It wouldn't be a picnic, then.

'To Blackwell,' Owen said cryptically. 'For an early wedding present.'

'Blackwell? Isn't that the docks?' She was determined to prise the secret out of him.

'Yes, and that's all I am going to say for now.' Owen laughed.

'Is it? Care to wager on that?' Josefina moved from her seat, straddling his lap, her skirts riding up on her thighs. 'I have ways of making you talk.' She kissed him on the mouth, her hand dropping low between them and finding him rousing.

'You don't play fair, minx.' Owen groaned, but he offered no real protest, happy to be persuaded if these were her methods. He loved this about her, her spontaneity, her ability to embrace passion openly. *Josefina will always be wild.* Thank goodness for that. A man needed a little wildness in his life. He certainly did. If wildness included lovemaking in a carriage, who was he to complain? There'd been little time for stolen moments since the night she'd decided to marry him. But there would soon be time.

She slipped her hand inside his trousers, having got his fall open, her hand warm about him. 'What's the surprise?' She leaned in for a kiss, her voice soft.

'It's the last piece of business I need to take care of before we can leave for Seasalter.' He chuckled when she made an exaggerated pout.

'You mean to tell me the surprise is business?' She stroked his length, calling him to complete arousal. 'I don't believe that for a moment,' she whispered against his mouth.

'Humour me, Josefina.' He laughed. 'It's not every day a man gets to spoil his bride-to-be.'

Humour him she did, with kisses, caresses and laughter until they pulled into a work yard beneath a sign: The Sutton Ship and Yachting Company.

Owen watched some semblance of comprehension dawn in her eyes as he righted his trousers. There were a hundred questions in her eyes, but she was guessing. He smiled as he handed her down from the carriage and she looked about at boats in varying sizes and states of completion in the yard.

'Your dream?' she asked reverently.

'Your dream and mine. They go together now,' Owen said quietly. 'I want you to meet Richard Sutton, shipbuilder and dream-maker.'

Richard Sutton was waiting for them in his office. A small girl of four or five played on the carpet at his feet with a carved toy ship. 'I hope you don't mind? I like to bring my daughter to work with me.' Sutton greeted Owen with a handshake.

'I don't mind at all.' Owen introduced Josefina, who bent down to speak to the wide-eyed child.

'What's your name?'

'Elise.' The child held up the toy boat for Josefina's inspection. 'I'm going to build yachts when I grow up, the fastest boats on the water.'

'Of course you are. Don't let anyone tell you otherwise.' Josefina handed the boat back to her with a smile. The scene touched something in Owen's heart. His bride was going to make a wonderful mother. *A family of his own.* The thought nearly choked him as he watched Josefina with the little girl. He'd not allowed himself to think beyond the proposal, the wedding. Josefina rose and smiled at him and he let his thoughts run a bit wild. He would have a family with this woman. A large one to fill up Baldock House, sons and daughters to inherit the business, to paint portraits and landscapes.

Richard Sutton cleared his throat. 'Would you like to see the plans?' His eyes were merry and Owen knew every thought he had was plainly written on his face for the whole world to see. He couldn't care less. Let the world see that he was madly, completely in love. Sutton unrolled a long sheet of paper and anchored it with paperweights. 'This is your ship, Mr Gann, and probably the last full-sized ship I'll build,' Sutton said. 'I think everything from here on out will be yachts for me.'

'Ship?' Josefina gasped, turning her dark eyes on him.

'Well, we need something to see the world in and to ship oysters.' Owen smiled, loving the surprise in her eyes. He had another surprise in store. He pointed to a space in the bow. 'Do you know what this is? It's our cabin.'

'It's huge,' Josefina breathed.

'It will be filled with all the modern luxuries one can have aboard a ship: a big bed, a table, chairs, a place for you to paint when you can't paint on deck. Do you see the big window? Perfect for an artist's light. We will live in comfort.'

'I can't believe it—this is your wedding gift?' Josefina was overwhelmed, he could see it in her eyes. 'We're really going to do it.'

'Yes, next year, on our anniversary, we'll sail away, just as I promised.'

'You're planning our anniversary already and we haven't even had the wedding,' Josefina laughed, but it was choked with tears of overwhelmed joy. Suddenly, she was in his arms, her arms thrown about his neck, kissing him hard while Richard Sutton laughed. It was good to be a man in love and he would be a man in love for the rest of his life.

It was good to be a woman in love, something that had taken Josefina a long time to admit to herself. But now that she had, she didn't want to fight it any more. She wanted to give in to it, every day. She stood outside the wooden doors of St Alphege's and drew a deep breath. This was her wedding day and the man she loved waited for her inside, along with her new 'family.' She touched the pearls at her neck. Owen had sent them to the farmhouse this morning with a note that read simply 'back where they belong.' The Gann pearls, collected over the years from various oysters, were a sign of Owen's love and the perseverance that was so typical of her husband-to-be. It had taken years to build this strand.

'Are you ready?' Darius approached quietly. He had volunteered to give her away. Addy and Artemisia were both acting as matrons of honour for her today. Addy had delayed her departure to Florence to come back to Seasalter for the wedding. Simon would stand beside his brother, all of them ready to witness their marriage, while back at the farmhouse his wife was overseeing the wedding breakfast alongside Mrs Harris. There would be cream cakes and ginger biscuits galore.

She nodded, her grip tightening on the spring bouquet of wildflowers in her hands, populated heavily with blue forget-me-nots to complete the old folk superstition that a bride must have something borrowed, something blue, something old and something new on her wedding day. Darius handed her a coin. 'Sixpence for your shoe.' He laughed. 'Can't forget that.' The strains of a violin came from inside the church, the final signal that it was time. Her stomach fluttered with nerves.

Darius took her arm. 'I've never seen Owen so happy. He's a new man thanks to you. He's going to melt, though, when he sees you. You make a beautiful bride.'

It was exactly the right thing to say. Josefina plucked at the skirts of the oyster-coloured silk with its lace and seed pearls—the ideal gown for the Oyster King's wife. It was her 'something new,' a gown that had been stitched at rapid speed and sent down from London just the day before. Artemisia had helped with her hair, putting it up in curls this morning and setting a simple tiara among them—her something borrowed sent down by Darius's mother. 'You're surrounded by family now,' Darius whispered as he opened the door and led her down the aisle.

There was a rustle of clothes as people rose in the pews. Seasalter was a small village and most had come. The girls from the school were there, excited for a day off, the oystermen and Padraig were there with their families. The little church was turned out in spring glory, clutches of wildflowers tied with pastel ribbons decorating the pews and a larger spray of flowers at the altar. A simple, spring wedding, a reminder that spring was a time of renewal, a time when all things were born again, even a reckless woman who'd nearly thrown away the richest happiness of all.

Owen waited for her at the end of the short aisle. His hair gleaming gold, his clothes—a blue morning coat and buff trousers—immaculate, his eyes shining. When he took her hand from Darius, she felt his grip tremble, saw his eyes glisten as they held on tight to each other as the words were said, as vows were spoken and she felt again the power and the intensity of his love.

At last, Owen kissed her, with a whisper in her ear as he took her in his arms for the first time as his wife. 'For ever starts today, my love.'

From this day forward he would be hers and she would be his, bound together with a love that no man would put asunder.

Epilogue

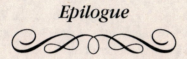

One year later

Josefina stood at the rail, a light breeze toying with her hair as the *My Josefina* made its way down the Thames towards the open ocean. London was already fading from view, the people on the wharf growing smaller, too far away now to see her if she waved. Artemisia and Darius had come to see them off, extracting promises that they would stop in Florence to see Addy and Hazard before going on to Greece and Egypt.

Strong arms came up behind her and drew her close. Her husband. Even after a year, she did not tire of saying that. She was more in love with Owen now than she'd ever been. It was hard to imagine how that could be, but her love for him grew every day.

'You'll miss them,' Owen surmised, dropping a kiss on her cheek. She leaned against him. Leaving was always bittersweet, there was the excitement of going, of setting out on this journey they'd so meticulously planned and yet there was the sadness of leaving behind a life and people they loved, even if only for a temporary time. They *would* be back, in a year or two.

'But I'd miss this more,' she answered honestly. As much as she loved her new life in Seasalter, working with Artemisia at the school, being Owen's wife and turning Baldock House into a home that was theirs, this journey remained important to her. It would bring closure to a chapter of her life. The art she'd create and bring back would be the opening of another. It would be the opening of another chapter for them as well in other ways, too. She laced her hands over Owen's.

'I don't think I wished you happy anniversary yet,' she said. Owen's word had been good—they'd set sail on the very date of their wedding a year ago.

Owen nuzzled her neck. 'There's champagne and a brand-new bed waiting for us to celebrate.'

She turned in his arms. She wanted to see his face when she told him. 'I want to give you your present first and to commend you on the foresight of building such a large cabin. Family-sized, one might say. We're going to need it.'

'We're having a baby?' Owen's face was a delightful mix of shock and joy, and then, as she knew he would, a moment of worry. 'When? We can sail for home whenever you like.'

She laughed up at him. 'Not until December and, no, we're not sailing for home. We've barely begun. Babies are born all over the world all the time.' She hesitated, second-guessing her gift. 'Are you happy?'

'Yes. More happy than you know, happier than words can express. Perhaps this will be a start.' He kissed her then, as London faded and the wind filled the sails. Happiness, peace, love filled her so completely, she thought in that moment she would burst. The world was her oyster, but Owen Gann was her pearl of great price. In loving him, she'd been rewarded a hundredfold and more.

* * * * *

If you enjoyed this story, be sure to read
the first two books in Bronwyn Scott's
The Rebellious Sisterhood miniseries

Portrait of a Forbidden Love
Revealing the True Miss Stansfield

And be sure to read her
The Cornish Dukes miniseries

The Secrets of Lord Lynford
The Passions of Lord Trevethow
The Temptations of Lord Tintagel
The Confessions of the Duke of Newlyn